Woman

of

Fairville

Rosemary,
 No rose is sweeter than the one
with a beautyful smile like yours.
thanks!
 Jn 4: 4
 Melodie

Woman

of

Fairville

MELODIE RAKES

TATE PUBLISHING
AND ENTERPRISES, LLC

Published by Tate Publishing & Enterprises, LLC
127 E. Trade Center Terrace | Mustang, Oklahoma 73064 USA
1.888.361.9473 | www.tatepublishing.com

Tate Publishing is committed to excellence in the publishing industry. The company reflects the philosophy established by the founders, based on Psalm 68:11,
"The Lord gave the word and great was the company of those who published it."

Book design copyright © 2012 by Tate Publishing, LLC. All rights reserved.
Cover design by Kate Stearman
Interior design by Nathan Harmony

Published in the United States of America

ISBN: 978-1-61777-908-4
1. Fiction / Christian / Romance
2. Fiction / Family Life
11.12.14

Acknowledgments

Mr. Rakes, for being so supportive of me in my endeavor to put my story in writing and for helping me in the editing of it. Thank you! I love you!

Marge, thank you for your encouragement and assurance that I wasn't just wasting my time.

Elizabeth Pence, thanks for the beautiful picture you so graciously drew for the cover. You are priceless.

Bradley Nicodemus (the best attorney in Ohio), thanks for letting me pick your brain.

Judge Haberman, thank you for taking the time to read my manuscript and for your input.

Zachary Arthur Huntington (the best car salesman ever), thanks for letting me use your most dignified name.

Preacher Carr, for encouraging me to write this book and for all your prayers.

Marcia, it's acceptable. Thanks for just being you.

Most of all, thank you, Lord Jesus, for the words you loaned me to write this book. May it enrich someone's life and bring them to you. If it does, then I know it will have been worth it. Amen.

All scripture references are from the King James Version Bible, which is the closest to the Hebrew and Greek translations.

Preface

Like the woman at the well, we are all seeking for something in our lives. As you read Bobbie Jo's story remember that the choices you make today determine your future.

Bobbie's story is not unlike your own. She could be the girl next door or she could be you.

Chapter One

"Bobbie, honey, it's time to get up," Mother said in her bright, cheerful little voice.

How she woke up so full of life in the morning was way beyond my comprehension, but she did. Every morning, she was up before the roosters, making coffee for Father.

Between the cracks of the blinds, the bright June sun peeked in at me, and I squeezed my eyes shut and rolled over, pulling the covers up over my head. I just wanted to stay there just a few more minutes. I could hear my parents rattling around in the kitchen, and try as I might, sleep would just not come.

"Bobbie Jo Patterson, are you out of that bed yet?" Mother yelled up the steps for the umpteenth time. "We're going to be late. You know Preacher Carr likes to start on time. What in the world is taking you so long to get ready this morning?"

What was taking me so long had to do with Marcia's midnight phone call concerning Dr. Tony Juxton, the new doctor in town. We have been without a doctor for quite some time since Dr. Adams died. Dr. Pitsmith in Barryville, about twenty-five miles from Fairville, was as old as the hills, and no one wanted to go to him unless they were dying.

Our conversation ended close to 3:00 a.m., and all night, I kept thinking about Dr. Tony Juxton.

What is he like? What does he look like? What kind of a woman does he like? I could not go back to sleep, for all of these questions kept me awake.

I finally got up and tried on everything I had in my closet, trying to decide what to wear. At last, I pulled out my favorite white sundress and matching crop jacket. If you looked closely, you could see the butterflies in the material. I always thought I looked good in white with my summer tan and long, black hair. I found my black sandals with wedge heels, and I was set. Being five-foot nothing, I could wear the popular two-inch heel.

I then carefully removed the dress and sandals and hung them on my closet door and slid back under my covers to get some sleep.

Marcia had talked until late, saying, "Dr. Juxton moved to town last week, and he is going to be at First Baptist Church this morning. He is very handsome, educated, and did I mention how handsome he is?" Marcia kept repeating. "We have to be there early. I have already alerted Danny to be sure we arrive early."

Marcia Sedders was my best friend. In elementary school, junior high, and high school, we were inseparable. We became blood sisters at age ten, when we stuck our thumbs with sterile needles heated by a candle, and then we pressed them together and said, "Blood sisters for life. Nothing can separate us." After that, we sucked our sore thumbs and laughed so hard that we were rolling on the floor.

Marcia was five-foot four with long, red, naturally curly hair. She was drop-dead gorgeous and had been trying to marry me off since she and Danny met. They were married the week after high school graduation, and now have a set of twins, Melodie and Harmony.

After three blind dates—I can't begin to explain the horror of those nights—I am a little leery of another "this is the guy for you" story, yet this guy intrigued me. I couldn't explain it, but I really wanted to meet Dr. Juxton. Maybe it was the whole doctor thing. I don't know. But I was hoping deep down inside that maybe this was the one.

I was quite content with my life. I was a unit manager at Beautiful Gardens Nursing Home, plus taking extra college courses online, studying for my bachelor's degree. I really didn't have time to even breathe. It's not that I didn't want to be married and have children, but just not then.

My dream of being a nurse started when Mother dragged me to Beautiful Gardens one day when I was young. I had heard the stories of how the people in those places were scary and mean and ate little girls. What I found was a roomful of the nicest, friendliest people I had ever met. It was like Halloween. When I left, I had at least two bags of candy. From then on, I went with Mother every week.

Beautiful Gardens paid my way through nursing school as I worked as a nursing assistant. I was obligated to them for two years of service, but I doubt they would have had to put a gun to my head to get me to stay. It was the most wonderful, fulfilling job.

I had just turned twenty-one, and I was still living with my parents, not that it was all bad living there. My parents were great, and I had managed to save a bit of money, even though I was quite a shopaholic.

Most of my friends were either in college or married, so when I decided to stay in Fairville, they just couldn't understand it. I was voted "most likely to succeed" in high school, and I felt I had achieved it. I had never wanted to move away from our little town. No, it's not a big town; it's sort of where two roads meet.

"Bobbie Jo, come on now. Your breakfast is getting cold." Mother's words reached my ears again.

Mother was one of those types who never wanted to be late. "It's not right to make people wait on you," she would say. Mother would be at church at midnight for the next day's service if Father would allow it. Mother was petite and beautiful with long, black hair streaked with a few gray ones, which she keeps up in a French roll. She and Father had been in love for thirty years.

Mother came from a very rich, respectable family who could never understand why she would want to marry a laborer. Mother and Father fell in love at first sight, dated for six weeks, and then ran off to the next county to get married, much to her family's disappointment. Mother serves on the school board and was president of the garden club and continues to visit at the nursing home. She accomplished all of this plus managed to keep a perfectly clean house and take care of a husband and daughter.

Father, on the other hand, is a machinist at the local paper mill, where he works six to seven days a week. We live in a white, two-story farmhouse with a wraparound porch that serves as the dining room most days, weather permitting.

Father could do anything and everything. He was my hero. He came home at 6:00 p.m. every night, and it was not unusual for him, right after supper, to have his head under the hood of someone's car or building something in his shed.

It seemed that he never sat still long enough to really talk to us, but when there was a problem to be solved, he was the first one everybody ran to. Father was a deacon at church, and now, it was him shouting.

"Bobbie Jo, you have ten minutes to get ready and get down here. Your Mother has made a breakfast fit for a king."

Down the steps I came, taking two at a time, brushing my hair as I ran. Sitting at my place at the table, I reached for my mirror, but Father gave me "the look." Returning the mirror to my pocket, I bowed my head for prayer, hoping Father would hurry so I could eat and then have another look at myself in the bathroom mirror before we left.

Father always had so much to say to God, even though he talked to Him three times a day at every meal. Sometimes, late at night, I would hear him through the floor register, asking God for things also.

After the amen, I inhaled a couple spoonfuls of egg, drank my orange juice, and asked to be excused to finish getting ready.

"You seem to be in a hurry this morning, little lady. Is there anything we need to talk about?" Father asked with a big grin on his face. He was chuckling like he knew a secret. "Mable, have you heard of something special happening at church this morning?"

"Leave her be, Henry, so she can get ready for church. I'm kind of looking forward to meeting Mrs. Juxton and her very handsome doctor son myself." Mother was chuckling too. "Go on, darling. You know how your father likes to tease. We're leaving in about fifteen minutes. By the way, you look lovely. That dress fits you perfectly."

Upstairs, I shut my bedroom door and started twirling in front of the mirror. My dress did not resist as it lifted up and swirled around me until I couldn't turn any more and fell on the bed, laughing. I remembered when I was a little girl, I wouldn't wear any dress that didn't swirl. I didn't feel like a little girl today though. I felt like a grown woman and, for some reason, a little anxious about meeting Dr. Tony Juxton.

Don't get me wrong. I dated, but all the guys in this town are bums or hicks. Donald, the last guy I dated, had blond hair, blue eyes, and roaming hands. The last I saw of him was when my milk-shake landed on his head at the drive-in theatre. For some reason, he has not called me since. Maybe he isn't as dumb as I thought.

Marcia was waiting for me as soon as we pulled into the parking lot. "Where have you been? They're already here, and you aren't going to believe what a knockout this guy is. Come on. Hurry up." Marcia was breathless from talking and running, pulling me along with her.

Mother and Father nodded agreement that I could go on, so into the church we went. I didn't want to look too obvious, but I didn't see him anywhere.

"They arrived about ten minutes ago, and Preacher Carr took them into his study to talk. This is the one for you, Bobbie. Just wait and see."

Finally, Marcia pointed to the door of the study. Opening up, Preacher Carr and his wife, Sandy, came out, followed by an older lady we assumed was Mrs. Juxton. She was a very well dressed and attractive woman. She was tall and wore a white jacket over her white dress with a double-strand black pearl necklace hanging around her neck to match her earrings.

We stood like a couple of statues staring at the man following them. He was very handsome with coal-black hair. He was at least six feet tall, and his suit fit like a glove, and all we could do was stare.

Preacher Carr saw us standing nearby and called us to come meet the newest members of the church. "Bobbie, Marcia, this is Mrs. Juxton and her son, Dr. Tony Juxton. He's opening the Fairville clinic again. They bought the old Adams estate and are remodeling. Mrs. Juxton, Tony, these are two of our young ladies, Bobbie Jo Patterson and Marcia Sedders."

"It's very nice to meet you, young ladies," Mrs. Juxton stated.

"Hi," Tony said as he shook our hands. "It's a pleasure to meet you both."

His brown eyes looked right into mine, and I couldn't turn away from his gaze. It felt like they were penetrating my very being. I wasn't sure whether to run or kiss him. Thank goodness Preacher Carr broke the silence.

"Ladies, would you please escort Dr. Juxton to your Sunday school class? We'll show Mrs. Juxton to the main class. Bobbie, are your folks here?" Preacher Carr said a little louder to get my attention, as I was still staring into those beautiful brown eyes.

"Yes, yes, they're here," I said shyly, looking away.

Preacher Carr and his wife took Mrs. Juxton into the main sanctuary for Sunday school, which left us standing there with Tony. I wasn't exactly sure of what to do next until I felt Marcia tap me on the shoulder.

"I need to make a phone call. Why don't you two run along, and I'll catch up with you," Marcia announced as she hurried away, digging in her pocketbook for her cell phone.

We stood for the longest time just looking at each other when, suddenly, he took my hand and started walking toward the back of the church. I couldn't resist, but it was probably because I didn't want to. Out the back door was a beautiful rose garden before coming into the cemetery. Along the side was an angel pouring water from a pitcher into a fountain. A red climbing rosebush almost hid the fountain from view. Someone had placed a cement bench beside it.

"Do you mind if we sit here for a minute and talk? Preacher Carr took us on a tour of the church, and I thought this place was a perfect spot to sit and chat. I wasn't sure who I would be chatting with, but then you came along," he said in a quiet, gentle voice. "Mom was determined to come to church today to introduce us to the entire neighborhood. She is quite the entertainer with no one to entertain except me. She misses her friends, but I'm sure she will meet plenty today."

My tongue wasn't working, and I was afraid to try to say anything, so I just sat and listened. His voice was so soothing, and his words were relaxing and inviting. I was hypnotized by him. I was also very conscious of his closeness on the bench and his leg touching mine.

"I'm so sorry, Bobbie. I didn't mean to sit here and do all the talking. Please tell me about yourself. First of all, why Bobbie? You're much too pretty to be a Bobbie." He spoke with such elegance.

"Thank you!" I said, hoping the words all came out right. Those big, brown eyes continued to pierce through me.

"There you are!" I heard Marcia's voice come up behind us. "We've been looking everywhere for you. You missed Sunday school, and your parents are hunting for you," she announced to me. Turning toward Tony, she said, "Tony, this is my husband, Danny."

We jumped up, and I said hurriedly, "Excuse me. I'd better go in. It was nice talking with you. I'm sorry we missed Sunday school." Before he could say a word, I rushed out. I knew Marcia and Danny would take care to escort him to the sanctuary. As for me, I had to get away from those beautiful brown eyes.

"Bobbie Jo, where have you been? We have been looking for you. The choir has already started practicing. Hurry now or you'll be late," Mother said.

After the special song, the choir sat down and a note was passed to me.

"Dinner tonight? I'll pick you up at five. Maybe a movie too?"

How exciting! Oh, wait until Marcia finds out. She'll be ecstatic.

Just then, I reread the little note, and in the corner, it read, "See ya tonight! Judd."

My heart sank to the floor. *How dare he write and send me notes in the choir.* Judd Carr was the preacher's son. Since we met, about ten years by then, he never failed to ask me out. He was persistent, that much I gave him, because the only answer he received was no.

Marcia and Danny were waiting for me outside. She asked me about the rose garden, and I told her we just talked when, in actuality, Tony did all the talking.

"Did he ask you out? Are you going to see him again?" Marcia inquired.

I shrugged my shoulders and shook my head. "I don't know."

"I need to talk with Judd Carr for a minute," I said, heading toward him. I threw the paper at him and said, "Don't ever pass a note to me in choir again." He looked at me and smiled his silly grin as I walked off.

Mother was in the kitchen, finishing dinner, when I heard her call me. I had run upstairs to change clothes as soon as we got home.

"Bobbie, hurry now. Get the plates on the table," she said as I grabbed our usual three plates. "No, no. We need two more for our guests," she announced.

Before she had time to elaborate on who our mysterious guests were, the doorbell rang and she told me to go see who it was. She was acting mighty peculiar, and then Father came in the kitchen and asked, "Are you going to let our guests in, or are they to eat with the dogs?" He kissed Mother on the cheek and waved me toward the front door. I wasn't sure what to expect when I opened the door. They both looked guilty of something.

There, standing on our doorstep, was Mrs. Juxton and Tony. They had apparently gone home first to change into more comfortable clothes. Mrs. Juxton was wearing a simple pair of green cotton pants and a blouse to match along with a cute pair of flowered sandals. Tony was wearing blue jeans with a blue shirt and black cowboy boots. He took off his hat as they entered, ducking as he came in. My heart was beating a mile a minute, and I was relieved when Mother came to the door behind me to welcome the guests.

I excused myself and ran upstairs to change from my ragged shorts and T-shirt to a black short set I had bought for vacation. I wasn't sure whether to thank my parents or be angry with them for not telling me, but either way, I had Dr. Tony Juxton in my house for dinner. Brushing my hair, I decided I didn't have time to pin it back up on my head, so I let it flow down my back.

Coming back down the steps, I noticed Father and Tony sitting in the front room, discussing cars. Tony looked up and smiled when I walked by. It was one of those up-and-down looks like when a man is checking you out. It gave me goose bumps, and I hoped he liked what he saw.

Mother and Mrs. Juxton were chatting in the kitchen, and I called the men into the dining room. Tony sat across from me and smiled. Father said the prayer, and this time, I wanted it to last forever because Tony had stretched his leg across under the table and was touching mine. I have no idea what Father said to God in that prayer, but I said, "Amen."

After we ate, Father asked, "Tony, would you like to see some of my woodwork?"

"If you wouldn't mind, sir, I'd like to take Bobbie for a walk. I promise we won't go far, and we'll be back before dark," Tony said simply.

"Of course, it's okay with me, but you better ask Bobbie Jo. She has a mind of her own." Father looked at me and winked.

"And a very beautiful one, I might add," Tony said, also winking at me. He politely bowed down. "May I have the honor of escorting such a lovely lady as you for a walk?"

"I would love to."

As stupid as that sounds, those were all the words I could muster. Tony Juxton actually wanted to take me for a walk all alone. He opened the door and gently took my hand. They were sweaty, but he wiped them on his blue jeans, and we laughed as we walked down the street.

Chapter Two

It was a beautiful evening for a walk. It was about seventy degrees and not a cloud in the sky. Tony held my hand as I showed him the sights of our little town. Fairville, Ohio, was a small town, but it had two gas stations and two traffic lights. On one corner sat the bank, and across from it was the pharmacy, and of course, two blocks farther down was Fairville Medical Clinic.

Tony asked questions, and I tried to remember all my history of the area so I could recite it to him, but some things I kind of left out. Nonetheless, we had a great time just walking and talking, and when we came to the park, we both grabbed a swing and raced to see who could get the highest. My little legs were pumping hard, and his long legs were only pushing once to my two or three. Finally, we were swinging side by side and laughing. We leaned back, and my hair almost swept the ground.

After the swing stopped, Tony took me in his arms and kissed me right smack on the lips. It lasted only a second, but it felt like forever. It was so gentle and warm. I experienced strange new feelings that I had never felt before. When he pulled away, I turned my head, hoping he wouldn't see the fear in my eyes. It was all new to me, and I wasn't sure how to handle it. I wanted to run down the street, jumping and screaming, "Did you see that? Dr. Juxton kissed me!" But I also wanted to just run. "Bobbie, are you all right? I'm so sorry. It seems I've upset you," he apologized. "You looked so beautiful with your hair blowing in the wind, and it just felt so right. Please forgive me. I would never do anything to hurt you."

"I'm fine. I just wasn't expecting that. Maybe we should get back home now, if that's all right with you," I said.

The way home seemed to take longer than usual. Neither of us said a word, but he held my hand, and I welcomed the touch. My head was spinning, and I could still feel the warmth of his lips gently pressing against mine. I wanted him to kiss me again.

Oh, Marcia, where are you when I need you?

At the front door, he gently lifted my face and looked into my eyes. I was so embarrassed I couldn't look at him. *What if he finds out? Does love happen like this? Is there really such a thing as love at first sight?* I remembered Mother saying it happened that way with her and Father, but I didn't know. I was so confused, and I didn't know what to say or do.

"I'm so sorry, Bobbie. I didn't mean to upset you. I hope this doesn't mean you won't see me again. I can't remember when I've had such fun. Thank you for a wonderful evening. Listen. Um… this week, I'm moving into my new office, and a lot of equipment and things are being delivered. I'll have to be there. Would you like to meet me there and have a pizza picnic on the floor in my office? How does that sound? Too corny?" he asked.

"No. It sounds like fun." I was so surprised the words actually came out of my mouth. "I had a great time this evening, and I'm not upset with you. A picnic sounds great. Just let me know which day."

"Thursday sound good? I would love to have your input about the clinic, you being a woman and a nurse. It'll really help me make some decisions on how things should be organized," he said.

Mrs. Juxton was saying good-bye to my parents, and then she hugged me and told me she hoped to see me again. Tony opened the car door for her and reminded me again about Thursday.

"I'm really looking forward to seeing you again. Can I call you?" he asked.

I wrote my number down on a piece of an envelope lying on the table and handed it to him. I walked with my parents to Tony's car to say good-bye.

Just before I walked back in, I turned around and, with a big grin, I said, "By the way, Dr. Juxton, you kiss great!" Then I turned and walked back to the house, but not before I heard him say, "Ditto!"

My cell phone was ringing when I got out of the shower the next morning. I knew it was Marcia before I answered it.

"Tell me all about it. I can't believe you didn't call me last night with all the details," Marcia said impatiently. "Is it true that Dr. Juxton and his mom had dinner at your house after church yesterday? I've been waiting for you to call and tell me. Come on now. I want to hear all the juicy details. Don't leave anything out."

I was laughing so hard I could barely talk. There was no way I could have talked to her or anyone else last night. When I went to bed, I laid there wide awake, remembering every detail of yesterday and the way it felt when he kissed me. The world was spinning out of control, and suddenly, my whole life was changed. In one day, everything was different.

"He kissed me, Marcia. He kissed me, and I liked it. No, I loved it. I've never felt this way before. What am I going to do?" I spilled my guts. We've always been able to tell each other anything. "He invited me to the clinic Thursday evening for a pizza picnic on the floor of his office," I continued.

"Oh, Bobbie, I just knew this was the right one for you. I'm so happy," Marcia said as if I were already marching down the church aisle.

"Wait a minute, Marcia. I can't base my whole life on one kiss. And yes, it was a great kiss, but what about my career and my family and my life…?" I just kept going on and on, not really making any sense and not coming to any real point.

"You're just nervous and anxious. Everything will work out. Just wait and see. I have to run. I hear the twins waking up. Call me tonight," she said and then hung up.

I was totally perplexed. It was the only time I could ever remember Marcia letting me down. She didn't offer any great advice, like what looks good on me when we go shopping or how I should fix my hair; all she told me was, "It'll all work out."

That's just unacceptable. Why can't she tell me what I'm supposed to do?

What in the world was, "It'll all work out," supposed to mean?

I grabbed a cup of coffee and a cinnamon roll and headed to my car. Mother and Father were still in bed, and somehow, I felt they had let me down too. I really needed someone to talk to, and so far, my best friend and my parents had abandoned me. I found my car keys, and as I was unlocking the door, I noticed a long, white box on the hood. Thinking the neighborhood kids were being ornery, I picked it up but was afraid to open it. It had a big, red bow on the top and a card that read, "You Kiss Great" signed by Tony.

I was laughing and crying as I ran back in the house to my parents' bedroom to show them the beautiful, long-stemmed red roses. They had the sweetest fragrance I had ever smelled. Mother went to the kitchen to find a vase to arrange them and then set them on the table. She handed me a hanky to wipe my eyes and smiled.

Running into work a half hour later, I apologized to the nurse, listened to the report, and started the morning med pass because one of my nurses had called out sick. With each pill I passed and each time I signed my name, all I could think of was Tony. Sometimes I had to sign my name twice because I placed it in the wrong box. Sandy, one of the CNAs, was following me, trying to tell me something, and until she stood right in front of me, I didn't even know she was there.

"Are you all right this morning, Bobbie? You seem a little preoccupied," she said.

"What do you need, Sandy?" I asked. "I'm sorry. I didn't mean to be so short with you."

Apparently Mr. Givens had fallen and had a skin tear. I locked the med cart and followed Sandy to investigate. He was fine except for the skin tear, so I cleansed it with normal saline and applied sterile strips to it and, of course, gave him a big hug.

As I walked to the nurse's station to call the doctor, it hit me. *Some of the patients will soon have Dr. Tony Juxton. He'll probably be making rounds here. How in the world am I going to make it through the day if he comes to my floor? I can't even do a simple med pass without having him on my mind. This has got to stop. He's just a man I met who kisses great, and I just have to quit thinking about him and get on with my life.*

Paperwork was piled on my desk, mostly medication administration records (MARs) that needed to be checked for the next month. I hated to go hide in my office with only one nurse on the floor, so I ignored the papers until later. The phone was ringing off the hook, which was nothing unusual, and as I picked it up, I overheard a conversation taking place down the hall.

"Did you get a chance to see the new doctor at church yesterday? What a hunk of meat," the first voice was saying.

"I also saw Bobbie making a fool out of herself with him," the second voice whispered.

"She is a pretty little thing," the first voice answered.

"Yes, but I think I'd like to try some of that myself," the second voice said.

Suddenly, from around the corner came the two voices that belonged to two nurses from another floor, Ashley and Linda. When they saw me sitting at the desk, they turned red and smiled, saying, "Hi, Bobbie," and then rushed to get into the elevator. As the doors were shutting, I could hear them ask, "Do you think she heard us?"

At six o'clock, I finally clocked out and drove home. Mother had supper all ready, and I set the table. Father came in, and we all sat down and bowed our heads. I was so tired it was hard not to fall asleep right there on the chair. Father must have known that because his prayer was shorter, or maybe I did sleep through it.

Mother had put the red roses on the dining room table. There were two dozen, and Father said, "Someone is trying to impress someone, buying two dozen roses."

The meatloaf was wonderful, but I just wasn't hungry. "I'll clean up, Mother. Why don't you go sit with Father?"

After the dishes, I rubbed some lotion on my hands and went outside on the porch to spend some time with Mother and Father. They were discussing, of course, Dr. Juxton.

"So, Bobbie, what do you make of the new doctor?" Father asked ever so slyly.

"I don't know yet. I haven't seen any doctoring being done," I answered him.

Father laughed, and Mother joined him. They were sure having a good time at my expense. I couldn't be angry with them though.

"Okay, you two. Enough is enough. I really do need some advice," I began as the phone started ringing. "I'll get it," I said as I ran inside, hoping to beat the answering machine.

"Bobbie, hi. It's Tony. Can you talk?"

When I heard his voice, it was as if I hadn't talked with him for months. I felt a blanket of doubt lift from my shoulders. I knew now what was bugging me all day. It was the fear he wouldn't want to see me anymore since I made such a fool out of myself over one kiss.

"Bobbie, are you there? Do you want me to call later?" he anxiously asked.

"Oh no, no, Tony. This is fine. I wasn't expecting to hear from you so soon. I'm glad you called." I was so nervous that my voice was shaking. I didn't know what to say, but I hoped he would just talk to me in that gentle, tender voice. Listening to him, I realized how much I had been missing him all day.

"I had a hard time waiting this long to call. I've wanted to call you all day, but I knew you were at the nursing home, so I made myself wait until I thought you would have had enough time to change clothes and eat supper. How's my timing?" he bragged.

"Your timing is great. We were sitting on the porch, talking about the new doctor in town. Have you heard? He's single, and all the girls are lined up at the Fairville Medical Clinic to have their annual physicals." I was laughing so hard I could barely get the words out.

"Yeah. So I heard, but I also heard he has his eye on one particular little lady with beautiful dark hair and brown eyes. I don't suppose you know who she is, do you?" His voice was sincere, and he was not laughing.

Suddenly, I stopped laughing and realized he was being honest and sharing his feelings with me.

"I did hear something like that, but then again, how much gossip can you really believe?" I couldn't stop joking. I was afraid if I did, he would see inside of me and know what I was feeling.

"I think in this case the gossip can be taken into consideration. It's coming straight from the horse's mouth." He then started making all kinds of sounds that were supposed to resemble a horse.

"Cute. Real cute," I was very thankful he wasn't being serious anymore.

"I can do a cow too. Moo!" he laughed.

"I think you need to work on both a little more," I suggested gently.

"Gee thanks," he said. "Maybe Thursday you can teach me since you seem to know a little more about cattle and horse language. We're still on for then?"

Of course we're on for Thursday. Are you kidding? If I don't see you Thursday, I think I'll die. I didn't let these thoughts escape through my mouth. Instead, I replied, "Yes, I'll see you Thursday. Have a good night." With that, I hung up.

———————————————

Tuesday night, after supper, Mother and Father were sitting on the porch, talking with Mr. and Mrs. Mountz, so I came out to join them. They are dear neighbors who have lived across the street since I was a baby. Mrs. Mountz had Alzheimer's and sometimes didn't remember who we were, but that night, she was talking coherently, and when I sat beside her on the swing, she asked about my job.

She listened intently, asking the right questions, and suddenly, she looked at me and said, "You'll be a good wife and mother if you want to." After that, she got up, took her husband by the hand, and walked across the street to her home.

Mrs. Mountz's words haunted me for some reason, and they were still playing around in my mind at work Wednesday, along with my date with Tony. After I finished the next month's MARs, I started doing the treatments for the nurses while they took their lunch breaks and was almost finished when I was called to John Maize's room. John was a favorite of mine. He was four feet, eleven inches tall and followed me everywhere, and at night, I would have to take him to his room and reassure him I would be back the next day.

That time, in his room, he lay on the bed, not breathing. One of the nursing assistants had started CPR, and another had called 911. I pushed the CNA out of the way and took over chest compressions, hearing his ribs crack with every push. The tears were streaming down my face as I counted and continued the chest compressions. After two sets of CPR, I felt a strong hand on my shoulder gently pulling me off, and I turned to see Tony standing behind me with the director of nurses, Ann Smith.

"He's gone, Bobbie. You can stop now." Tony took me out of the room into the hall and wiped the tears from my eyes.

"No. He can't be gone. He's been following me all day until I started doing treatments and one of the girls took him to the dining room to eat. What happened?" I was out of control. I couldn't understand how he could be gone. That was unacceptable.

Ann Smith came out of the room, and Tony went in to pronounce Mr. Maize dead just as the emergency team came off the elevator.

"I'll take care of it, Bobbie," Ann said and started walking toward the EMTs.

"No. This is my floor and my responsibility. I'm fine. Thanks," I said to Ann.

I saw her and Tony get on the elevator, and Tony smiled and nodded at me.

Chapter Three

On Thursday morning, I woke up with a headache, probably from the trauma the day before at Beautiful Gardens. I hadn't realized how much Mr. Maize's death affected me. Slowly, I got out of bed, showered, and went downstairs for coffee. As I was pouring my coffee, I remembered my date with Tony.

He had been so kind the day before, stopping me from making a fool of myself in continuing CPR even though the patient was gone. It was tough washing Mr. Maize and preparing his body for the funeral home, but I always tried to do it for each of my patients when they passed away. I felt like it was the last gift I could give them.

━━━━━━━━━━

Tony called late the night before, when I was getting ready for bed. For some reason, he knew just what to say to cheer me up and encourage me.

"How are you doing?" he asked.

"Okay."

"You did a great job today. I've never seen a nurse care about her patients as you did. You're quite remarkable." He was trying to make me feel better.

"Thanks."

"Will I see you tomorrow? I've been practicing my barnyard sounds." He laughed.

His laugh was contagious, and before long, I was laughing too. I could just see him walking around the clinic, mooing and acting like a horse.

"Don't worry. I make sure all the blinds and curtains are closed," he added.

"That's good," I said. "I'd hate to think what the good people of Fairville would think of their new doctor walking around in the clinic late at night, mooing."

I was laughing, and it felt great. I couldn't believe the effect he had on me. It was almost scary but delightful also. Nothing made sense anymore when it came to Dr. Tony Juxton.

"I'll see you tomorrow, Dr. Juxton. Good night," I said before hanging up.

A new patient was admitted to room 7, Mr. Maize's room.

"Man, the bed isn't even cold yet," the nursing assistant stated.

"An empty bed doesn't pay the bills," I told her.

As cold and callous as that sounds, that's the nursing home business, and I didn't like it any more than they did, but we had fifty-nine other patients on the floor who needed to be taken care of.

At lunchtime, I was surprised to get a phone call from Marcia, who was waiting downstairs in the lobby. She had brought me lunch, so I told the charge nurse where I would be if they needed me.

Marcia would never come to the floor. "It's just too depressing," she would say. She sat outside at a picnic table, waiting with a ham salad sandwich, chips, and iced tea.

"Hey, girl. What a nice surprise." I kissed her on the cheek and sat down beside her.

"I haven't heard from you, so I figured I'd better come over and see if you were still a nurse here or if you'd turned into one of the patients." She laughed. "How are things going with Dr. Juxton? Are you still having a pizza picnic tonight?"

"Yes, we're still on for tonight. He was so wonderful yesterday." I then told her the story of what happened with Mr. Maize.

"This guy sounds like he really likes you, girl," she said.

"I know, but what am I supposed to do?"

"What do you mean supposed to do? You aren't supposed to do anything. Just let it happen. Everything will be fine."

There she said it again. I had no idea what that was supposed to mean, but Marcia didn't seem to want to elaborate on it either.

"Thanks for lunch," I said as I cleaned up the table. "I promise I'll call you tonight, no matter how late it is. Poor Danny will never get any sleep."

The afternoon dragged on, and finally, it was four o'clock and I made rounds with the oncoming nurse. I wanted to make sure I had time to run home and change clothes before going to the clinic.

"I hear you're seeing the new doctor in town," said Mary, a big, robust nurse. "It's about time you got your skinny little butt out there and started dating. You're too old to still be living with your parents. You need half a dozen kids following you around."

"Gee thanks, Mary," I said as I entered the elevator.

Mother was in the kitchen when I came in the door, so I kissed her on the cheek and ran upstairs. What in the world do you wear to a pizza picnic in the office of the new doctor in town? I couldn't choose, so I showered and then opened my closet doors again. It was seventy-five degrees outside, so I chose a pair of white shorts and a white blouse with black flower silhouettes. My white sandals were perfect, so I found them and then tried to decide what jewelry to wear. Mother bought me a beautiful shell necklace when she and Father were in Hawaii the year before, and I found some earrings to match. My hair was still damp, so I towel-dried it and brushed it up into a pony tail.

"How do I look?" I asked Mother.

"Beautiful, as always. I wouldn't expect my daughter to be any less. Have a good time, darling. Tony is a very nice man, and if this is to be, then it will be."

Mother was great. She always knew what to say.

"Thanks. I shouldn't be too late. I love you." I kissed her on the cheek and ran out to my car.

Tony was waiting at the door for me when I pulled into the parking lot. He opened my door, took my hand, and helped me out. Turning me around a couple of times, he nodded his approval, and with a smile, he took my hand and we walked into the clinic.

Everything was in disarray, with equipment, papers, desks, chairs, and unpacked boxes in every room and in the lobby. The only orderly room was Tony's office. In the middle was a huge cherry desk that took up half the room. Bookcases filled with books lined the room. In the middle was a beautiful bay window with a seat that opened for storage space.

I walked around the room, examining the books and the desk. He had pictures of his father and mother in the middle of the desk, and then I happened to notice a picture of him with another woman about his age. She was tall and very beautiful with dark eyes.

Before I could inquire about the picture, Tony showed me the picnic area that consisted of a blanket on the floor behind his desk. He had a pizza, pizza cutter, two paper plates, napkins, and two glasses of iced tea all spread out on the blanket. There was even a candle in the middle of it. We sat on the blanket, and he handed me a glass of tea and put two huge slices of pizza on my plate.

"Thanks for coming, Bobbie. You look great. Would you mind removing the combs from your hair? I love the way you look with your hair down around your face. I hope you don't mind."

"No. That's fine," I told him.

Fine? It was wonderful. No one had ever told me those things, and he seemed so genuine. He wasn't saying those things just to impress me. He probably knew he didn't have to. I was already impressed.

We ate our pizza and drank our tea and talked about the clinic and Fairville in general. "Well, I dragged you over here to show you the place, so if you are ready," he said and reached out his hand to me. As he helped me up from the blanket, I fell into him. When he caught me, he gazed into my eyes for the longest time but then took my hand and led me to the lobby.

The lobby was a nice size with dark green carpet. The walls were windows from the ceiling to the floor, and light green vertical blinds had been hung to protect the furniture from the sun. Tony unpacked a box of the lobby chairs. They were dark green and light green flowered leather chairs. He started placing them up against the windows and set a small table between every three to four chairs. A magazine rack was built onto the front of each table. We pulled a big mahogany table into the center of the room that was to have information and magazines on it.

The front desk was behind a large window that could be opened and shut as needed for privacy. The nurse's station was located down a small hallway next to the four examining rooms, each equipped with examining tables, thermometers, and blood pressure cuffs. The rooms were a nice size to accommodate family conferences.

"I'm going to start the hiring process next week. The applications have been pouring in, and I have decided to hire locally. Two nurses and two front desk people should be enough. I'll also need an office manager and an assistant. I hope I'm not boring you."

There was no way I could have been bored. Tony was like a little boy, so enthusiastic, and he wanted everything just right.

"I'm thoroughly enjoying myself. You have some great ideas. I think you should have the stock room closer to the examining rooms though, so the nurses won't have so far to walk for supplies." I suggested.

"I never thought of that. I liked this room for supplies because it was so big, but I could make this the main supply room and have a smaller one here beside the rooms. Do you think that will work?" he asked.

After the tour, we returned to his office and sat down on the blanket, putting our backs against the window seat and stretching our legs out. It was such a comfortable moment and so relaxing. I felt like I could actually help him with the clinic. It was exciting talking about it and helping him plan. His enthusiasm was contagious.

"Tell me about Tony Juxton," I began after a long silence.

"What do you want to know?"

"Everything, but for now, you can give me the short, condensed version."

"Okay. We moved here from Tally, Texas. Dad died a couple of years ago of a massive heart attack. He too was a doctor, a surgeon, the best in Texas. His death was a great loss not only to Mom and me but Tally also. Mom didn't know what to do with herself. She was all alone for the first time in her life. I was away in med school. The next thing I knew, she was moving to Fairville, Ohio. She told me she just liked the name.

"After graduation last year," he continued, "I came here to bring her back home to Tally, but she refused to leave. She was a pillar of society, entertaining and president of the garden club. Without Dad, though, nothing had any meaning. She'd built her whole life around him."

"Okay. That tells me about your Mom. Now what about Tony Juxton?" I was hoping he would get around to that picture on the desk, but he needed some encouragement.

"Well, that's a very boring story," he said teasingly. "Let's see. I wanted to be a doctor like Dad, so I applied to all the right schools and was accepted right out of high school. I was hoping to practice medicine with my dad, but God had other plans."

Looking at his watch, he jumped up. "Oh my goodness, Bobbie. It's one in the morning. I'm so sorry. Your father is going to kill me. Let me walk you to your car. Then I'll clean up this mess."

As I drove home, I kept wondering about the mysterious woman in the picture. Is she an old friend or something more? Has he been married before? Thinking over all he had told me, he never really told me anything about himself. Is there something about Dr. Juxton I need to know before this relationship goes any further, and is it going to go any further? He was nice enough tonight, a real gentleman, walking me to my car, opening the door, and kissing me on the cheek, for Pete's sake. What man kisses you good-bye on the cheek? Maybe he's lost interest after that first kiss, and all he wants now is someone to help him with the clinic. He did say he would like my input, being a woman and a nurse.

Marcia was waiting for my call, and I told her everything, as usual, and she just said, "Everything will be fine. Why would he have a picture of an ex-wife or girlfriend on his desk and then invite you to a pizza picnic? You're worrying about nothing. Stop fretting. I'll talk to you tomorrow. Remember, we're going to that new mall. I'll pick you up at ten. You do remember, right?" she reminded me.

Actually, I had forgotten, but I didn't tell Marcia. I said good night, telling her I would see her at ten. I was taking the day off to go shopping at the new mall in Thorn City. It was all she had been talking about for weeks until Tony came to town. I welcomed the chance to get away for the day. I needed some time to shop and just enjoy myself. Marcia was right. I was fretting. When I laid down, I think I was asleep before my head hit the pillow.

Chapter Four

Loaded down with packages, I could barely make it through the door. Father took a few of the parcels and put them on the couch. I didn't realize I had bought so many things until I tried to carry them all at once.

"Your day seems to have been very successful," Mother said as she came out of the kitchen, wiping her hands on a dish towel. "I just finished dishes, but if you're hungry, I can warm something up for you."

"No, no. We have been eating all day. I probably put on ten pounds," I said, patting my flat belly. "Look at this new shade of nail polish. It's called Red. I love it. The girl put my legs in a whirlpool and massaged my calf muscles. All the tension and stress from everything just kind of floated away with the water. I had a great time. Of course, with Marcia, it's hard to have a bad time, especially shopping. I'm exhausted."

As I carried my packages up to my room, Mother said, "Oh, Tony called. He said it wasn't urgent but he would like you to call him."

"Thanks, Mother," I said.

Tony Juxton was the last person I wanted to talk to right then. Between him and work, it was no wonder I was so stressed out. When did my life get so complicated? As I was putting all my goodies away, I tried on my new Sunday dress. It was a baby blue sundress with butterflies on the bottom flying through some flowers. It was a perfect fit and the last size four on the rack. Marcia said it was meant for me to have it.

My mind immediately wondered if Tony would like it. It was amazing how much that man invaded my thoughts. Every time I picked something up, my first thought was whether he would like it.

What in the world is happening to me? Am I going crazy?

"Bobbie, phone call," Father hollered up the steps.

"Thanks, Father." I picked up the phone and heard Father hang up on his end. "Hello?"

"Bobbie, hi. How was the shopping trip? I look forward to seeing you in all your new duds," he said, laughing.

"It was great. I spent way too much money, and I'm exhausted. Marcia is so much fun to go shopping with," I told him.

"I called to see if you would like to catch a movie tonight, but how about tomorrow? It's that new romantic comedy. Maybe we could grab a bite to eat beforehand," he said.

"That sounds great. All the reviews have been fabulous for that show. What time were you thinking?"

"Six o'clock sound all right?" he suggested. "There's a new Chinese restaurant that opened last week. I'll make reservations for two."

"It sounds like you have it all planned."

"I figured after our pizza picnic, I'd like to show you I do know how to entertain a beautiful woman. I'm sorry Thursday became a work night. Your suggestions were valuable, and I took them into consideration. I could use some more help, if you wouldn't mind, but not tomorrow night. I promise this is going to be a real date."

"I will be ready at six sharp, and mind you, I love Chinese food, and I have a very big appetite," I added.

━━━━━━━━━━

Saturday was cleaning day around the house, so I gathered all the dirty clothes and took them to the wash room and started the washer. Mother was cleaning the kitchen, so I found all my cleaning supplies and headed up the stairs for bathroom duty. Most of the dirt in my bathroom was long, black hair. Father got very upset when it stopped up the drain and he had to snake them.

Mother came upstairs with some folded towels, and while she was putting them away, she started acting peculiar. She would go from the bed to the closet and back to the bathroom, and finally, I asked her what she was doing.

"I'm trying to find the right words so my daughter will not think I am interfering in her life," she said.

"Mother, you know you can ask me anything you want. We're friends too. What do you want to know?" I asked, unsure of what she had to say.

"Are you in love with Dr. Juxton?" she blurted out.

She was never one to beat around the bush or mince words, so she was being true to form. I loved her for that.

"I'm not sure, Mother. I think about him all the time. Yesterday, when I was shopping, with everything I picked up, I kept asking myself, 'Is Tony going to like it?' I've never been in love before, so you tell me."

"Head over heels," was all she said, and then she went downstairs.

Why can't I get a straight answer out of anybody? Has the whole world gone mad? Even my parents are acting weird. Love. Okay. What am I supposed to do now if I am in love? Maybe tonight will help answer some questions. The pizza picnic was great, and it was fun giving him my input about the clinic. He made me feel important, but does he just want a consultant?

At five o'clock, I took my shower and put on my new blue sundress. Why wait until church when I had a real, honest-to-goodness date? Too excited and nervous to fix my hair, I pinned it back away from my face, remembering that Tony said he liked it better down. My new blue sandals fit perfectly and were also comfortable.

As I was putting the finishing touches to my makeup, I heard the doorbell. Running to the window, I saw Tony's blue sports car in the driveway, and I heard Father speaking to him downstairs. I gathered my things and stuffed them into my dark blue purse.

"Wow!" was all Tony said as I walked down the steps.

Father joined him, and I am sure I was a pretty shade of red to match my toenails.

The Chinese restaurant was fantastic, and I had no idea of some of the things I ate, but everything was delicious. The movie was slightly boring, but we sat through it. Tony put his arm around me and held me close. I felt like a queen, and he was my king. He was very attentive when I talked and seemed to hang on to every word, afraid he might miss something, and he always looked into my eyes when he talked with me.

After the movie, we did a little window shopping, and we heard music coming out from one of the stores. It was a familiar tune, and Tony stopped to listen to it. Then he turned to me and bowed down, holding his hand out for me. I curtsied, and then he swept me up in his arms and twirled me round and round. We didn't notice when other couples joined in dancing beside us. When the song ended, he drew me near and kissed me gingerly on the nose.

On the way home, we talked and sang to the radio, and I finally found enough nerve to ask about the woman in the picture. I just had to know. The suspense was killing me. If he had been married before or just broke up with someone, that made a big difference. I was hoping he would understand.

"Tony, who was that woman in the photo with you?" I asked.

"I'm sorry, Bobbie. I saw you looking at the picture but didn't think to explain. I'm not hiding anything from you. She's my sister, Rose. She's a lawyer, and I can't wait for you to meet her. She's coming next weekend, and Mom is planning to have a few guests. I hope you and your parents will be able to attend."

When we walked to my door, he lifted my chin so I could look deep into those beautiful brown eyes. I was lost in a dream when he kissed me. The world was spinning, and I was hanging on for the ride. What a ride it was too. After he let me go, I couldn't think straight.

"Bobbie, I just want you to know I have my sights set on you. You're the prettiest girl I have ever met. You're charming and fun. I love spending time with you. So, until you tell me you don't want me around anymore, you're my girl." His eyes were dead serious. There was no mischievous smile on his lips.

"Okay, Dr. Juxton. I'll be your girl if that means being treated like a queen like tonight. I'll see you tomorrow at church." I found my key and unlocked the door.

He turned me around toward him and said, "No. I'll pick you up tomorrow for church. I want the whole town to know you're my girl." He was smiling now and kissed me on the cheek before he turned and whistled all the way back to his car. He waved as he drove off.

My feet were floating when I climbed the stairs. I was light as a feather. If I were on the roof, I would have bet I could fly. Sleeping was impossible that night. All my thoughts were on Tony and how he held me in his arms and we danced on the sidewalk. I was still thinking of him when my alarm went off at eight for church.

Mother was making pancakes when I came down, so I set the table and found the butter and syrup. Uncle Gerald, Father's brother, always made sure we had homemade maple syrup. He had a friend who made it, so every year, he gave us a gallon. Store-bought syrup just never could compare.

"How was your date last night?" Mother asked. "I didn't hear you come in."

"Of course you didn't. I was floating. I had such a wonderful time. We actually danced in the middle of the sidewalk, and there were two or three other couples dancing alongside us."

"It sounds like you're really falling for this guy." Father had snuck into the kitchen and put his two cents in. "I just want you to be happy, Bobbie Jo. He seems to be a nice man."

The doorbell rang, and I ran to answer it. I saw Mother and Father look at each other and smile. Tony was standing there in a three-piece light tan suit holding a long, white box. He ducked as he entered the doorway and kissed me on the cheek. When we entered the kitchen, he gave the box to Mother, and she was just as tickled as she could be. It was full of the prettiest sunflowers, big and bright yellow. Mother thanked Tony and found a vase to put them in next to the window.

"How did you know Mother liked sunflowers?" I asked him as we drove to church.

"It wasn't too hard to figure out, considering her kitchen curtains and tablecloths are sunflowers."

"You really amaze me, Dr. Juxton. Most men wouldn't take time to notice such things."

"Something else I noticed too, Miss Patterson, is you look quite lovely this morning."

Marcia and Danny were waiting for us in the parking lot.

"Do you two have any plans this afternoon? The high school band is having a symphony at the lake. Would you like to come? Danny's mom is going to watch the twins," Marcia was saying.

We both agreed, so plans were made to meet at the lake.

Chapter Five

After church, Tony drove me home, and while I changed into some shorts, he talked with my parents in the kitchen. Afterward, we drove to his house and I talked with Mrs. Juxton while he changed into shorts and a T-shirt.

Mrs. Juxton offered me a glass of iced tea and showed me her rose garden. She explained how she brought all of her roses from Texas and replanted them. She hired a special van with temperature control to transport them. Every rose had a special white wire around it with its name written on a small card encased in plastic. As we walked from plant to plant, she told me a little bit about raising roses and compared it to raising children.

"These are my children, Bobbie," she said, proudly waving her arms to indicate she was talking about her plants. "I think Tony and Rose are jealous of them because I spend more time here than with them. I transported each one from Texas and replanted them here."

"They are beautiful," I said.

"My daughter, Rose, will be coming next weekend. She's a lawyer, and I couldn't convince her to move along with us. She loves the excitement of a big city, and her law practice has done well. You will be joining us, won't you?" she asked.

"I would love to, Mrs. Juxton," I said politely.

"Please call me Catherine. I hope we can become close friends. It seems my son has taken quite a liking to you, and I agree wholeheartedly with his choice. You are a very sweet girl coming out here and allowing me to ramble on about my roses. They are my passion."

"Aw. I should have known Mom would bring you out here. Sometimes, I think she loves these roses more than her children," Tony said as he hugged his mom.

"Are you all ready?" he asked me.

"All set! Thank you, Mrs.—I mean—Catherine. I enjoyed talking with you and seeing your beautiful roses."

The field was packed with other couples and families coming to enjoy the concert. With no cloud in sight, Mr. Williams, the band director, had picked a beautiful day to perform. The band was warming up when we arrived, and walking through the crowd, we were stopped several times by friends and coworkers welcoming us. Finally, we saw Marcia and Danny and unfolded our blanket, laying them side by side.

Marcia had fixed a picnic lunch with tuna sandwiches, chips, and iced tea. I helped her make the sandwiches and handed the plates to Danny and Tony and then sat down next to Tony to enjoy the concert. We sang along with the songs we knew, and when we didn't know the right words, Tony would make up words to it.

"Twenty-five or six to four, I'm running late but I want more," he sang.

We tried to hush him, but we were laughing too hard to say much. Danny and Marcia and everyone sitting near us learned the new lyrics quickly, and soon, the whole section was singing Tony's new song.

When the band took intermission, we took a walk to the restrooms. Tony held my hand as we walked and told me how beautiful I looked. It was so nice to be close to him, just to smell him and touch him.

Finally, we made it back to our blanket as the band started playing. Tony grabbed me, and we started dancing. He twirled me around, and at the end of the song, he dipped me low and kissed me. The crowd started clapping, and I think it was more for us than the band. I was in my own little fantasy world, and I loved it.

"You are crazy, Tony," Marcia said.

After the concert, Marcia and I cleaned up while the boys went to talk with Mr. Williams.

"He is really a lot of fun," Marcia said.

"Yeah. I really had a great time. Thanks for inviting us. Maybe we can go to dinner together sometime."

"Sure. How about a nice, quiet dinner at our place? I will take the twins to Danny's mom's house, and that way we will have more time to talk."

"That sounds great. Tony's sister, Rose, is coming in next week, and Mrs. Juxton is planning a big party. She is a lawyer, and I have heard a lot about her from Tony and Mrs. Juxton," I told Marcia. "Mrs. Juxton actually asked me to call her Catherine and said she hopes we will become good friends."

The boys returned to carry everything to the cars, and we all decided we did not want the day to end, so we headed for the ice cream parlor. Marcia called her mother-in-law to notify her that she would be late picking up the twins.

The ice cream parlor was packed. It seemed that we weren't the only ones with ice cream cravings. Marcia and I found a picnic table and gave our orders to the guys, who then fought their way through the crowd, pretending to be pirates with swords. They were laughing and kidding with all the other patrons but finally made it in the door.

"You look beautiful today, Bobbie Jo. That is what love does to you," Marcia said.

"I don't even know if that is the case, Marcia. We have only been dating a week now. I know I enjoy being around him, and we always have such fun."

The ice cream pirates appeared with our treats, and we all sat silently enjoying the taste and the beautiful evening.

"My sister, Rose, is coming into town next weekend. I would love it if you two could come to the party. Mom is quite the entertainer, and this will be her first get-together. I guarantee anybody worth knowing and some who aren't will be there," proclaimed Tony in between bites of ice cream.

"That sounds like a wonderful evening. We will be looking forward to it. Just let us know the details," Marcia said.

After we said good-bye to them, Tony took my hand and we walked to his car. The full moon was bright enough that I could see his face. Before he opened the door, he turned me around and gently kissed me not once but three times. They were hungry, passionate kisses, and each one was more satisfying. I did not want him to stop.

He took my face in his hands, and trying to catch his breath, he looked at me with the most loving eyes. "I fell in love with you the first time I saw you when we sat in the rose garden at church. I hope I don't scare you away because these are not just words. I am going to prove it to you."

Before I had a chance to say anything, he opened the car door and I slid in. He was quiet on the way home. We listened to the radio, and at the house, he walked me to the door and kissed me good night.

"I am going to be busy with interviews this week, but I will stop by on my way home a couple of nights if that is all right."

I don't know why he asked. Of course it was all right. I wanted to see him the next day and the next day and the next day and the one after that.

"Yes, that will be fine," was all I managed to say.

He kissed me again and then drove off. I stood for the longest time, just watching as his tail lights finally disappeared.

I sat on the porch swing and thought about everything that had happened that week. *Yes, it has only been a week since I met this incredible guy, Dr. Tony Juxton. So much has happened this week. I'm not sure how I feel about any of it except I like it. I like how he makes me feel. I don't know if that is love or not, but it's right close to it.*

Tony called me every night after work and stopped by a couple of nights as he had promised. We would sit on the porch with my parents and talk of the day, and then my parents would go in the house to give us some privacy, and he would kiss me and ask how my day had gone. We would stay cuddled up on the swing until we knew it was time for him to go.

On Thursday, he seemed really tired. He was excited about the clinic. It was starting to come together just as he had hoped it would.

"I hired two nurses today. One of them works at the nursing home, Ashley Boone. She has a great personality but not much experience in a doctor's office. The other is Lillian Bibson. She was Dr. Adams's nurse, so I was very thankful she wanted to work for me. She has some great ideas and agrees with your idea on moving the storage closet." His enthusiasm was exhilarating. He was putting everything he had into the clinic, and he wanted it to succeed.

"Lillian is a great nurse. I hope you two won't butt heads with her telling you that Dr. Adams did it this way."

I was afraid to comment on Ashley. She was a good nurse, but I didn't like the idea of her working there.

"Yeah. I thought of that, but even if she does, maybe they will be some ideas I could use. I will take anything into consideration," he said.

"Do you think you will be ready to open September first?"

"I certainly hope so." He was beaming.

I loved to watch his face as he talked about the clinic. He was so proud of it and was anxious to get started. I hoped I could help as much as possible.

He continued on about the clinic, telling me about the new desks that would be arriving the next day. More equipment, an autoclave, and instruments were going to be arriving Friday.

"Lillian is going to be there Friday to see they get put in their right places. I don't think she trusts me."

I kissed him good-bye at his car and slowly walked into the house, waving to him as he drove down the road. It seemed like all we talked about was the clinic. He hadn't said anything about the weekend.

The next morning, I couldn't think straight. All I could think of was Ashley and Tony.

"Bobbie, are you all right?" Mary asked. "You have been sitting there, staring at that same chart for an hour now."

"An hour, huh? If you have been watching me sit here for an hour, that means you have not been doing any work for an hour, right?"

"Well, I guess you got me there. Are you ready to do rounds? It is six o'clock. I'm sure that doctor friend of yours will be upset if he doesn't get to see you tonight," she teased.

Tony had called and said the autoclave was delivered, but so were a lot of other things he didn't order, so he was going to stay and try to figure it out. Here it was Friday night, and I was alone. Marcia and Danny had gone out to eat with some friends from DC, so I decided to go to the clinic and see if I could help.

The weather was warm, so I rolled down the window and turned on the radio, singing with the songs I knew. I wished Tony was there, but maybe I could kidnap him and take a midnight ride. As I turned the corner, I saw the clinic door open and hoped maybe he was finished for the evening.

Before I could pull into the parking lot, Tony walked out of the door with the nurse, but it wasn't Lillian. It was Ashley. She was holding his arm, and they were laughing and having a good time. He opened the car door for her, and she kissed him on the lips, *my lips*.

I just sat there, not moving, just watching as she got in the car and drove off, waving as she went. The car behind me started honking, and I looked up in the mirror and noticed that I was blocking the road. I put the car in gear and saw Tony walking toward me. The car continued honking, and I looked at Tony and drove off.

Chapter Six

I drove until I couldn't drive anymore. I was exhausted. All I could think about was Ashley kissing Tony. The week before, he was in love with me, and this week, he was kissing Ashley. I didn't understand. I didn't want to be in love anymore. I hated being in love. I wanted my life back. I wanted to get up in the morning, go to work, and come home at night to spend time with Mother and Father. I didn't want Tony Juxton in my life anymore.

The louder I cried, the faster the car went until I saw blue lights in the rearview mirror. I pulled the car over to the side of the road and found my wallet. I pulled my driver's license out and had it ready when the cop came to the open window.

"Were you going to a race, Bobbie? Because if you were, I think you could win. Do you know how fast you were going?" The voice was Barry Williams, one of the deacons at church. "Are you okay? You look like you have been crying. Do you want me to take you home?"

"No, Barry. I'm fine. I just thought I would go for a drive, and I sure didn't mean to be speeding. How fast was I going?" I asked.

"Too fast. Now, you get on home before I call your father, and try to slow down. Okay?" he said.

"Okay," I said meekly.

He got back in his car and pulled out, driving on down the road. I put my license in my wallet and started the car, making a big U-turn in the middle of the road. I turned on the radio, but all it played was songs Tony and I had sung to, and I did not want to think about him. It was about two o'clock in the morning when I finally pulled into the driveway. I got out of the car and walked up the steps, and then I saw him. Tony was sitting on the porch swing.

"Hi," he said.

I didn't have anything to say to him, so I kept quiet. I was too angry and tired.

"Do I even get a trial, or do you just convict people with circumstantial evidence?" he asked.

"I saw you kiss her. Are you going to deny that?" I said angrily.

"No! You saw her kiss me. That I won't deny," he replied.

"There's a difference?" I asked.

"I would say there is a pretty big difference. You can't see that?"

"I just want to go in and go to bed. I'm tired. We'll talk about this in the morning." I turned to unlock the door but couldn't manage to get the key in the lock.

"Well, you can do that, but I will be right here when you get up in the morning. We need to talk about this now. I'm sorry we haven't been together as much as I have wanted to this week, and I am very sorry you saw Ashley kiss me. I promise I did not return the kiss, and I told her you were my girl," he explained.

He got up from the swing and stood beside me. The tears were streaming down my face, and I didn't know whether to believe him or not. He took my hand, and I let him lead me to the swing. We sat down, and he put his arm around me and pulled me close to him. Gently, he wiped my tears away and kissed me.

"I love you, Bobbie Jo Patterson," he began. "I have never said those words to another woman. I told you the other night that you are my girl, and until you don't want me around anymore, I am going to continue to be your man." He kissed me and held me tightly.

"I'm sorry, Tony. I don't like feeling like this. I feel so vulnerable and scared. What is happening to me? I have never been this way before. If this is what love does to you, Tony, I'm not sure I can handle it," I confessed.

"Let me handle it for you," he offered. "I promise no more Ashley or any other woman kissing me. I told her she needed to find another job. When I looked up and saw you sitting there and knew you had seen her kiss me, I thought I had lost you. I too felt vulnerable and scared. Here. I want you to have this. Every time you look at it, I want you to remember that you are my girl, my only girl."

With that, he took off his medical school graduation ring and handed it to me. It was even too big for my thumb, and we started laughing. Then he took me in his arms and kissed me again and again.

"Wait. I forgot this," he said, and he handed me a small, white box with a big, red bow on top. Inside was a beautiful gold chain. He took the chain and put it through the ring and then fastened it around my neck. I touched it, and smiled.

"Okay, Tony Juxton. I really am your girl now," I told him.

"If I had known that a ring and a gold necklace would seal the deal, I would have given it to you last week," he teased.

"Very funny," I said and leaned into him.

Lying in bed that night, I kept going over in my mind about Ashley kissing Tony. Why did they come out of the door with her arm around him, laughing? No, I can't do this. I touched the ring and remembered what he said about how every time I saw it, I was to remember that I was his girl.

On Saturday morning, as I finished my chores, I called Marcia to remind her of Mrs. Juxton's party. Actually, I needed to just talk to her. She and Danny arrived home late the last night from DC, so I waited until noon to call.

"Of course I am up, silly. I have twin two-year-olds. They get up at six o'clock in the morning every day, Sunday to Saturday." Marcia sounded sleepy. "We didn't get home until late. What's up with you? I can't wait to see you tonight. What are you going to wear?"

"I thought maybe I would wear those peach-colored culottes I bought at the mall. I really like them, and they are so comfortable. How about you? Are you bringing the twins?" I said.

"No. Danny's mother wants to watch them." She sounded relieved. "I have heard that anybody worth knowing is going to be at this party tonight. Do you have any inside gossip?"

"Sure I do. Danny, you, and me are going to be there. How about that?" I laughed at her.

"Okay. I'll get you for that. See you tonight," she said as she hung up the phone.

As we drove to the party, we noticed that there were so many cars that they had to hire some of the teenagers to park them. As Father handed one of the boys his keys, Tony came out of the house. He kissed me on the cheek, and he smelled so wonderful. He had just shaved, and his face was smooth. I didn't know the name of his aftershave, but I made a mental note to find out for Christmas gifts. I couldn't believe I was thinking like that. It was as if an alien had come and taken up residence in my body.

Tony escorted us in the house, where Mrs. Juxton was waiting for us. She had on a long, yellow dress with sunflowers. She was charming as she introduced us to everyone. She was having a grand time entertaining. It was fun to watch her as she captivated the guests. She treated each one in such a way that they felt they were the only one present. She was quite intriguing.

Marcia and Danny arrived a few minutes later. Marcia was fussing about how hard it is to care for three children, Danny being number three. He stuck out his lower lip, and she kissed it. Tony wanted to show Danny his 1965 candy-apple-red Mustang he had been trying to restore. As we entered the garage, I was amazed. The car looked brand new, with no scratches.

We left the boys in the garage and went back in the house just as Mrs. Juxton was introducing the governor of Ohio, and we clapped for him. He seemed quite embarrassed, stating that he had not come to campaign but to be entertained. With that, a piano could be heard from the back of the room. It was a beautiful sound. We couldn't see who was playing, but suddenly, the garage door opened and Tony came out, pushing his way through the crowd to the piano.

"You little hussy!" I heard him exclaim.

The piano stopped, and everyone was clapping. Marcia looked at me, and I shrugged my shoulders. Then Mrs. Juxton introduced her daughter, Rose, and her son-in-law, Rob Negate.

The people began chanting for her to finish the song, and she obliged, sitting back down with Tony at her side. The music was beautiful, classical jazz and even a little modern mixed in. Everyone was quiet until she finished, and then the room exploded in applause. Tony came through the crowd and introduced us to Rose.

After talking with us for a while, Mrs. Juxton ushered her back to the piano. Rose played for at least another hour, and no one moved or made a sound. Finally, she got up to take a break. Tony took my hand, and Marcia and Danny followed us as we went outside to the rose garden. In a little box by the fountain were several blankets, and we spread them on the ground to sit and talk.

We had a fun evening talking, laughing, and getting to know Rose and Rob. They were delightful. Rob never seemed to run out of jokes. Each time I thought he was being serious, another joke would come flying out of his mouth. They made a wonderful couple.

Finally, Mrs. Juxton found us and ushered us all inside to bid adieu to the guests. As the last ones drove off, Mother and Father said their good-byes and headed home. After Marcia and Danny left, we all went back outside to the rose garden. Tony pulled a lawn chair close for his Mom to join in. She was exhausted.

"That was an amazing party, Mrs. Juxton. Everybody will be talking about it for months," I said.

"Well, they will only be talking about it until the next one," she exclaimed. "Rose, you are a sly one, just like your dad. Tony, did you know she was coming?"

"I was as surprised as you. It was a nice surprise though. Thanks, sister dear. How long are you staying?" Tony asked.

"We are flying back tonight. Our flight leaves at midnight. I just had to come and see this quaint little town Mom has chosen. It is quite appealing. Everyone treated us like old friends. I have never met people like them. And this little lady," Rose said as she put her arm around me, "where in the world did you find her? She is an angel in disguise. You had better hang on to this one."

We drove Rose and her husband to the airport and watched until their plane was too small to see. We walked hand in hand through the terminal, and Catherine stopped and bought us a milkshake. As we sat, Tony kept slurping his shake, making it sound louder and louder. Finally, Catherine and I got up and just started walking away.

"Okay, okay. I will behave. Please come back. It is mighty lonely here," he said with big puppy dog eyes.

Finally, we came back and sat with him until we finished, and then they drove me home.

Chapter Seven

July and August were the hottest months on record, and the rainfall was far below average. Tony and I spent all the time possible together between work and getting the clinic set up. My BSN (Bachelor of Science in nursing) studies took a lot of my time, but it was only six more months until graduation. Tony was excited and kept hoping I would change my mind and work with him at the clinic. I assured him I was going to continue at Beautiful Gardens.

We learned a lot about each other, our likes and dislikes and even our favorite colors. Tony liked blue, and my favorite was yellow. Picnics were our favorite thing, and most of them were in the park. After eating, we would swing and try to get our swings as high as possible. We would laugh and kiss, and he would tell me he loved me.

I hadn't said anything about love. I wasn't exactly sure what I was feeling, and I felt I had better make sure before I went blurting something as important as, "I love you," without really meaning it. Tony showed me more each day that he loved me. At least two times a week, flowers were delivered at work, always two dozen red, long-stemmed roses. The girls were drooling each time they were delivered.

Tony did keep his promise that Ashley would not be working there. Lillian's daughter, Pam, had just lost her husband to cancer and came back to live with her Mom. She was slightly overweight with a very pretty face. Bonnie Jones and Jean Simmons were hired as receptionists, along with Joyce Carr for insurance and Kristy

Prince for payroll. Tony hired each one himself, interviewing them over and over until he made his decision.

September first, opening day, finally arrived. I called Tony to wish him luck and went to work hoping to see him that night. His schedule was full, and he was to start seeing patients at 9:30 a.m. I sent two dozen long-stemmed roses to the clinic, hoping they would be delivered before the first patient arrived. All day, I thought of how things were going and couldn't wait until the time I could clock out and see for myself.

Tony was sitting behind his desk with a pile of charts in front of him when I walked in. I hadn't bothered to change before coming over, so he must have thought I was one of the nurses and held out his hand, asking the name of the patient.

"Bobbie Jo Patterson," I said, laughing at him.

He looked up and smiled and came around his desk to hug me.

"I'm sure glad to see you. What a wonderful first day."

He went around and opened a drawer on the desk and opened a bottle of champagne he had on ice. There were two glasses on the bay window, so we sat down as he filled them.

"I was hoping you would come by and rescue me from all this paperwork. Everything went smoothly. Lillian and her daughter are both hard workers and reminded me today why I hired them. They were great," he boasted.

He went on about the clinic and the patients, being very careful not to break confidentiality. The schedule was full. He saw sixteen patients that day and even one little boy who had fallen in front of the clinic. After a lollipop that Lillian gave to each child, he was up and ready to go.

Lillian came in and notified Tony that they were leaving, and Tony offered her a glass of champagne.

"Lillian, please have a drink with us," Tony said. "If it weren't for you and your daughter, this day could never have gone so smoothly."

"No thank you, Dr. Juxton. We will see you in the morning."

"Good-bye, Lillian. Thanks for a great job!"

We talked a little longer, and then I decided I had better leave so he could finish his work. He seemed anxious to get back to it. I really was glad the first day was such a success. It was fun to watch him get excited about all the minute details of the clinic, but for some reason, I felt left out. He didn't ask about my day or anything concerning me. The clinic was the main topic of conversation between us, and it seemed to be the only topic.

Thanksgiving was only two days away, and I had a four-day weekend. Tony and Mrs. Juxton were coming to our house for lunch. Mother and I had been baking for weeks it seemed. Pumpkin, mincemeat, and apple pie aromas filled the house. Father put the leaf in the dining room table, and I laid the white plastic tablecloth on it. The ends were decorated with pumpkins, and I placed orange candles on the table for decoration.

As I set the table, I wondered about the next year and if I would ever be decorating my own table as Mrs. Tony Juxton. Those thoughts had been invading my thoughts for weeks. *What would it be like to be married to Tony?* I voiced those ideas to Marcia the night before.

"Oh, Bobbie Jo, I didn't think I would ever hear those words come out of your mouth. Has Tony said anything about marriage?" she asked.

"No. He has not even mentioned or hinted at it. Do you think maybe he doesn't want to marry me? He has been so busy with the clinic that I feel I have been kind of pushed to the side," I whined.

"Yes, I know the clinic is taking a lot of his time, but it can only get better," Marcia encouraged.

Leave it to Marcia to always be positive about things. As I finished setting the table, the doorbell rang. While Father answered it, I cut up the homemade bread. Tony and Catherine walked into the kitchen with a couple of surprise visitors: Rose and Rob.

"I hope it won't be an imposition for you if they stay. I just didn't want to cancel this dinner date, and I had nothing prepared," Catherine said sweetly. "I really just wanted to snoop at your recipes and see if I could pick up some new ones."

"Uh huh! A recipe thief! There is one in every crowd." Mother was laughing as she showed us each our spot at the table.

Father began his prayer, and Tony reached under the table for my hand. He was very attentive. I guess he just had a one-track mind. The clinic was just invading our lives too much, and I needed to figure out where I fit in.

The meal was excellent, of course. Mother is a great cook. Rose and I cleaned up while the men watched football and Catherine and Mother poured over recipes.

"How long will you be staying?" I asked.

"Only until tomorrow," Rose said. "I love popping in and surprising Mom. I'm sorry about all the extra work we caused for you and your family."

"It was great having you here. Thanks for coming," I told her.

"How are your studies coming? Tony says you are going to be graduating soon and then work at the clinic with him," she stated.

"He did, did he? We have been having this conversation for weeks, and I keep telling him I am going to continue working at Beautiful Gardens," I informed her.

After we finished, we joined the men in the front room. We inquired about the game and discovered that the men were cheering the team in black uniforms, so we decided to cheer for the team in blue uniforms. They looked at us like we were crazy, but we were enjoying ourselves and our team won. They acted as if it were our fault their team lost, so we decided to leave them in their misery.

Around eight, everyone left and we made plans to have Christmas at Catherine's house. She went on and on about how she celebrated Christmas, so the arrangements were made.

Our families were becoming one, and our relationship was growing stronger with each passing day.

On Christmas morning, the snow was falling, so I went to the window to watch it. It was 6:00 a.m., and already, the kids were up, sledding down the big hill. After some coffee, I thought I would find my sled and join them. I figured I could at least go down a couple of times.

With that thought in mind, I dressed and headed to the kitchen, where the coffee aroma led me. Mother and Father were already up, and I kissed them both on the cheek and poured myself a cup of hot coffee.

Oh, it smelled great. Mother had made some cinnamon rolls and was just taking them out of the oven when the phone rang.

I picked it up and said, "Merry Christmas."

Ann Smith, the director of nursing at Beautiful Gardens was on the phone. It seemed they only had three nurses in the whole building and eight CNAs. She sent the SUV to pick them up, but it couldn't make it down their roads due to the road conditions.

"Bobbie, I know you probably already have plans, but four of my nurses can't get in. The plows haven't had a chance to clear the back roads. Is there any way possible you can come in?" she pleaded.

"I'm on my way. I will get Father to bring me," I said.

Mother said, "Bobbie, we are supposed to spend the day with Catherine and Tony."

"I know, Mother, but the patients need someone to take care of them." I ran upstairs to get dressed and call Tony.

"I thought we were spending Christmas together? Why can't they find someone else to do it? You spend enough of your time there." Tony was actually angry with me.

"I beg your pardon, Dr. Juxton. This is my passion, just like the clinic is yours. If it is a little inconvenient for you to not have your way for Christmas, then I am just as sorry as I can be. Merry Christmas," I said angrily.

With that, I slammed the phone down and finished dressing. *The nerve of him, being upset. He spends twenty-four hours a day at his clinic, and if he isn't there physically, his mind is there.* I was so mad I could have spit nails.

Father drove me to work, and I started getting things organized. After the first medication pass, I helped bathe and dress the residents, trying to make them as presentable as possible. Family members were coming to visit, and the floor was buzzing with people. The CNAs worked as hard as they could to make it a Merry Christmas for the residents.

As I was wheeling Mrs. Thomas to the dining room, the elevator doors opened and Dr. Juxton stepped out. I nodded my head to him and walked on to the dining room. He followed me but didn't say anything. I put Mrs. Thomas in her place at the table and then went to the kitchen for her tray. Sandra, her daughter, took the tray and started feeding her.

Tony was standing in the middle of the floor, watching me. The staff, residents, and family members were all watching us.

"Bobbie Jo Patterson, I want to apologize for being such a jerk this morning," he began as loudly as he could.

Everyone quieted down, so he continued.

"I love you very much," he said, and then he got down on one knee in front of me and reached in his pocket, pulling out a little black box.

As he opened the box, the ring sparkled in the lights, with a one-carat diamond centered on five small ones. "Will you marry me, Bobbie? I want to be your husband, and I want you to be my wife."

When I looked at him, tears were flowing down his cheeks. I wasn't sure what to do until I heard everyone start chanting, "Yes, yes, yes."

"Yes." I said it so low nobody could hear it, and then I yelled, "Yes! Tony Juxton, I will be your wife. I love you."

The whole room burst into applause, and Tony picked me up and swung me around, kissing me. He put the ring on my finger, and it fit perfectly. We spent the rest of the afternoon putting people in bed, and finally, the roads had been cleared enough for the next shift to come in and Tony drove me home.

Rose, Rob, and Catherine had a surprise party for us. They were all waiting at the house. They had cake and punch, and Marcia and Danny even brought the twins. When we walked in the house, they all shouted congratulations, and Marcia started singing the wedding song, which, when everyone joined in, sounded like a cat fight, but I loved them all for it.

After we were stuffed to the max with cake, we all sat in the front room with calendars, trying to decide what day the wedding should be to accommodate everyone's schedule. No date seemed to work out, so Tony stood up and asked me when I wanted to get married.

After thinking about it for a minute, I said, "I have always wanted a June wedding, and, Father, do you think we could have it in the backyard? I don't want to upset Preacher Carr."

"If you want it in the backyard, then that is where it is going to be," Father assured me.

"Mother, I want to be married on your wedding day, June twenty-first, solstice. It looks like it is on a Saturday next year," I suggested.

So everyone agreed, and the wedding preparations began. You would have thought it was Marcia's wedding all over again. She was just like a little kid. Of course, she was going to be my matron of honor. She made a list of everything we could possibly need, and it kept getting longer and longer.

My BSN finals were four weeks away, and I stayed up late every night, studying. Tony helped me go over things and tested me on the things he thought were important, anticipating they would be on the test. I was so nervous, but he assured me it was going to be all right. Everyone was so encouraging, even the girls at work. The wedding preparations were on hold until after the test.

Marcia drove me to Columbus for the test, and when we walked in, the place was packed. I soon found a place and learned the procedure for taking the test. I was so nervous that I couldn't think straight. I rubbed my engagement ring, twisting it around on my finger, trying to remember what we had gone over.

As the time wore on, I was becoming more familiar with the questions, and the answers seemed to flow. This scared me because it had never happened before, but I figured, *What the hey? I am going to pass this test.* As soon as time was up, the computers turned themselves off and we were asked to leave the room. Marcia was waiting for me outside the door, and we found a nice restaurant to have supper before heading home.

"So how do you think you did? You were in there forever. I did some shopping though and found the most perfect wedding gown. We can go see it when we're finished if you want."

"Oh, wow! I should have known you would keep yourself entertained somehow. Yes, let's hurry and eat. I can't wait to see it."

Marcia paid the tab, and I hurried to the restroom. Then we took off, walking the two blocks to the boutique. When we found the store, we discovered that it closed at five. They had a beautiful wedding gown in the window that went way too low in the front, but I loved the way the sequins caught the light. We read the sign on the door that said they were closed on Sunday. We made plans to go the next Saturday to see the dress and maybe do some shopping.

Chapter Eight

The week seemed to crawl by, but finally, Saturday came. I was so anxious to see the dress that I made Marcia get up at five in the morning to drive to Columbus. We stopped at a little restaurant for breakfast and went over the wedding list. It kept growing, and I wondered how we were ever going to have everything ready by June twenty-first.

We found a parking place a couple of blocks away and walked to the boutique. It was February, so it was still cold, and I wrapped my heavy coat tighter as we walked into the wind.

The only one in the store was the owner, Bessie. She was delightful and eager to assist us. Marcia described the dress she had seen in the window only a week earlier, but it had been sold.

"About twenty-five brides have an order in for that dress. It is a Bessie Love original," she said, bowing down. "Let me see. Take your coat off and let's have a look at what we have to work with."

I took my coat off and laid it on a chair, and Bessie led us to a back room, where I stood naked except for my bra and underwear as she measured one way then the other. Each time she removed the tape measure from around me, she would exclaim, "Yes! Yes!"

She handed me a beautiful, white silk robe to wrap around me, and we went to her office. There, she sketched the most beautiful wedding gown I had ever seen. We were in awe of her talent. Not only could she create beautiful gowns, but her pencil sketches lined the walls of her office.

"Do you like?" she asked, holding it up for us to see. "I think it is perfect for you. I will have it ready in one month. Of course, you will have to come in for a few fittings in that month so it will be just right. I don't want your handsome groom to take a look at you and run. But, no, you are too beautiful for that. Now, these are the bridesmaids and maid of honor dresses I have in mind."

"They are beautiful. What's not to love? Thank you so much, Bessie." I was stunned. The wedding was actually coming together.

We set up appointments, and I put a down payment on the dresses. As we sat in the restaurant for lunch, we again looked at the wedding list. It might have gotten longer, but it was nice to check off one of the important items.

"That dress is perfect, Bobbie. Tony is not going to be able to say, 'I do,' because his mouth is going to be hanging wide open when he sees you," Marcia teased.

"In that case, maybe I had better not buy that one. I definitely don't want him not to be able to say, 'I do.'"

We stopped at the small flower shop in Fairville called Edie's, and the owner welcomed us with open arms.

"I was so hoping you were going to allow me to do the flowers for the wedding. It is the talk of the town. What are your colors?"

She took a sheet of paper and wrote everything down. "Sunflowers can be placed in your bouquet and, let's see, it is an outside wedding, so we will have them wound around the archway also. Blue and yellow will be beautiful. Blue ribbons and bows, and I will put yellow all in them. Oh, Bobbie, you have made my day. Thank you so much for coming to me for this most important day of your life. I feel honored to share it with you. I hope I can do you proud." With that said, she left us standing there, and, whistling a song, she went to the back of the shop to work on her ideas.

Marcia and I looked at each other, shrugged our shoulders, and went out to the car. We crossed *flowers* from the list. It still looked like a long, impossible list to fill, but at least two of the major things were off. Invitations needed to be ordered, so I called Tony while Marcia drove and told him about the flowers and my dress. He said he was going to the clinic to finish some paperwork, and I was to meet him there.

"Thanks, Marcia," I said, getting out of the car. "I'll see you tomorrow at church. Hello, Dr. Juxton. How has your day been?"

He was sitting at his desk, so I walked behind him and started massaging his neck.

"Your muscles are really tense. Here. Let me rub them for you."

He grabbed my arms and pulled me around, and I fell onto his lap. He lowered me to the floor, and his hands were all over me. I wasn't sure whether to fight him or enjoy it, but before I had to make that decision, he helped me up and looked at me rather oddly.

"I am so sorry, Bobbie," he said, pulling me to my feet. "I have been sitting here, thinking of you, and I am not sure I can wait until our honeymoon to make love to you."

"A cold bath will do you some good, my dear almost-husband. I will see you tomorrow at church. Pete Nelson is going to open his shop for us at one so we can decide on invitations. See you." With that, I walked out before I changed my mind.

It seems I had been having the same problem. Lately, Tony's kisses were hungry, more passionate too. I started thinking about the honeymoon, and then I started worrying.

I wasn't really a virgin, virgin, per se, but I had never really made love to a man either. A little petting was about the extent of my lovemaking knowledge, and it was really not much.

After the petting, what is supposed to come next? What if I don't please him?

I had no idea what turned a man on, so I went to the authority.

Of course, it was Marcia. She was the authority of almost everything. I found her in the front room, playing dolls with the twins. Melodie was the prince, and Harmony was the princess. They looked so cute, and all of a sudden, I got this funny urge to have a baby of my own.

Oh my goodness. That is what making love is all about.

Then I wondered what would happen if I didn't do it right and I couldn't have a baby.

"Hey, girl," Marcia said as I walked in the front room. "Girls, go get your nighties. Okay. What's up? You never come over this late at night without calling me unless something is wrong."

"Nothing is wrong. I just want to talk to you about some things," I began.

"Sex?"

Marcia said the word, and I think everybody in Fairville heard her. I was so embarrassed I put my finger to my lips to hush her.

"I'm right," she said knowingly. "I knew this would come up sooner or later. Okay. What happened? Did Tony start something you didn't want to finish?"

I told her about what Tony had said and about all my doubts. I just blurted it all out. I was so glad nobody could hear our conversation.

Marcia looked at me like I had just dyed my hair green and orange. "You aren't serious, are you? And I didn't know you and Jim did any petting either."

"I was so mad at him that night I just forgot about it, and then, the next day, at school, he announced he was leaving for another city. I was so relieved," I told her.

"Bobbie, everything is going to be fine. Tony loves you, and he will teach you whatever it is that turns him on. Every man is different, and every man is alike. I know that won't make any sense until after you've experience it. So you will just have to trust me. Are you afraid you won't be able to have a baby?" she asked. "That was one of my fears, but look at this," she said as the twins ran and jumped on her lap for bedtime stories.

"I love you, Marcia. See you later. Thanks!" I said and walked home.

Chapter Nine

In April, we gathered at the house around the dining table, addressing the wedding announcements. Both our parents had made guests lists, and we poured over them, adding and subtracting. Now we needed to get them ready to mail.

The invitations had sunflowers mixed with roses on the outer edge of them and simply stated:

Mr. and Mrs. Henry Patterson

Are pleased to announce the wedding of their daughter

Bobbie Jo Patterson

To

Dr. Anthony Michael Juxton

June 21st at 2:30 p.m.

The wedding will take place at 13341 Pine Road Fairville, Ohio

We would be most honored if you would take the time to celebrate this union of our children.

"Okay. What else is on that list of yours? What about a cake?" Tony asked.

Before I could speak, Mrs. Juxton said, "Oh, Bobbie, I make the loveliest wedding cakes. I would be honored if you would allow me to do this for you. I feel I am not contributing at all to this wedding."

"That would be great, Catherine," I told her. "Thank you so much for offering, but I'm afraid you will have too much on you just being a mother-in-law."

"Oh no. I have experience at that. Please, I would really like to make the cake. Come with me and let me show you something." And with that, she jumped up and went into the kitchen with me on her heels like a little puppy.

In the kitchen, I found her climbing on a ladder to reach something on the top shelf. The book almost fell, and I was worried she was going to be next. She set the book on the table and sat down beside me, opening the book, which showed page after page of beautiful wedding cakes she had made. There was no way I could tell her no.

I drove into Columbus the next Saturday for another fitting of my dress, and Marcia was fitted for hers. It was so much fun trying on the beautiful dresses and pretending to be getting married right in the shop.

As soon as the weather was warm enough, Father made a sidewalk up the middle of the backyard and then built a temporary altar, adding an archway at the front. He planted red climbing roses, and as they grew, they wound themselves around every board. They made the archway look as if it were an archway of roses. He worked on the back yard every night after work, and sometimes, I would come out and see what he had done. I was so proud of him for all the hard work. I loved him so much. He and Mother were wonderful parents, and I hoped they would continue that even after the wedding.

Father was sitting on the step, drinking his iced tea. "I can't believe my little girl is actually getting married," he said, pulling me close. "I love you, Bobbie Jo, and you will always be my little girl. I am very proud of you. Here you are, the almost-wife of a doctor, and you have worked so hard to earn your BSN degree."

"My BSN degree!" I shouted. "Father, I haven't heard anything from them. I have been so busy trying to plan this wedding that I haven't even thought about it. Wait a minute. Do you know something I don't know? Did I get a letter today?"

He was sitting there, grinning from ear to ear, nodding his head up and down and laughing. Out of his pocket he pulled the envelope from the Ohio State Board of Nursing. I was scared to death to open it, but Father handed it to me and I eagerly ripped the envelope open.

There in my hands, in black and white, was my degree. Oh, I couldn't believe it. I had actually done it. I jumped up and hugged Father and kissed him on the cheek and ran inside to tell Mother. Marcia was next, and we talked for hours.

"I got it!" I yelled into the phone. "I am now Bobbie Jo Patterson RN, BSN."

Tony was silent for a moment and then said, "You'll have to fill out an application and go through the hiring process like everybody else, but I will take you into consideration."

When I hung up I wondered if he was joking.

On Friday night, Tony picked me up at five o'clock. We both left work a little bit early. He had tickets to the new Broadway play in Columbus, and we had great seats. They were given to him by a patient. I wore my blue sundress with its polka-dot blue-and-white crop jacket. Tony was dressed in blue dress pants and a blue-and-white-striped shirt with matching tie. We looked quite the couple.

The play was exquisite, and we stopped at Maxie's cocktail lounge on the way home. Tony ordered a wine called Rose Petals and a cheese plate. I went to the restroom to freshen up. The piano was playing when I returned to my seat, and Tony got up and took me in his arms and led me to the dance floor. He held me tightly and pressed his body close. My head rested on his chest, and his heart was beating hard and fast. After the song, we went back to our table to enjoy the wine.

Tony took his glass and stood up, raising it in the air, and said as loudly as possible, "May I have your attention please?"

Everyone was watching him, and no one dared say a word. They probably thought he was a lunatic or drunk.

He continued, "I want to make a toast to this beautiful young lady. This young lady has just earned her BSN degree and is also going to be my wife. Please hold your glasses high and help me celebrate such a joyous occasion."

I could hear glasses clanking all around the room, and some of the patrons came to our table to toast us firsthand. I was hoping my glass wouldn't break. I'm sure at least a hundred people must have hit my glass. After that, the manager came to the table with two free dinner passes and told Tony, "Tonight's meal is on the house."

At the house, we sat on the porch swing. He put his arm around me and kissed me and told me thanks for not giving in to him the other day.

"The cold shower did the trick. I still want you, Bobbie, and if you have any doubts about you turning me on, forget it. All you have to do is be in the same room with me, and, well, we'll talk about this on our honeymoon."

At the end of May, Tony picked me up early, saying he had a surprise for me. I couldn't believe it when he pulled in at Mr. Thompson's old house a block away from my parents' home. I was so excited. Mr. Thompson unlocked the door, and I fell in love with it.

The foyer was huge with polished wood floors. To the left was the library with bookcases lining the walls. On the right was the kitchen with a cooking island in the middle and a separate dining nook off the side by a bay window. The dining room came off the back of the kitchen, and a door also opened into the foyer. The stairway came down from the right and the left of the foyer, leaving a huge space with a vaulted ceiling.

The balcony ran in front of the three upstairs bedrooms, each with their own full baths. The master bedroom was in the middle, and it too had a bay window and window box, and I could just picture getting up in the morning and having coffee there, looking out over the countryside.

It had a full basement that was recently carpeted and contained the laundry room. Tony talked about getting a pool table and dart board and making it his game room. I laughed and hugged him.

"It will only be your game room until the kids decide it is theirs," I reminded him.

"Hold out your hand," he said and gently took my hand and placed a key in it. "This is your wedding gift. I wanted to surprise you. I closed on it a week ago."

I was so surprised and a little disappointed too that he would not let me help with the decision of where we were to live, but I dismissed it from my thoughts, thinking only of how much he loved me and wanted to make me happy.

On the way home, Tony leaned over and kissed me, "I love you, Bobbie Jo. I just want to tell you over and over so you don't forget."

"I love you too, Tony," I said somewhat hesitantly.

Father and Mother came with us to look at the house again, and Father, knowing Mr. Thompson for a long time, asked questions concerning the plumbing, electric, septic system, and well. He and Tony walked through the house, examining each room thoroughly. Mother and I talked about decorating, of course.

"I have never had a house to decorate before, Mother. You will help me, won't you? And I am sure Marcia will have to put her two cents in also. This is going to be so much fun."

Mother looked at me and said sincerely, "Bobbie Jo, being married is not about having fun. It is about loving each other and putting the other one first before your needs and wants. Too many marriages end in divorce because one becomes selfish. You have to wake up each morning and fall in love with that man fresh and new each day. The troubles and heartaches will come, but if your love is strong, you can get through anything and everything."

Chapter Ten

June 21, solstice, was a wonderful day for a wedding. I picked that day because it was my parents' wedding anniversary. The sun was shining, and I got up early to walk around the backyard and admire all of Father's handiwork. Everything was perfect. Father came out with me, and we sat and drank our coffee in silence. There was too much to say to put anything in words, and we both understood what we were feeling. He hugged me, and then walked to the house to get ready.

As I walked in the house, I looked back at the yard, remembering all the years playing grown-up and pretending to walk down the aisle to meet my groom at the altar. Now it was real, and my dreams were coming true.

The music began, and Marcia's daughters slowly walked down the sidewalk Father had made in the backyard. Their dresses were long, blue, velvet gowns, and they entertained the crowd as they delightfully tossed red rose petals along the way.

Marcia gave me a kiss on the cheek and did the finishing touches on my veil. "You look gorgeous, Bobbie." Her dress matched the twins' dresses, and they all looked stunning as they waited for the bride at the altar.

The bride… That was me. I was shaking and so nervous I couldn't think straight. *The bride! Wow! I am actually going to be Mrs. Dr. Tony Juxton's wife.*

My father stood at my side and held his arm out for me. I held on tight.

"I love you, Bobbie Jo. You have never looked more beautiful," he said with a tear in his eye.

The trumpets sounded at the beginning of the wedding march, and I kissed Father on the cheek and placed the veil over my face. I felt like a princess, and when we entered the backyard and started on our way down the sidewalk, our friends and relatives rose to their feet and smiled.

My eyes were on Tony. He looked so handsome in his white, three-button notch lapel tuxedo with a blue satin shirt and white bowtie. Rob was standing next to him in his blue velvet tuxedo. Tony had an "I love you" smile on his face.

We sure had come a long way in a year. I thought about how we met and that first day sitting in the rose garden at church. Then I thought of the park and that first kiss and how scared I had been. The clinic opening and obtaining my BSN degree were two accomplishments last year, but getting married one year after we met was like *wow*. There was just no other way to describe it.

On my birthday, June sixth, Tony had taken me to the park for a picnic, and when we had finished eating, he got down on one knee and asked me again if I would marry him. He did not want there to be any doubts. He gave me a beautiful set of tanzanite earrings and a necklace to match. I put my hand up to touch them as they lay around my neck.

As we slowly made our way down the sidewalk, I saw Mother crying, and I looked at her just in time to see her mouth the words *I love you*. She was fantastic. She had made sure everything was ready for that day, and Catherine did, indeed, make the cake. It had three tiers, and the top was full of red roses.

Preacher Carr asked who was giving the bride away, and I heard Father reply, "Her Mother and I," and then he linked my arm in Tony's and sat down next to Mother. Tony took my arm and gently held it. Preacher Carr went on with the ceremony, but honestly, I wasn't sure how much I really heard. I was thinking about Tony and our honeymoon.

We had decided to fly to Hawaii for our honeymoon. Catherine, Rose, and Rob gave us the trip as a wedding present. My bags were packed, and Marcia and I had gone shopping for a few new things to wear.

Marcia bought me a red lace nightie that had less material than a handkerchief. She told me not to worry about it because I wouldn't be wearing it long. Another pep talk and I was ready for anything, or at least that is what I kept telling myself.

It was my turn to say something, and I heard Preacher Carr say my name.

"Bobbie, repeat after me."

I repeated, or I hope that is what came out of my mouth. I really wasn't too sure. Tony then repeated his words, and the two wedding rings were handed to Preacher Carr from Marcia and Rob.

Preacher Carr told the story of the ring and how it is a symbol with no beginning and no end. They represented God and his love for us, and our marriage too should have no end. Finally, he asked the audience if there was any reason why we should not be married and then said, "This ring symbolizes not only Tony and Bobbie's love but Jesus's love for us. It has no ending and no beginning." He then said, "I now pronounce you man and wife. Tony, you may kiss the bride."

Tony did not need a written invitation. He grabbed me, lifted my veil, and laid one on me that was almost embarrassing. "I love you, Mrs. Juxton."

We then walked hand in hand back down the sidewalk, and the people greeted us and congratulated us. I think the whole town was there. The backyard was packed with people. After the greetings, we stood for what seemed like hours, getting all the wedding photos taken and retaken and retaken. I was exhausted.

Marcia helped me change into a white sundress. Downstairs, I found my husband dancing with Catherine in the backyard. After the dance, he told the band to play a nice, slow song. He bowed in front of me and held out his hand.

"May I be the first to dance with my lovely wife?"

I curtsied and then took his hand. He led me to the middle of the yard and held me tight as we danced like two lovers who could not get enough of each other. Our feet were floating, and I know we had angel wings on our backs because our feet never touched the ground.

The beautiful cake was cut, and we fed each other before Rob, Danny, and Tony had a cake fight. Catherine shook the knife at them and told them to behave, and Marcia grabbed Danny's ear and drug him inside. We were all laughing so hard. There was cake everywhere, but Catherine was laughing too. It was such a wonderful time of everybody being together.

I threw the bouquet, and Melodie caught it. Marcia took it away from her and said, "Young lady, you are not going to be married anytime soon."

Melodie was so upset that Marcia finally gave it back to her, and she and Harmony ran outside, pretending to be married. Someday, they would both be beautiful brides.

Tony and I grabbed our bags and headed to the car, trying to give our information to our parents in case of an emergency. The car had been decorated with shoe polish announcing "Just Married" on the back window. A string of cans was attached to the back bumper. Everyone jumped in their cars and followed us through town, honking their horns. People standing on the street corners waved and whistled and shouted, "Congratulations," as we drove by.

At the airport, we barely made our plane. We found our seats, and Tony put our luggage in the bin over us. I took the window seat and was shaking with excitement. I had never been on a plane, and I wasn't quite sure what to expect. Tony held my hand and kissed me, telling me how much he loved me. The stewardess stood in front, showing us how to fasten our seat belts, showing the exit doors, and explaining the oxygen masks. Finally, the captain was heard over the speaker to welcome us aboard and explain the flight details. He had a very smooth, reassuring voice, and I wondered if that was a qualification for a captain.

The plane's engines were running, and the sound filled the plane, making it impossible to talk. As the plane started moving down the runway, my heart beat faster and faster. Suddenly, I felt weightless as the big, huge plane lifted up off the ground. My ears popped, and I laughed. I loved it. It was an awesome feeling.

The flight seemed short to Dallas, Texas, and then from there, we had a twelve-hour flight to Hawaii. At the airport, we found the gate for our next flight and then sat down for a snack at one of the restaurants. The airport was huge, and I was worried about missing our flight, so we walked back to the gate and sat there, watching the planes land and take off.

When they announced our flight, we got our carry-on bags and walked to the ticket agent. She took our tickets and stamped them, and then we walked down the long hallway to the plane. Once again, we found our seats and Tony let me sit by the window. The stewardess did her thing, and the deep-voiced captain gave his speech, and I think we had the same captain because he too had the same soft, reassuring voice. That time, I knew what to expect at takeoff, and I waited anxiously for it. I was not disappointed.

Hawaii was absolutely beautiful. We were met at the airport by two natives, a man wearing shorts and a tank top and a very beautiful girl with long, black hair wearing a grass shirt and coconut bra. She could sure shake those hips. Of course, when I tried it, everyone started laughing. They put beautiful leis over our heads made from plumeria flowers grown there. They had the most beautiful smell, and I thought of Catherine and how much she would love them.

Tony found the car rental booth and finally arranged for a car for the week. A week didn't seem like very long to spend alone with my new husband, but I was determined to make every minute count. We found the resort, and a gentleman came to the car to park it for us, and another was there to carry our baggage. Inside, the place was simply gorgeous with high ceilings, and only native Hawaiians worked there. They were very nice and practically granted our every wish.

A beautiful girl named Beth showed us to our room, and the balcony (*lanai*) looked out over the ocean, and the sun was just beginning to set. Tony grabbed the camera, and we watched as the red, yellow, and green lights brightened the sky and then the water and then faded away as it set. "The legend goes that if you see the green flash of the sun just before it sets in behind the horizon, it is good luck," she said.

The room was rather large. It had a kitchen and two bedrooms and two bathrooms. After making love, we took a nice, hot shower together, enjoying the intimacy. I never knew it could be so wonderful. Afterward, we got dressed and took a walk.

We found a sidewalk running all along the ocean and followed it, walking hand in hand. It was lit, and many other people were walking or jogging on it. Everyone was very friendly, and we stopped and talked to quite a few of them.

The next day, after our shower, we found a cute little bagel shop downstairs at the resort. Beth was there, and she gave us a map of things we might be interested in seeing. We sat outside on the picnic table and watched the sun come up. The birds were singing, and there was the scent of flowers everywhere. The air was so fresh and clean.

We toured the island of Hawaii that day, shopping at different shops and window-shopping at others. We ate at a local restaurant. The food was delicious. We had our bathing suits under our clothes, so we put our blanket on the sand and went to walk along the beach. The water was the prettiest blue. It was so blue it looked like somebody had dumped millions of gallons of blue dye in it.

There were a lot of people swimming, so we dove in and raced to the buoy. Tony, of course, beat me and helped pull me up on the floating dock. We were the only ones on it until a couple of teens made their way up, so we dove off and swam back to shore. It was such a nice, relaxing time.

We went souvenir shopping the next day and found some cute earrings for Marcia, some Hawaiian dresses for the twins, and a shirt for Danny that read, "My Friends Went to Hawaii and I Got This T-Shirt." On the back, it said, "Wow." I bought Mother a beautiful shell necklace and a silk robe. Tony bought Rob and Rose lookalike Hawaiian shirts, and he liked the shell necklace so much he bought one for Catherine.

Our week was going by fast, but we were having a great time. I called home every night, sometimes forgetting the time difference. My parents were both okay and couldn't wait to hear all about our trip.

Every evening, we would walk along the ocean, watching the sunset; and on our very last night there, we watched the sun as it slowly sank into the water, and suddenly, there was a bright green flash of light seconds before the sun disappeared. We couldn't believe we had actually seen the green flash. Everybody around us started clapping and dancing. It was some kind of good luck to experience it, and now we were part of it. We danced with them until we were too tired to walk back to the resort.

We knew it was our last night there, and we wanted to make the best of it. I went to the bathroom and changed into the red nightie Marcia had given me. I hoped Tony would like it. I combed my hair and walked out. Tony looked at me and was actually speechless. He grabbed me and gently laid me on the bed. In the morning, I woke up to find my red nightie on the floor beside me and remembered Marcia's words: "Don't worry about it because it won't be on long."

Everybody was at the airport when we arrived home. Mother and Father, Marcia, Danny, and the twins, and Catherine came to welcome us home. We hugged and kissed and then drove to our new house. We hadn't had much time to do anything with it, but we hauled our suitcases upstairs to our bedroom.

Danny and Marcia stopped for pizza, so we sat down on a blanket from Tony's car to eat. Paper plates and plastic forks were passed around, and I found some paper towels for napkins. We gave everyone their gifts after we ate and talked about the trip. Tony showed the pictures we had taken, and we told them the story of the green flash.

"I have heard of the green flash," Danny said. "We studied it in school. I think it is supposed to be good luck if you see it."

"After we saw it, all the people around us started dancing and singing, and they too said it was good luck."

We were both exhausted from the trip, so after saying good-bye to everyone, we headed upstairs to our bedroom. We blew up the air mattress Danny gave us and made up the bed with some of our wedding gifts. The next day, the furniture was supposed to be delivered, and we needed to open the rest of our gifts; but for then, we lay down on the air mattress and, tangled in each other's arms, fell right to sleep.

Chapter Eleven

The furniture delivery truck came at eight the next morning, and I rushed down the steps, trying to dress as I ran. Two big, burly guys were standing there, eyeing me when I opened the door. They showed me their invoice, and I showed them where everything was supposed to go.

Tony came downstairs, sleepy-eyed, and said he was going to the store to get a couple cups of coffee and some donuts and kissed me on the cheek.

"A captain is supposed to go down with the ship. You are abandoning your crew." I laughed at him.

"Yeah, but my first mate is a mighty fine sailor, and I have confidence she can handle the job." He said this in his best pirate's voice and then got in his car and left.

The men were very efficient and handled everything with care. The furniture was exactly what we had chosen, and everything looked great. I signed the papers as "Mrs. Tony Juxton," and it felt great. I wanted to write it over and over.

Tony returned with the coffee, and we had just enough time for a couple sips before the next moving van pulled into the drive. This was supposed to be our bedroom suite, so I took the men upstairs to explain to them where everything was supposed to be. Tony took the air mattress downstairs to let the air out and take it back to Danny.

In the meantime, our wedding gifts had been placed in one of the extra bedrooms. Tony helped write people's names down with the gift so we could send thank-you cards. We were both happy to see a coffee pot with two big mugs.

It seemed everyone in town had given us a gift because the room was full. We had toasters, china, sheets, silverware, and money. We unwrapped until we decided we had better get something to eat. Mother had invited us over for lunch, but the next delivery truck was due at any time, so she and Father brought lunch over for us. Mother wanted to see all the new things, and we walked from room to room, discussing ideas of how to decorate.

The next day, Tony was up early and had coffee waiting on me when I could finally tear myself away from the bed. He said he needed to get back to the clinic. It had been two weeks, and even though Dr. Joe from the hospital had been covering for him, he needed to resume his position. I kissed him good-bye, and we made plans for him to come home for lunch. I sat down with another cup of coffee when the phone rang.

The furniture for the spare bedroom would not be delivered until the next day, and when I hung up, I was very grateful for the broken rear axle of their truck. I had a whole day to myself. I took my shower and then unpacked the rest of the gifts, being very careful to write down the names of the givers and the presents.

Two hours later, Marcia came strolling in with the twins. They marched to the backyard with their new toys and were running and jumping.

"Someday, that will be your children out there," Marcia said proudly.

"Yeah. Maybe someday," I said.

She helped me finish the gifts, and then we had a minute to sit and talk.

"How is everything with the good doctor?" she asked.

"Fantastic. We had such a wonderful time in Hawaii. I didn't want to leave. He went to the clinic this morning, but he's coming home for some lunch. Let's get together Saturday for a cookout. We can have it in the backyard. It will be our first party. Come here. I want to show you this huge cook stove Catherine gave us. Tony loves to grill out."

While we were making arrangements for Saturday, Tony came in, kissed me, and asked what was for lunch. Marcia laughed and took the twins by their hands and skipped to her car.

"What is so funny?" he asked, looking perplexed.

"You are my handsome husband. Come on in the kitchen and I'll make you a sandwich," I told him.

He grabbed me and started kissing my neck and running his hands over the front of me. I guessed lunch was going to wait. He picked me up and carried me to our room.

After he left, I showered and walked to my parents' house. It seemed so funny that it was no longer my home, but it was great to share a home with Tony.

Mother was in the kitchen, trying to find her lasagna recipe. She said Preacher Carr and Sandy were coming for dinner. I helped her prepare everything and mopped the floor, taking out the trash, and then went back home to my mess.

On Monday, I went back to work. I was so thankful to be out of the house. I needed a break. A couple new CNAs were starting that day, so I assigned them to my best CNA, Vera. She had been on Two Main since I went to work as an LPN, and once they had asked her if she would move to another floor, she told them flat out, "No."

Ann told me about the nurses' meeting at two, so I figured I had time to do some of the treatments. I needed to check on Ms. Maxine's decubitis on her left hip. I had been gone way too long.

She was bedridden and only weighed ninety pounds, and that was probably stretching it. I gently turned her over and loosened the bandage. The area was small and clean looking, so I measured it and placed a dry, sterile bandage on the area after cleansing it with normal saline.

Everyone was already at the meeting when I walked in the room, and Ann had just walked to the platform and announced she was retiring.

"I have worked here from the beginning. Some people claim I dug the first hole to start construction on this building, but I can assure you I did not. I just want to thank each and every one of you for forty years of service. You have all been wonderful, and again, I say thanks."

Ann was one of the most compassionate nurses I had ever met, and her leaving would definitely put a void in this place. Before Ann left the platform, she introduced the new administrator, Jeb Hardy. He was a big man, probably over six feet tall, with blond hair and blue eyes. He was maybe ten years older than me and very distinguished looking in his navy blue suit.

As he began his speech, I felt he was talking directly to me, the way his eyes kept searching for mine. His voice was very kind yet demanded attention, and I couldn't help but hang onto every word. He was saying that he would do everything he could to make Beautiful Gardens live up to its name. He was going to personally meet and talk to each employee and hopefully obtain some ideas from them. After the meeting, a small party was given for Ann's retirement and for Jeb Hardy.

Ann took me aside and hugged me. "You have been such a blessing to me, and I have thoroughly enjoyed watching you grow as a person into a wonderful, caring nurse. I want you to apply for the director of nursing position."

I thought she was kidding, so I kind of laughed it off, but she took my arm and said, "I am very serious, Bobbie. You would be a very good D.O.N. You know the ins and outs of this place, and you are so well organized. I want you to be my successor. Please go home and talk to Tony about it."

"Think about it," she had said. *How could I not think about it? What a privilege to have the opportunity to follow in Ann's footsteps. I never dreamed of being anything more than a floor nurse or a unit manager, but this wasn't a dream. Ann sincerely thinks I can handle the job.*

That night, I couldn't wait until Tony got home. Finally, around seven, he came in and I told him the news. I was so excited I could barely get the words out.

"What?" he shouted. "You have got to be kidding, Bobbie. Do you know how much of your time it would take up? Being a DON will consume you. I thought you were happy just being a unit manager."

I felt as if he had just punched me in the stomach and all my air had been driven out of me. If he had slapped me in the face, it could not have hurt as badly. I was so hurt I couldn't say anything.

"We'll talk about this later. Is supper ready?" He changed the subject, putting his arms around me to escort me into the kitchen to hasten the meal.

That night, when we went to bed, I feigned a headache, so he rolled over and went to sleep. I was so empty and hurt inside. The opportunity of a lifetime was being handed to me, and I felt like I was not allowed to accept it.

The next morning, Tony left for work and the subject was never mentioned. I went to work feeling defeated, like it was something bad. It was not bad. It was good, very good. All he kept talking about was my quitting and working at the clinic with him. *Work for him.* Now those words just went all over me. I was not just some paid help. I was his wife. I was not going to work for him.

———

Jeb Hardy called me into his office. I wasn't exactly sure what was going on, but I remembered him saying he was going to meet with all the staff for their input. His office had been remodeled with dark-and-light-blue-intermingled carpet that sank when I walked on it. He was sitting behind his big desk when I entered and came around holding his hand out to me.

"Please come in, Bobbie. I am very pleased to meet you. We have been discussing your floor, and I must say the numbers are quite impressive. It seems Two Main has the lowest number of pressure areas and falls. I also hear there is a waiting list just for this floor."

He ushered me to a chair when I noticed Ann sitting behind the door. She nodded and winked, and Jeb continued.

"Ann has been telling me how you started here as a CNA and have worked up to a unit manager. I understand you have recently obtained your BSN degree also. It just so happens that I am in need of a DON, and Ann seems to think you are the best qualified. Actually, she thinks you are the only qualified applicant."

I wasn't sure what to say, so I just sat there. Jeb was so easy to listen to with his smooth voice. I was taking it all in, but then I remembered Tony and his being so against it. I felt like I was between a rock and a hard place.

Jeb handed me an application and said that an AD would be placed in the paper and he would try some inside interviews, but he pretty much had his mind made up. "This is not to leave this office though," he quickly added.

Outside the office, I hugged Ann and told her thank you and then went upstairs to finish up some paperwork before heading home. My mind was full, and I had no idea what to do. Jeb and Ann had already made up their minds, and, somehow, I was going to have to get Tony to change his.

Chapter Twelve

A whole month went by with Tony and I being at odds. We barely spoke, and we slept on separate sides of the bed. One Saturday morning, I woke early and went downstairs to make coffee. I thought about what I should do. I just wanted him to listen to me, even though he already had his mind made up that I was not going to be DON. I couldn't understand why he was so against it and would not even talk to me about it. I think that was the worst part of it.

Tony came downstairs, and I poured him some coffee. He took my hand and turned me around. "I can't stand living in the same house with you and not touching you and talking with you. We have got to work this out. I'm sorry I have been so upset with you. I should have sat down with you and discussed this whole thing with you. I really am sorry. I am new at this husband thing, but I promise I will get better. Tell me about this position."

I sat down at the table across from him. I explained that Ann was retiring, and she thought I was the best qualified applicant. Even Jeb thought so and brought me to his office to encourage me to take the position.

"Wait a minute. Who is Jeb?" Tony asked.

"He is the new administrator. Mr. Jones left when his wife died. Anyhow, Ann and Jeb have been so encouraging and confident that I could handle the job. Yes, it would be a lot of work, but I really think I could make a difference there. Ann is going to train me before she leaves."

I knew I was talking too much, but now that he was listening, I wanted to tell him everything. I didn't want to leave anything out. "It will require a lot of my time, just as the clinic requires your time, but this is something I really want to do," I included.

"I guess my biggest problem is I was trying to make you like Mom," he finally said. "When Dad had his practice in Texas, she was there every day, doing the bookkeeping or checking people in, whatever needed to be done that day. I'm sorry. I just always hoped you would come to work with me and be by my side. I never dreamed I would have a wife with her own mind and desires. If this is what you really want to do, Bobbie, then by all means go for it. I do not want to stand in your way. I am your husband, and I want to encourage you, not hinder you."

I thought I was going to fall off my chair, so I held on to the table. The tears started flowing, and he got up and kneeled down in front of me with a napkin and wiped them off. I hugged him and told him I loved him, and he picked me up and carried me back to bed.

We had dinner at Marcia's house that night. The guys were watching TV while we cleaned the dishes. The twins kept running in and out, so Marcia told them if they didn't behave, they would have to go to bed.

I told Marcia about the DON position, and I was shocked when she said, "Bobbie, you've got to be kidding. Why on earth would you take that position now that you are married? What did Tony think about it?"

Never had Marcia Sedders turned against me until now. All I could do was stand there and look at her. She had not only upset me, but she hurt me to the core. She made me feel like I was abandoning my marriage.

"Marcia, this is a great opportunity for me to do something wonderful, to make a difference there. I can't believe you are acting like I am doing something wrong," I told her.

"It is wrong, Bobbie, and you know it. Your place is with your husband, not in some career. You are married now, and that changes everything. You belong to him now, not the nursing home. It's about time you got out of there before you become one of the patients," she announced.

I was so upset I couldn't say anything else. I went to get Tony and told him I needed to leave. He looked at me strangely and said, "Okay."

Marcia followed us to the car. "I'm sorry, Bobbie. I have to tell you how I feel or I am not much of a friend."

On the way home, Tony asked me what happened, and I told him Marcia's reaction to my taking the position. He didn't say anything, so I knew that he had not changed his mind. He just gave in. I was determined right then that I was going to prove them both wrong. I was going to be the best DON Beautiful Gardens had ever had, and I was going to be the best wife also.

On Monday, I met with Jeb Hardy in his office and applied for the position. He said he had only one other applicant from inside, but he would not tell me who. The AD was to go in the paper that day, and I was afraid they would find somebody more qualified.

Tony never asked if I got the position. It was like I had never said anything about it. We just went on with our lives on the outside, but on the inside, we were growing further away.

Two months passed, and Jeb called me to his office and handed me a key. I followed him to the next office. The key fit, and when we walked in, there was a plaque on the desk that read "Bobbie Juxton, RN, BSN, DON." All the administrative staff was in there, and Jeb led me to my chair, a big, brown, overstuffed chair that sucked me in when I sat on it. The office had been remodeled, and it was beautiful. Ann was there, ready to train me, and my director of nursing career began.

The only trouble was I was not in the least bit happy. My marriage was falling apart, and the only thing that gave me any pleasure at all was my new position, which seemed to be the center of all the problems. I just didn't understand. I had no idea what to do about it, and I had no one to talk to.

I hadn't called Marcia since that night she betrayed me, and yes, that is exactly what I called it. My best friend turned against me. How could she? I was so angry with her that at church, we sat on the opposite side instead of in our usual places. Mother and Father had even turned against me and sided with Tony. Everybody seemed to think that Tony had the only say in this marriage. Somehow, that had gotten all twisted up.

Around the middle of November, Tony was called to the hospital for an emergency. After he left, I was hugging the toilet, puking my guts out. It was the third morning I had woken up sick as a dog. I sat there and tried to figure out why people compare getting sick with a dog, but right then, it didn't really matter. I was sick. There was a virus going around, and two or three of my nurses had called out sick the last couple of days. I hoped that was what it was, but I knew deep down that it wasn't. I had missed the last couple of months' menstrual cycles, but I hadn't told anyone, especially Tony.

After I got up from the floor, I showered and dressed. I was going to make coffee, but as soon as I smelled the grounds, it made me sick and I made a mad dash to the trash can. I found some saltine crackers and sat at the table, eating, and drank some cold water.

How in the world was I going to go to the pharmacy and get a pregnancy test without the whole town knowing before I could tell Tony? It was still early, but I decided to drive to Columbus. I could go shopping too while I was there. Tony's birthday was coming soon, so I could pick something out for him. I wished I could call Marcia, but she hadn't called to apologize, and I refused to call her. I couldn't believe she was being so hard headed about this whole thing. She was supposed to be my best friend.

The little pharmacy carried three types of pregnancy tests, so I bought all three. I decided I would rather be sure than make a fool out of myself. As I paid the cashier, I happened to see movement out of the corner of my eye, and when I turned my head, there stood Jeb Hardy. I wanted to just die right then and there. The cashier handed me my receipt and my bag.

"Hi, Bobbie. What brings you to Columbus today?" he asked charmingly.

"I just thought I would do a little shopping today." I hoped he had not seen what I had purchased. If he did, he didn't say anything.

"There is a little restaurant around the corner. Come on. I'll buy you lunch," he offered.

"That is so sweet of you, but I think I will just head on home." I was anxious to get home before Tony so I could do my three tests.

"Come on. I promise I will not bore you with work."

He kept his promise. Work did not enter the conversation, not even once. He was very charming and talked a little about himself.

"I am originally from California. I moved to Ohio about ten years ago after my divorce and found the people to be quite friendly, so I stayed. I moved to Fairville when Larry Greenfield asked me to be administrator of his new nursing home he had just purchased. I was intrigued by the name, so I came and visited and made my decision to join the staff."

Our sandwiches came, and I couldn't believe how hungry I was. I was ravenous. I ate my entire sandwich and wished I had another, but I didn't want to be impolite.

"I guess I had better walk you back to your car so you can finish shopping," he said as he went to find the cashier.

At my car, he thanked me for having lunch with him and hoped maybe we could do it again sometime. As I drove home, I thought about Jeb and how understanding he seemed to be. For the last two months during my training, he overlooked my mistakes, and if there was another way of doing something that was easier or more efficient, he would take me to his office and explain it patiently to me until I thoroughly understood it. He was a great boss, and I really enjoyed having lunch with him to get to know him better.

When I finally made it home, I was so thankful Tony was not there. With my bag of pregnancy tests in hand, I made a beeline for the upstairs bathroom and, one by one, watched as the test strips turned blue. I was definitely pregnant. Blue meant positive according to the directions on the box. *Great. I'm not really ready to be a mother. I want to wait a couple of years until I'm well established in my career. Now Tony wants me to quit and stay home to be a full-time mother. Sure, I want kids, but just not now.*

I found the phone book and called Dr. Hansen, my GYN doctor, for an appointment. She was booked for a couple of weeks, but then the secretary found an opening, and I made my appointment.

After supper, I told Tony about the tests. He picked me up and then gently put me back down, patting my belly.

"I can't believe you are pregnant already. It will be great to have a son or a daughter. I don't care as long as they are healthy. Have you told your parents? We need to find you a good OB/GYN doctor and get you an appointment." He was so excited. It had been a long time since he was this happy.

I told him I had already made an appointment with Dr. Hansen. She had been my gynecologist for years. He wanted to call Catherine, but I told him it would be better if we went over there and told her firsthand and then drive to my parents' house.

Catherine hugged us and patted my flat stomach. She was so happy. She called Rose and Rob and put them on speakerphone so we could hear their reaction. Both of them congratulated us and asked when I was due. Since the boxes don't give you this information, I could not tell them anything except there were three positive pregnancy tests. I assured them I had an appointment with Dr. Hansen on Thursday.

My parents responded about the same way. I had never heard my father talk baby talk before, but he got on his knees in front of my chair and patted my flat stomach, telling the baby he was "Gwampa." I just looked at him like he had gone mad and thought maybe we should call for an ambulance. Mother asked if I had thought of names, and I told her I just found out that day so I hadn't really thought of anything except telling Tony and them. Really, all I had been thinking was, Great. Now Tony will want me to quit my job and stay home to raise babies.

Chapter Thirteen

Dr. Hansen confirmed the three pregnancy tests, and now I could proclaim to the world that I was pregnant. Proclaim was not quite the idea that came to my mind though. I waited every day for Tony to tell me I was finished with my career.

At Christmas, both families met at our house for dinner. Thank goodness for Mother and Catherine. They prepared the whole meal and even cleaned up afterward. I wasn't able to even lift my head from the pillow. After they left, Tony kissed me good night, saying that someone was waiting for him at the clinic. He did give me my present before he left, and when I opened it, I found a big, blue, fuzzy robe. Merry Christmas.

I was getting bigger and bigger and started waddling when I walked. I picked out which room would be best for the nursery, and every night after work, I could be found there. I painted it bright yellow and stenciled farm animals on the walls because at my first sonogram, they told us it was definitely a boy, and he wasn't shy in letting us know. I immediately named him Michael Henry and talked to him constantly. One of the books I purchased stated that the baby can recognize his mother's voice even while in the womb.

I was a frequent visitor at the town library and sat for hours, reading about babies and delivery and how to take care of them when they wake you up, screaming with colic. I really was getting excited, but I had the feeling I was going to raise him all alone.

Tony was spending more and more time at the clinic and making hospital rounds. He was up at four every morning and didn't come home until ten or eleven at night. We never talked unless it was to answer a question, and our lovemaking had simply disappeared since I became pregnant. He barely pecked me on the cheek when he walked out the door, and I wondered if he still loved me, and if I still loved him.

Going to work was the highlight of my days. I loved my job, and I was good at it. The CNAs were doing a wonderful job, and the nurses pitched in to help. We met weekly to discuss things they thought was important and make the necessary changes.

One day, sitting at my desk, going over the report sheet for the day, I discovered that the floors were short staffed almost every day by at least three CNAs. Their main excuse was they had no one to watch their children. Almost immediately, an idea started formulating in my head. *Why couldn't we have a day care center?* There was an empty storage room downstairs that would be perfect. I went to Jeb's office to run the idea past him.

Jeb was very receptive of the idea. We worked for hours trying to put it on paper to present it to the board. I was so excited and anxious to get started. It would be my baby in that day care too. Arrangements were made for Jeb and me to meet with the board on Thursday at ten.

"This is a great idea, Bobbie. I know a lot of companies that have opened their own day cares, and they have proven very beneficial. Let's hope this one does too. I want to see the storage room you have in mind and maybe do some measuring." Jeb was so encouraging. He took the idea and ran with it, yet he made sure the credit was given to the right people.

We found the storage room locked, so Jeb had to find the key on a ring of about a hundred different keys. We were laughing as he tried one after the other and, finally, one fit the lock. The room was dusty, and I sneezed as I walked in.

"Maybe you shouldn't be coming in this nasty room. I wouldn't want anything to happen to you and that precious baby."

He said it in such a way you would have thought the baby was his. I was stunned that he would care so much.

"I'm fine. Look at this mess. Where in the world did all this equipment come from? Is any of it worth keeping?" I asked as I entered.

The room was full of old beds, tables, and blood pressure machines. They looked ancient, and I wrapped a cuff around Jeb's arm and tried to pump it up, but it made a funny noise like passing gas, and we started laughing again.

"Bobbie Jo!" he said, accusing me.

When we went back to his office, I noticed it was time to go home, and I hated the thought. Today had been such a good, productive day. I was anxious to get started on the day care. That was, if the board approved it.

"Are you ready to go before the board? They are pretty tough, but we will put the hard sale on them. In your condition, how could they say no?"

"Very funny, Mr. Hardy. I think when they see me waddle in the door, they'll know how to vote. Thanks a lot for not thinking my idea was stupid and for working everything out. I really appreciate it. This really is a good idea," I told him.

Jeb put his arm around me, and I started to cry. He held me until I stopped and then led me to a chair.

"What's going on, Bobbie? I have noticed you have not been your sweet, fun-loving self lately. Is it just the pregnancy or is something going on at home?" he asked carefully.

I told him about Tony's reaction to my job and the situation at home. It was so nice to be able to tell someone who actually seemed to care. I had bottled all this inside me for months. It needed to be dealt with because the stress was killing me. I must have talked continuously for thirty minutes, but he sat there, patiently listening and asking all the right questions. Finally, I just sat there, exhausted.

"Bobbie, you are doing a fantastic job here. The patients love and adore you, and I hear nothing but praise from the staff. This idea for the day care is not only going to benefit the staff and you, of course, but the facility itself. I can't believe no one has ever thought of it before. Everything is going to be fine. After that baby is born, everything will get back to normal, or as near normal as it can be with a new baby to tend to," he added.

He hugged me again before I left, and I thanked him. I felt like a load had been lifted from my shoulders, and I walked out of his office with a feeling of accomplishment. I hadn't felt that good in months.

Before I went home, I wanted to take another look at the future day care center. No one was around, so I opened the door, thankful that Jeb had not locked it. I tried to find the light switch, but I stumbled on something on the floor. I tried to catch myself, but it happened so fast, I couldn't find anything to grab. I found myself lying on my back with my feet over top of a table. I couldn't call for help because no one would hear. I finally picked myself up and felt Michael kicking me to let me know what a klutz I was.

Tony wasn't home, so I grabbed a peanut butter and jelly sandwich and headed up the stairs to the nursery, but just then, the doorbell rang. I turned around and opened the door, and Marcia was standing there. She asked if she could come in, and I stepped aside for her to enter. She just stood in the foyer, and I didn't offer her a chair. By the look on her face, I was not going to like what she had to say.

"Bobbie, I'm not sure how to say this, so I am just going to say it. You are heading for trouble. I saw you and that new administrator having lunch in Columbus. You seemed to be enjoying yourselves, laughing and talking, so I didn't come over to the table. You are married, Bobbie, and you are going to have a baby. You need to get your priorities back in order before you lose everything," she said with her usual flair.

I walked to the door, opened it, and told her she needed to leave. Before she walked out, she turned and looked at me, but instead of saying anything, she just shook her head and left.

I locked the door and ran upstairs to the nursery. *How dare she tell me my priorities are out of order! I don't know why she continues to accuse me of doing wrong. I figured she'd tell Tony about my lunch with Jeb, and I don't care. I really don't care.*

I was trying to make curtains for the windows when I heard Tony come home. I closed the door and went downstairs to greet him. He ran past me up the stairs, saying he had forgotten his bag this morning and he needed to get back to the clinic.

"I don't know how long I will be. Don't wait up." With that, he slammed the door, and I heard the car peeling rubber all the way down the road.

Okay. I guess that means I will have time to do some more sewing, I thought to myself.

The curtains had barnyard scenes, and I embroidered animals on them. The black-and-white cows looked very fat. *Like me,* I thought. And the little pigs were as cute as could be. I got up to find the blue thread when a sharp, piercing pain brought me to my knees.

Chapter Fourteen

When the pain finally subsided, I was scared to death. My water had broken, and it was everywhere. I couldn't find the phone, and all I could think of was going to the clinic to find Tony.

I made my way downstairs before another pain shot through me. It felt like somebody was stabbing me and twisting the knife inside. I tried to time the contractions, but I couldn't even stand up.

"Michael Henry, please stay put until I can get your daddy," I begged.

I didn't know what to do. I found the car keys and drove to the clinic, hoping the baby would not be born on the way. There was another car beside Tony's, and I assumed it was the patient he was seeing. The back door was unlocked, so I walked in holding on to the wall trying not to faint. I was so dizzy. I looked down and saw the blood pouring down my legs.

Slowly, I walked to his office and saw that it was closed, but I heard him talking and laughing. When I opened the door, there were Tony and Ashley, lying on the floor. I couldn't move. I just stood there with blood gushing out from between my legs, and then I passed out.

The lights were blinding as I tried to open my eyes. I could hear my mother calling my name, but I didn't want to answer her. I just wanted to go back to sleep. I felt so tired. Again and again, I heard her.

"Bobbie Jo, please wake up. I love you."

She was holding my hand and brushing the hair out of my eyes, and I heard Father. He was holding my other hand. It was so nice to have them both with me again. I felt so safe and secure, and I went back to sleep.

"Bobbie, wake up. Everything is fine, and I need you to wake up and look at me so I can check you." The voice was Dr. Hansen's. "Come on now. You can do it."

I opened my eyes and tried to focus, but everything was blurry. Slowly, they cleared, and I could see Dr. Hansen's face a couple of inches from mine.

"Can you squeeze my hand?" she asked.

I squeezed it as hard as I could. I felt so weak.

"Good," she continued. "Now, tell me how you are feeling."

"I feel fine, but why are you here?" I had to strain to get the words out. I just wanted to go back to sleep. I looked around and saw Mother standing behind Dr. Hansen and she took my hand. "Where am I?" I asked.

"You are in the hospital—"

I wouldn't let her finish. I jumped up and felt my stomach, and it was flat. My heart sank.

"Where is my baby? Where is Michael Henry?" I screamed.

"Bobbie, you need to lie down and rest," she said as she gently pushed me down onto the bed. "We will talk about this later. I want you to rest."

"I don't want to rest. I want to see Michael. Mother, where is he? Did Tony take him away? Please tell me where my baby is."

"He was born a little too early, Bobbie. He is in prenatal ICU, and when you are strong enough, I will take you there."

"You will take me there now," I said as I tried to get up out of the bed.

The IV popped out of my arm, and blood flew everywhere.

I have to see my baby. I can't let Tony take him away. I will never see him again.

"Bobbie, if you don't calm down, I will give you a shot, and that will make it even longer for you to see your baby. Now, lie down and be still."

I lay down, but I couldn't be still. I planned to wait until they all left and then go find my baby. I knew they were hiding him somewhere, and Tony was going to take him away.

The nurse came in and re-inserted the IV and asked if I would like anything to eat or drink. I tried to be as polite as I could and told her, "No thank you." She fluffed my pillow and changed my pads and then told me to sleep tight. My parents were in the waiting room, and I watched the clock until I thought no one was around.

Slowly, I pulled the IV out of my arm and held the site tight until the bleeding stopped. All I had was a hospital gown, so I secured it in the back and quietly got out of bed. When I walked to the door, I saw no one, so I slowly pulled the door open and hurried down the hallway. I found a lab coat hanging on one of the doors and slipped my arms into it. I tried to remember where the prenatal unit was and punched the eighth floor.

As the elevator opened, there were a lot of people waiting to get on the elevator. They looked at me oddly, but I continued down the hall. I found the nurse's desk and asked to see my baby. One of the nurses looked at me and picked up the phone to call security. The next thing I knew, I was falling to the floor.

When I awoke, the nurse was putting my bed up, and a breakfast tray was set in front of me. "I'm not hungry. Thank you," I told her. "Please take me to see my baby."

She smiled and opened the milk and the plastic wrap containing the fork. I ate the eggs and toast and was drinking my juice when my parents came in with Tony.

I threw the tray at him, just missing his head as he ducked out of the way. The coffee, however, found its mark and it dripped down his face.

"Get out of here, and you leave my baby alone! I don't want you anywhere near him! Do you hear me? You go back to your little slut, and leave me and Michael alone!" I screamed.

I looked for something else to throw, but Dr. Hansen came in and told Tony that it would be best for him to leave.

Mother looked at me like I had gone mad, but I assured her I was okay.

"I want to see Michael now. Now! I want to see him now."

The nurse brought a wheelchair into the room and helped me into it, wrapping a blanket over my bare legs. Slowly, we made our way to the nursery. I was so scared of what I was going to find. No one would tell me anything, and I needed to see him for myself. They wheeled me into a tiny little room and put a net on my hair and a mask over my face, along with a sterile gown.

I sat in the waiting room, anxiously waiting for what seemed like hours until the door opened and the nurse wheeled in a tiny incubator with the most beautiful baby inside. He had dark hair, and he was so tiny. The nurse said he weighed two pounds five ounces when he was born, but he was losing weight. The prognosis was not good. He just had too many things wrong.

I put my hand on the glass and looked at him. He had tubes coming out of his mouth, and his little arms weren't as big as my fingers. The IVs had turned his little arms blue and purple. He drew his little legs up and turned his face toward me.

I just sat there, watching him. He was so beautiful. I ached to hold him, to just feel him in my arms, smell him, and kiss him. The tears were pouring down my face, and I started to sing to him. I told him how much I loved him. The nurse came in and told me she had to take him back now. It was time to feed him and give him some medicine.

"No! Please let me hold him. I just want to touch him."

"You can't, Bobbie," the nurse said.

I turned to Dr. Hansen, "You told me the prognosis was not good, well if he is going to die, then he is going to die in my arms. Now, give me my baby!"

Dr. Hansen told the nurse to leave, and as soon as she was gone, she walked over to the incubator and gently lifted him out and placed him in my arms. I took off my gloves and mask and held him up to my breast, where he tried to latch on. He was so small and weak that he was unable to nurse, so I put my little finger in his mouth, and he sucked on it.

"Little Michael, I am so sorry. I am so sorry." I cried and kissed him. I held him as close to me as I could. I kissed him one last time on the forehead, and he stopped sucking my finger. His eyes closed.

I knew he was gone, but I didn't want to let him go. I continued to hold him and sing to him for another fifteen minutes, and then I kissed him good-bye. Dr. Hansen took him and gently laid him back in the incubator. Taking her stethoscope, she tried to find a heartbeat. I knew that it was in vain because he was gone.

Chapter Fifteen

On a warm, sunny day with the temperature around seventy-two, they buried my precious Michael. Mother said it looked like the whole town was there, but as for me, while they were putting him into a deep dark grave, I sat in the nursery reading books and rocking on the new chair I had bought. I was so thankful for those few moments Dr. Hansen had given me to be with Michael. That was how I wanted to remember him.

"Bobbie, the church people have been bringing in food all day," Mother said, handing me the plate. "Why don't you try to eat a little?"

"I'll eat it later," I said. "I just want to be alone now."

Marcia kneeled down in front of me and took my hand. "Bobbie, everything is going to be all right," she said. "Do you want me to sit with you for awhile?"

"No, I'm fine," I told her. I was so relieved when they finally left and the house was once again deserted.

"Oh, my precious Michael," I cried. "I'm so sorry I hurt you. I'm so sorry." I walked around the room gently running my hand along the crib. Folding the tiny shirts, I tucked them away in a drawer and picked up the little brown teddy bear that was lying on the crib.

> "Michael was a little boy,
> Who never got to play with toys.
> For his Momma she fell one day
> And took Michael's life away."

Over and over I sang this song as I walked around the room. It grew louder each time, until I was screaming. I swept my arm along the top of the dresser, watching as lotion, soaps, blankets and a little nursery light crashed onto the floor. I turned over the crib and the changing table and grabbed the paint can, throwing the contents onto the walls.

I was screaming and crying, and anything my hands grabbed went flying across the room, breaking into a million pieces onto the floor. Finally exhausted, I fell to the floor.

"Michael was a little boy," I whispered.

"Bobbie, are you all right?" I heard a voice ask. "Bobbie, its Father. Mother wanted me to bring you some cards that people have been sending."

"Who never got to play with toys," I continued softly.

"Everything is going to be all right, Bobbie," he said, picking me up like he did when I was a little girl. He laid me on my bed and pulled the blanket up around my shoulders.

"Because his Momma fell one day," I couldn't stop. "And took Michael's life away."

"It wasn't your fault," he said, brushing my hair out of my eyes. "Everything is going to be okay."

Softly he hummed a song and held my hand until I fell into a fitful sleep. The sun was shining high in the sky when I awoke. I poured a cup of fresh-brewed coffee and walked around the big empty house, now with no hopes or dreams of a future. The den was quiet, so I sat on the couch, thinking about how my life had changed.

I noticed a book had fallen off the shelves, and when I picked it up, it was a Bible. I chuckled to think God would want anything to do with me, and I knew for certain I didn't want anything to do with him.

As soon as I felt stronger, I went to see Nat Apecs, who was Father's attorney. He was a strange little man, and his fancy designer suits hung on his emaciated frame.

"Bobbie Jo, I feel honored you would allow me to serve you in this capacity," he said in his squeaky, high voice. "As you know, your father and I have been friends for many years now."

"Yes, Mr. Apecs, that is why I chose you," I explained to him. By the time the meeting was over, I felt confident my divorce would be short, sweet, and to the point, just like my marriage.

"Thank you very much," I told him, and when I went to write him a check, he refused it.

"This is for your father," he said as he walked me to the door.

My first day back at work, I was introduced to Frances Capri, a mousy little lady who was about forty-something, with thick-lens glasses that overemphasized her brown eyes.

"Bobbie, this is your new secretary, Frances," Jeb Hardy introduced her.

"Good morning, Ms. Juxton," she said pleasantly. "I have your schedule ready for your approval, and there are quite a few papers on your desk that need your attention."

"Thank you," I said. And then to Jeb I said, "I don't need a secretary."

"Now then," he said, "We have a surprise for you." With that he took a handkerchief from his pocket and wrapped it around my eyes.

"What is going on?" I asked. I could hear people talking as we walked.

"Here she comes," they said. I felt the elevator taking us downstairs, and then Jeb led me down a hallway.

"Okay, now you can open your eyes," he said, removing the blindfold.

There before me was the daycare center. Jeb and the staff had been working on it the whole time I was gone. The walls had pictures of children swinging and laughing, and there were swings, cribs, and a play area.

I couldn't say anything. I was so touched that they cared enough to make all this happen. Jeb handed me the blindfold/handkerchief, and I wiped the tears from my face. A lot of the staff was there, and they introduced me to Mary Hale, who was hired as director of the daycare. After some cake and ice cream, I was anxious to get to work. Frances was wonderful, and I soon learned that she ran the place. It may have been my signature on things, but Frances was the brain behind it all. We became good friends, but it took me months before I could get her to call me Bobbie.

Chapter Sixteen

Another June came as beautiful as ever. It was my favorite time of year, and not because of my birthday, but because it was almost summer. The birds were singing, and every night I would sit on the back steps and listen to them along with the night sounds. I had a hard time sleeping, so I spent a lot of time thinking.

My birthday was on a Wednesday, and when I arrived at work, a huge banner was hung in the lobby that read "Happy Birthday, Bobbie." I was serenaded by the staff and patients. The kitchen made a huge cake, and everybody helped blow out the candles.

On Saturday Mother and Father came to wish me a happy birthday and gave me a gift certificate to the new shopping mall in Columbus. While we ate cake and ice cream, Danny, Marcia, and the twins came in.

"You two are getting more beautiful every time I see you," I exclaimed as they ran up and hugged me. "The boys will be following them around soon."

"I am prepared for them." Danny laughed as he pulled his pocketknife out and pretended to be fighting.

"Put that thing away before you hurt yourself," Marcia teased.

Mother started talking about the new couple that had joined the church last Sunday.

"They are a very nice couple. I believe they moved here from California," she said. "They are hunting for a house. They have four of the most precious little boys."

"I haven't really thought about it, Mother," I said, pondering the idea. "I'll let you know."

"You can't stay here in this big house all alone, Bobbie," she continued. "You can't take care of a big house like this."

"Someone told me those new apartments on King Street were really nice," Marcia said. "We could go see them next week if you would like."

Danny added, "Yeah, I helped build them, so you know they are good and sturdy." I threw a pillow at him.

"I remember when you helped us build a tree house, and when all three of us climbed up in it, we all came tumbling to the ground." I laughed.

"One little mistake and my reputation is tarnished for a lifetime," he said, sticking out his lower lip for sympathy.

"Well, darling," Mother continued as if no other conversation had taken place. "You really should look into moving. This house is just too big for you."

"I'll be just fine," I said, and Father took the hint.

"Come on, Mable," he said, kissing me on the cheek. "We need to get on home."

"Yeah, us too," Marcia said, looking at her watch. "Come on, girls." Melodie and Harmony came running back in, and after quick hugs and kisses, they piled in the car.

"Call me," she said. "I miss spending time with you. It would be fun to go see those apartments, even if you aren't interested in moving."

"I'll think about it," I said and waved as they all headed to their homes. I closed the door, and it echoed through the house.

Maybe Mother is right. Maybe I should look into moving. This house would be perfect for a couple with four children.

I spent a lot of time at the graveyard talking to Michael. It gave me a sense of peace and sometimes for just a minute or two, the loneliness and emptiness inside me would dissipate. Funny thing was, no matter how hard I tried, it always came back.

Chapter Seventeen

I received a call from Mother that Father was taken to the hospital with a massive heart attack. I immediately drove to the hospital after asking Frances to clear my schedule.

Father looked pale when I walked in the room. He had IVs in both arms, and monitors beeped a cadence with the rhythm of his heart. Mother was standing at his side, holding his hand.

"He has not opened his eyes since they brought him in," she told me. "He was out in the backyard trying to turn the lawn mower over so he could sharpen the blades. The next thing I knew, I heard a strange sound, and I ran outside. Henry was lying on his back, and he couldn't talk. He just kept holding his chest and making that awful noise. I didn't know what to do. I called the ambulance and then I called you."

She looked scared as the nurse came in and wheeled him down the hall. We followed them to the elevator and then took the next one up. Gently they lifted him off the gurney and placed him on a monitor bed. Once again all the machines and heart monitors beeped with their incessant noise.

I held Father's hand, and when the doctor walked in, Mother ran to him and hugged him. Imagine my surprise when I saw who it was. Tony Juxton was my parents' physician.

"What are you doing here?" I demanded, getting up in his face.

"Bobbie, Tony is Henry's doctor. We did not stop seeing him as a doctor just because you are divorced," Mother explained.

Seething, I took my place by Father's bed. Tony nodded and took the chart from the bottom of the bed and wrote down the blood pressure and pulse, which was recorded on the heart monitor. He then walked over next to Mother and squeezed her arm. My blood pressure hit the ceiling, and all I wanted was a chance to squeeze his neck.

"Henry has had a massive heart attack," Tony began.

No duh! I wanted to scream at him.

He continued, "I am not sure how much damage has been done. He is scheduled for tests that will give us more information."

Biting my tongue so I didn't spit the words, I asked, "So what is your prognosis?" I couldn't believe Mother and Father continued to use Tony as their personal care provider.

"I would say not very well, Bobbie, but Henry is a strong man and a fighter. He has a great wife who loves him very much," he said.

I got the dig, but I wouldn't give him the satisfaction of knowing he got to me. When he left, I was so angry I couldn't even look at Mother, so I told her I needed to get some air.

"Is there anything you need?" I asked her.

"I need for your father to be okay and come home," she said with tears in her eyes.

I walked out the back door of the hospital and found a quiet place to sit where I could just be alone and think. The tears poured down my cheeks, and I felt so helpless. I had no idea how to help my own father. He was dying, and with all my nurse's training, I could do nothing. A few minutes later I returned to find Mother asleep on the chair, so I stood by Father's bed, holding his hand.

"I love you, Father. I love you so much," I told him.

Mother woke up with a start when they came to take him for the tests. She kissed him, and then we walked to the waiting room. I glanced through the magazines, but I couldn't keep my mind on them.

The hospital smelled like bleach, and the longer I sat there the more nauseated I felt. Mother nodded when I told her I needed to get some fresh air.

"I'll be right back," I told her.

A small garden was located right outside the east door, and that's where I headed. I needed to get away from the smell of death. Warm air hit my face when I exited, and it felt so good. I hadn't realized how cold I was in the air conditioning. I walked around the little garden, reading the signs that gave the plant's information.

One sign read "Bleeding Heart" plant. I thought that would be a good plant for me, for I felt like my heart had been pierced and the life-giving blood was being poured out on the ground.

I became aware of someone's presence and turned to see a young couple holding each other and crying. I left, so as not to disturb them, and made my way back to the waiting room where Mother was still seated.

Two hours later, the surgeon came out of the operating room and talked with Tony. He had been hanging around the nurse's station and keeping in contact with mother. Now, as he walked slowly toward us, I knew something was wrong. He looked me straight in the eye, and I knew Father had died.

I took Mother's hand, and we met him halfway across the room. "I'm sorry, Mrs. Patterson. Dr. Munson did everything he could, but the bleeding just wouldn't stop. I am so sorry. Henry was a good man, and he loved you very much."

Mother hugged Tony and told him thank you and then collected her purse and walked to the nurse's station to make a phone call.

I was frozen in time. My mind would not, could not comprehend Father being dead. Mother was acting like nothing was wrong. After the phone call, she told me she was going home to get some rest and freshen up.

"I have an appointment at Brown's Funeral Home at nine tomorrow morning." Then she turned and left me standing there by myself.

―――――――――――――――

Before going home I stopped at the graveyard. I sat on the grass and cried. I didn't stay long because the sky was turning an ominous gray, and I could hear the thunder rumbling in the distance. On the way home, I stopped by the store and picked up a couple bottles of wine, and by the time I pulled into the driveway, the storm was in full force.

I found a glass in the cupboard and poured the wine into it. Sitting on the back steps, I watched as the lightning ripped the sky in two, and then the thunder would boom out into the stillness. I sat there sipping my wine. Suddenly I felt all alone. I had no one I could run to for help.

"Oh, Father," I cried into the black clouds, hoping he could hear me. "I love you, Father. I am trying to be a good girl, but for some reason everybody has left me all by myself."

I woke up on the couch the next day, and when I looked at the clock I took my shower and drove to the funeral home. Dressed in my black pantsuit with a little short jacket, I grabbed my pocketbook and made myself ready to welcome the mourners.

For two days people I hadn't seen in years came pouring in to say their farewells to my father. I listened to stories from old friends when he was young and stories about the paper mill from guys he worked with there.

Preacher Carr officiated the funeral, and Mother and I sat on the front row. Tony came in and was standing in the back when Mother motioned him to sit by her. I jabbed her and gave her the dirtiest look I could summon up at a funeral. She ignored me, and Tony sashayed to the front and placed himself by Mother's side, which was where he stayed through the entire funeral.

When Preacher Carr said, "Amen," I was ready to go. Mother didn't say a word, and I didn't bother to either. She had what she wanted, and I guess she didn't need me anymore.

"Bobbie," Marcia said, walking beside me to my car. "Bobbie, I'm so sorry."

"Did you know Mother and Father were still seeing Tony as their doctor?" I asked ferociously.

"Why yes, Bobbie. Tony is a great doctor, and he is right here in—"

"I can't believe you'd do that to me, Marcia," I said. "Stay away from me. Just stay away from me."

At home I found the other bottle of wine and sat on the back porch. What a beautiful day for a funeral, I thought as I swirled the wine in my glass and inhaled its fragrance. I drank it slow and easy, and it didn't disappoint me. The worries and sorrow of the past week seemed to float away with the white, fluffy clouds in the sky.

Chapter Eighteen

The next Saturday, I decided to take a ride. The weather was beautiful, so I threw on some cut-off shorts and an old T-shirt and jumped in the car. I rolled the windows down and let my hair blow in the wind. Soon I passed a sign for the Little Country Store.

The place was packed with tourists, and I noticed cars with license plates all the way from Texas. I guess everybody liked to just take a drive in the country. I found a pink hat with "Little Country Store" embroidered on the front and paid for it. I looked around a little more, and then I noticed a sign in the rear: "Puppies for sale."

A wooden pen had been erected in the rear of the shop, and four tiny, white fluff balls were in it. One of them was trying to sleep in the corner, and I picked him up, and he snuggled into my arms. He whimpered, and I pet his soft fur and rubbed him on my cheek. He was so soft and smelled just like a puppy should. I sat down on one of the chairs to see what the puppy's face looked like. He was so cute. He was all white with big, brown eyes.

The owner came over to me and told me he was a Bischon Frise. "They don't shed, so they have to be groomed regularly. They're very smart dogs."

"This one here is very smart," I said. "He knows exactly what to do to get a girl to buy him. He sits in her arms and whimpers like a baby. No girl can resist that."

After inquiring about the price, I bought cute little dishes with puppy tracks painted on them, a blue leash and harness to match, and everything else the proprietor thought I would need. By the time I left, my bill was over a thousand dollars.

"So, what are you going to name him?" the man asked.

"How about Butch?" I suggested. "I kind of like that. It makes him sound tough, so the bully dogs in the neighborhood won't pick on him."

Butch proved the salesman right. He was a very smart dog. He was housetrained in a week, and the board said that as long as his shots were up to date, he could be a regular visitor at work. Jeb bought a cute little bed for him and put it in my office along with a water and feeding bowl for home and my office. He walked right beside me everywhere I went. When we made rounds, he would go to every resident to be petted and then was right back at my feet when I was ready to leave.

One day I stopped at Al's gas station to fill up. Al was the only station anywhere in the country probably that still filled up the car, checked the oil, and looked under the hood. He was about sixty-something. His wife had died about two years before. She and Al built the station and ran it until she died. Now he ran it by himself. I asked him why he didn't hire somebody to help him, and he said, "Can't find no one to do it the way I want it done."

I went inside to pay for my gas. Al also did not take credit cards, and it was cash only. He always liked a few extra dollars for the trouble of pumping the gas himself, and I always obliged. When I turned to leave, Mother was coming in the door.

She reached to hug me, but I just kept walking to my car. I heard her calling me, but I didn't stop.

"Bobbie Jo, please let me just talk to you!" I heard her calling after me. I didn't want to hear anything she had to say. *Maybe she should call Tony. They were such good buddies.*

Seeing Mother upset me more than I thought. The tears started falling as soon as I pulled out of the gas station. I couldn't find a hanky, so I used my sleeve, and I was a sight by the time I walked into my office. Frances was right behind me and quietly closed the door, handing me a box of hankies.

"Thanks!"

"Anything I can do?" she asked.

"No. I stopped for gas, and Mother was there," I told her. "I didn't realize how much it upset me until I started driving away. It really hurts what she did to me, and I don't know if I will ever be able to forgive her. She just said she wanted to talk with me. I just can't." I cried.

"Bobbie, it's almost two. Everything is ready in the boardroom," Frances interrupted.

"You are the greatest, Frances. Do I look okay, or do I look like a blubbering fool?" I knew the answer before I asked.

"You look like a beautiful woman who has been crying," she said.

"That was not the right answer," I said as I found my pocketbook and powdered my nose, adding a tad bit of lipstick.

When I walked in the boardroom, the nurses were talking and laughing and getting their lunches. They all quieted when I walked in.

"Okay. This makes me feel like you have been talking about me. Does that mean you are giving someone else a break?"

They all started laughing and talking, and as we sat down to eat, someone asked, "Is it true we are finally going to get unit secretaries?"

"Yes, but I need your help in the selection of them," I informed them. "I want you to pick them out for your particular floor. Do you think we should hire from within or place an AD in the paper or both? I really need your input on this."

"What exactly will their responsibilities be?" Sherrie, unit manager of one east asked. "I would hate to have my best CNA be a unit secretary when I really need her to be on the floor."

"They'll work Monday through Friday, nine to five and be responsible for organizing the paperwork and handling your work schedules. They will answer the phones and fax documents," I said, reading the list of responsibilities.

"I think I'd like to apply for the job. It sounds great to me. When do I start?" Judy asked. Judy was unit manager of Three Main.

After a lengthy discussion, we decided to try to hire from the inside first. I was going to put up a notice and see if anybody applied. If not, then we would hire outside help. I hoped it would work. I knew it was a great idea, but we all had to work together.

I cleaned up the boardroom, when Frances came in to tell me I had a call in my office. "I'll clean this mess up," she said as she started throwing away trash and wiping down tables.

Chapter Nineteen

The seasons changed, and soon it grew cold. One Sunday, and I heard the church bells ringing, begging people to come in. I wondered if maybe this wasn't such a good idea to come to the graveyard, but I really needed to just talk with Michael. A couple inches of snow blanketed the ground, and big huge flakes were still floating down. I picked Butch up and wrapped him up in the blanket I was sitting on, and he went to sleep.

"Didn't your mother teach you to get in out of the rain?" Danny asked as he sat down on the blanket.

"You need to get out more often, Mr. Sedders," I laughed, trying to make a snowball so I could throw it at him. "This here is called snow." The snowball landed on his head, and I laughed at him.

"You scared the bejeebies out of me," I said. "What are you doing here?"

"I saw your car and wanted to make sure everything was all right," he said and looked away.

"Is everything okay?" I asked.

"Sure. Marcia is raising the twins, cleaning the house, and being a pillar of society. What else could a man ask for?" he said sarcastically.

"Is there actually trouble in paradise?" I asked. I had never in all the years I had known them heard them argue or even raise their voices.

"I'm not sure if I would call it paradise," he said.

"Wow, I thought you had the perfect marriage. Marcia was so busy trying to tell me how to have a good marriage that she forgot about her own," I said. "I'm sorry Danny."

––––––––––––––––––

When I got home, the door was unlocked, and inside sat Mother. I could tell she had been there awhile. She had fixed up the den and hung my bath towels. I nodded my head when I came in, and Butch growled at her. I laughed at him and told him to behave himself.

"Her bark is worse than her bite, Butch." I laughed. "What brings you to my humble abode? Don't you have better things to do than come in here and clean?"

"I just came to ask you to please come back home, Bobbie. I realize you have been through a lot of heartache after losing your husband, but your place is home now so you can heal." She sat on the couch, wringing her hands and turning her wedding band around.

I looked at her and asked, "Why did you really come over here now, Mother? I know it wasn't just to ask me to come home. This is my home."

"Bobbie, you need someone to help you and take care of—" she stopped.

"I can take care of myself!" I yelled at her. I calmed myself down before I spoke again. I am doing just fine, Mother."

"I love you, Bobbie, and well, what I really came over for was to give you this." She handed me a set of keys on a key ring. "These belong to your father's truck. You never did come around to hear the reading of the will, so I finally decided to stop waiting and get over here and give you Henry's truck. It's brand new. He bought it a week before he died. He wanted you to have it."

I was touched by her generosity. I never even considered Father to have a will, and I just assumed everything would go to Mother. Now here she was, giving it to me. Uncertain of what would come out of my mouth, I accepted the gift and hugged her. She was crying when I released her, and I didn't know what else to say.

"Here is a copy of the will. It would be in your best interest to read it. Even now, your father is taking care of you. He loved you, Bobbie Jo. I guess I need to go now. Please call me. I love you," she said hurriedly.

After she left, I sat down and started reading Father's will. Somebody knocked at the door, and when I answered, Danny was standing there with a bottle of wine and two glasses.

"How did you know Rose Petals was my favorite wine?"

"Because it is mine too," he said. "Is everything all right? I saw your mother walking down the sidewalk so I circled the block a couple of times. Are you okay?"

I handed Danny the key ring and told him it was to my father's truck. "Mother said he bought it a week before he died. He told Mother to give it to me."

"Wow. That's a nice truck!" Danny exclaimed.

I showed him the papers Mother had left. "She also left me a copy of Father's will. When he died, it didn't even cross my mind that I needed to know what was in the will. I just assumed everything went to Mother. I don't really understand all of this, In the meantime, let's have some wine. Thank you."

Danny poured the wine, and then we sat down on the floor and talked. "What brings you back here tonight? I thought I wouldn't see you until tomorrow."

"When I got home, Marcia lit into me about being with you all day and not going to church. She accused me of all kinds of things, so I turned around and walked back out. I didn't want to drink alone, so I was hoping you would join me," he said sheepishly, handing me a glass.

"Through the lips and over the tongue," he said and locked his arm around mine.

"Look out, tummy," I said, laughing so hard I could barely get the words out.

"Here it comes," we said in unison and tipped our glasses emptying the contents.

I fell back on the carpet, laughing, and Danny fell on top of me. Suddenly he leaned down and kissed me. It was not a friend-to-friend kiss; it was a deep, hungry passionate kiss that took my breath away, and I drank it in like the wine, wanting to get lost in it.

When I awoke, the clock said 1:00 a.m., and Danny was gone. Butch jumped up on the couch and nestled beside me. A deep void came over me, and all the heartaches and loneliness came crashing in. I took a hot shower, trying to wash away the guilt and shame I felt. How could I have made love with my ex-friend's husband?

Chapter Twenty

Father's truck was wonderful, and I was so thankful for it. It was four-wheel drive, and I could go anywhere. Sometimes after work, Butch and I would take off and go for a drive and find a beaten path to turn on to. We got ourselves in a couple tight situations. One time we got stuck in the mud so deep I couldn't open my door. The next time, we went over a hill and started heading down on the other side, when I noticed a gulley at the bottom. I couldn't stop because we were going so fast, so I hit the gas and we flew over top of it. I yelled, "Yeehaw!" and Butch cuddled up close to me on the seat. The landing was kind of rough, but the truck just kept on going. I nicknamed it Henry and thought Father would like that.

Turning left onto Cedar Road, I noticed a truck pulled off to the side with the hood popped open. I pulled over to see if they needed any help and recognized Garrett James. He owned and operated the Car Repair Shop right outside Fairville.

When I walked up to him, he said, "Hi, Bobbie Jo. I haven't seen you in a while."

"Yeah, it has been a while. What's up with your truck?" I asked.

"I'm not sure. I have been working on it for months now. It seems like I get one thing fixed and something else falls apart," he admitted.

While he talked, I kept noticing how much he had changed. Garrett was a year ahead of me in school and used to date a girl named Phyllis. After graduation, she ran off with some guy she met on the Internet. Garrett was tall and looked like he had been working out. He played football in high school, and he and Danny were good friends. His hair was bleached blond from the sun, and his eyes were such a hypnotizing blue.

"Bobbie, are you all right?" he asked.

"Sure. I'm fine," I said, shaking my head to bring me back to reality.

"I was asking if you would mind taking me back to the shop. I'll pick up my tow truck and come back for the truck," he repeated.

"Sure. Hop in."

I walked back to the truck with him, and Butch growled when he opened the door. I picked him up and assured him that Garrett was a good guy and there was no reason to be afraid.

"It's all right. He probably wouldn't taste very good if you bit him." I laughed.

"I heard about Tony, Bobbie. I'm real sorry about all that trouble in your life," he said.

"Thanks, Garrett. Everything is going to be all right," I said.

"You sure look good," he said shyly, looking away before I could catch his eye.

"How about you? Anyone special in your life now?" I asked curiously.

"No. I moved into my parents' old house. They both died last year about two months apart. It's not much of a house, but I like it. I'm building a porch on the front. I stay pretty busy," he added.

When we arrived at the shop, he hopped out of the truck, shut the door, and started walking in. Suddenly, he turned around and came over to my window and said, "Bobbie, I'd sure like to take you out sometime. Would you like to go to Columbus and see the fireworks for New Year's Eve? They always have a big to-do every year. There are usually booths selling hot dogs and pop too."

He couldn't have shocked me more if my finger were in a light socket. He looked so cute standing there, playing in the snow with his foot and afraid to look at me. I was actually flattered.

"Garrett, I would love to. Here is my phone number," I said, writing it on a piece of napkin I had in the truck. "Just let me know what time and where to meet you."

"Thanks. You know, I always thought you were the prettiest girl in Fairville, and nobody has come along to prove me wrong. You be careful now. Don't get stuck out there four-wheeling." He smiled.

That time, he walked all the way to his shop, and I put the truck in gear and drove down the road. I wasn't really in any mood to go four-wheeling anymore, so Butch and I grabbed a couple hamburgers and headed to the house.

I couldn't get over Garrett asking me out. That was so sweet. Maybe there are some good men left in this world. He sure has changed in looks. I remembered when he was shorter than everyone and had braces on his teeth. He was still kind of cute, but back then, he only had eyes for Phyllis. It's funny how we all seem to change as life goes on.

I knew my life had changed. It seemed like only yesterday I was looking forward to going to church to meet the new doctor in town.

I got up to pour another glass of wine when I heard a knock at the door, and there stood Danny, looking guilty with snow all over him. I hadn't seen him since that night. I opened the door for him to come in, and he stomped his boots off and entered.

Chapter Twenty-one

"Good afternoon. Would you like a glass of wine?" I asked him rudely. How dare he come in here without calling?

"I just want to talk to you about what happened. I mean between us. I'm so sorry, Bobbie. It just happened. I didn't mean for it to happen."

He was talking faster and faster with each word, and I have to admit I was enjoying his insecurity. I had been feeling used and abused. When the husband of your used-to-be best friend makes love to you and then just walks off without saying good-bye and no phone calls—yes, I was definitely enjoying this.

"Bobbie, I love Marcia and the twins, and I have never ever cheated on them before. I don't know what came over me. Please forgive me. All I wanted to do was help you," he said over and over again.

"Yeah, well, you helped me all right and yourself too. If you are here for forgiveness, you need to be talking to your wife. I am considered the other woman in this case. She's the one you need forgiveness from."

"Marcia doesn't know. I didn't tell her," he began.

"So," I interrupted, "you are here to beg me not to tell Marcia. That is the whole purpose of this visit. Am I right?"

"I also wanted to tell you how sorry I was. I really didn't mean to treat you like the other woman. I really like you, Bobbie," he said.

Of course, I had to interrupt again. "You really like me? Isn't that a hoot? Great. Now you tell me. What exactly I am supposed to do with that information?"

"Bobbie, please. I just—"

"Why don't you go on home to your ivory palace and perfect little life and quit complicating mine. I don't need your friendship," I told him.

He turned and walked out, and I cried. I cried because I had lost a friend, two friends; and I cried because I lost Michael; I even cried for the cat that was dead on the side of the road. It didn't matter what it was; I cried for it. I grabbed a hot shower and inhaled the rest of the bottle of wine.

Garrett called me Wednesday night when I got home from work. "The fireworks start at six p.m. if you'd still like to go."

"Of course. I'm looking forward to it. Are blue jeans okay?" I asked.

"Make sure you have a good heavy coat, hat, and gloves. Sometimes it gets pretty cold sitting out there in the field. I'll bring a blanket for us to sit on. I'll pick you up at five thirty p.m. Is that okay?"

"Five thirty it is. See you then," I said before hanging up.

I stopped by the grocery store on my way home, and Marcia and the twins were standing at the checkout counter. Guilt was written all over my face, I was sure, but she saw me before I could turn around.

"Hi," she said, smiling.

"Hi," I said back and then turned to the twins. "You two are getting so big and, of course, beautiful."

They both said thank you and Marcia reminded them I needed to get a hug and kiss.

"And where are my hugs and kisses?" I asked, extending my hands and sticking out my lip.

They rushed over to me at once and nearly knocked me over, but I hugged and kissed them.

"How are doing, Bobbie?" she asked. "I sure miss you. Maybe we can get together sometime."

"I'm doing great, Marcia," I lied.

"I hear you and Garrett are going out Saturday night to see the fireworks. He is a very nice man, Bobbie." She relayed the gossip.

"What exactly is that supposed to mean, Marcia?" I asked.

"It doesn't mean anything, Bobbie," she said. "Don't be so paranoid."

"Right," I said and left my groceries on the counter as I walked out of the store.

When I climbed in the truck, I was fuming. *Marcia just thinks she knows everything and she knows nothing. Why can't she just leave me alone? I don't like the idea of her snooping around in my life. Maybe going out with Garrett isn't such a great idea after all.*

On Friday, Frances asked if I had any plans for New Year's Eve, and I told her I was going out with Garrett James.

"Oh, you mean that adorable man who owns The car repair shop?" Her eyes were as big as softballs. "He is quite a hunk. I see him at his house all the time since I have to pass it on my way home. He is always building something there."

"What about you? What are you doing tomorrow night?" I inquired.

"I am babysitting my friend's little boy, Jerry. He is two years old, and his parents want to go out and celebrate, so I volunteered. It will be a lot of fun."

On Saturday, Garrett picked me up at exactly at 5:30 p.m. He held Butch while I finished with my hair, and then we locked the house securely and walked through the snow to his truck.

"Is this truck going to get us there and back?" I asked, remembering the last Saturday.

"I hope so. I have been working on it all week. Come over here. You have to get in on the driver's side. The passenger door doesn't open."

I climbed in and stayed in the middle. He didn't seem to mind, and we headed to Columbus. He turned up the heater a little bit, asking if I was warm enough. He kept both hands on the steering wheel and didn't look at me when he talked. I turned on the radio, but it didn't work, so I turned it back off.

"What do you like to do for fun?" I asked, trying to get some kind of a conversation started. I would hate it if we just stared at each other all night.

"Fun? I like to build things and work on cars. How about you?" he asked.

"I have learned to love four-wheeling. Father's truck is great. The trails are endless, and we are determined to find them all," I told him.

"You're going to have to bring in the truck for me to have a look at it. I hope you didn't tear up an axle or something. It sounds like you are a little wild," he suggested.

"Maybe just a little," I admitted.

When we arrived, there were hundreds of people. Garrett held my hand as we made our way to a hot dog stand, where we ordered three hot dogs and two pops. We carried them with us along with the blanket until we came to a huge field. They had scraped off all the snow so we could lay our blankets down over the top of the plastic sheet. There we sat and ate.

"It is sure a beautiful night," I said once more, trying to start a conversation.

"Just right for seeing fireworks. They put on quite a show. Have you ever been here before?" he asked.

"Not that I can recall," I answered.

"Did I tell you how beautiful you look tonight, Bobbie? Your hair looks really nice when you wear it down like that," he quickly added.

"Thanks," I said, watching him turn red.

As soon as it was dark enough, the fireworks started. Green, yellow, orange, and red splashes of color burst into the air. They filled the darkness with light and colored the whole world. Some of them whistled as they soared up into the sky, and some popped. It was a spectacular sight.

Garrett sat back and pulled me to him. He would point at the ones that most impressed him, and soon, the splashes of color were everywhere all around us. People everywhere were "oohing" and "aaahing," and we watched not only the light show but the people as well.

When the last one finished, Garrett looked at his watch and said, "Midnight! I'm sorry. I forgot to tell you how long they lasted. It is already midnight."

"I kind of figured they would last this long. Why don't we just stay here for a while as the crowd thins out," I suggested.

"Are you warm enough? That breeze has a chill to it." He sat down and patted the blanket beside him and then wrapped us both up in it. A band started to play, and Garrett started singing. His voice was so smooth and nice.

After a couple of songs, he stood up, pulling me along with him, and we started dancing. The band was playing, and people were running around everywhere, yelling, laughing, and talking; but we were holding each other tight and dancing cheek to cheek, hip to hip. We danced a couple slow songs, and at the end of the second one, he gently kissed me on the cheek and then looked me in the eyes and gently kissed me on the lips.

He wrapped me in the blanket as we walked back to the truck. The night was still beautiful, and it had started snowing again. He opened the door, and I slid into the middle of the truck. Garrett hopped up behind the steering wheel and started the truck. He looked at me and put his arm around me, pulling me near. I laid my head on his shoulder, and he sang as he drove me home.

Gently, he kissed me good-bye. "Thank you for being my date tonight. I hope you had a good time."

"It was wonderful, Garrett. Thank you," I said.

"Could I see you again sometime?" he asked shyly.

"I would like that," I admitted.

"I'll call you," he said and then drove off.

Chapter Twenty-two

A wave of nausea sent me flying out of bed, and I barely made it to the toilet. I made an appointment with Dr. Hansen before going to work.

"Don't forget your appointment with Mr. Apecs," Frances reminded me.

"Thanks," I said as I headed to the truck.

Mr. Apecs handed me a key and a lock box. "I have an appointment. I thought maybe you would want a little privacy. Take as long as you like." I thanked him and opened the box. I thought of Father and how much I loved him and missed him. He was such a good father, and I wished I would have spent more time with him to get to know who he really was.

There was a letter inside in Father's handwriting. It read:

> My precious Bobbie, I love you so much, and since you are reading this letter, I know you are grieving for me because I have passed on. Don't fret, my child, because I am in the arms of my Lord and Savior, Jesus Christ. Death is only hard for the ones left behind. I love you, and I hope this will help you in your life. I have tried to think of everything necessary to help you, but you will have to make the right choices. Sometimes that is the hardest thing to do. Remember, the choices we make now determine our life tomorrow.

Within the box was a roll of money. When I removed the clip it contained ten thousand dollars, all one-hundred-dollar bills. The will put the house in my name but stated Mother would have a place to live as long as she wanted.

Dr Hansen was less than excited about the possibility of my being pregnant. She took a urine test and checked my lungs and everything else doctors check. When the nurse came back in with the report, Dr. Hansen said, "Bobbie, you are definitely pregnant. I'm not sure if this is good news or bad news for you, but you know if you want to end this now, I will help you find the right—"

"Dr. Hansen, I'm not thrilled about having another baby, but I'm not going to kill it either. Do you think I will be able to go full term this time?"

"I foresee no problem. We determined that Michael came early due to your fall. You will have to be very careful. If necessary, we will put you on bed rest for the last six weeks," she suggested.

"No thanks!" I told her.

"Do you know who the father is?" she asked.

"No," I lied, and then I paid for the visit and headed back to work.

Frances greeted me with the mail and a cup of coffee when I walked into my office.

"Is everything okay?" she asked.

"I'm just pregnant. That's all," I said, not even looking away from the mail I was sorting through.

"Pregnant!" she hollered.

"Yes, that is what I said. Do you want me to turn on the loud speaker so everyone can hear you?" I asked.

"I'm sorry, Bobbie, but isn't this bad timing on your part?" she hesitated.

"Frances, it is not as if I planned it this way, but thank you for your concern. I think. I—I mean—I think 'we' will be just fine."

The rest of the day, everybody I passed congratulated me and asked when it was due.

"August is what Dr. Hansen is predicting," I told them all.

Mr. Greenfield came to my office to congratulate me and asked if I thought I would be able to work. "I just don't want anything to happen to this precious bundle of joy."

I drove to Mother's house after work. I figured I had better tell her before she heard it somewhere else. When she opened the door, Marcia and the twins were there. I told her I would come back later, but Marcia said, "Nonsense. You have been the subject of our conversation, so now, Mable, maybe we can hear it from the horse's mouth."

"What are you talking about?" I looked at Marcia with a frown on my face.

"Bobbie Jo, are you pregnant?" Mother blurted out.

"How in the world? News sure travels fast. Yes, Mother, I saw Dr. Hansen this morning, and she confirmed it. I was coming over here to tell you."

"Bobbie Jo, you should be ashamed of yourself," Mother said. "Whatever are you going to do with a baby? I think it would be a wonderful idea for you to place it in a family where it will have a father."

"Mother, this is my baby, and I am going to have it and take care of it myself. How dare you try to get rid of my baby? I think that's my exit cue. Come on, Butch," I said and scooped him up in my arms.

Garrett called Saturday morning and asked if I would like to go to the new restaurant in Gittland. It was a Japanese buffet. I told him I was sick and hoped he would ask me again sometime.

"Is there anything I can get for you, Bobbie? I'm not much of a nurse, but I can drive to the store for you," he offered.

I assured him I was fine, and he asked if he could call me later. "Maybe in a couple of weeks."

Marcia brought the twins over Saturday. When I opened the door, I must have looked a sight because Marcia told me to sit down and she was going to make me some breakfast. I tried to protest, but she wouldn't listen.

"Marcia, really, I don't need someone to take care of me," I told her.

She made me some toast and butter and a glass of orange juice. It smelled really good, so I ate it slowly.

"How was your date with Garrett?" she asked.

"It was nice. You were right. He is a nice man," I assured her.

"Does Dr. Hansen know if you are going to have a boy or girl yet? I guess it is really too early. I hope you are doing the right thing by keeping this baby. There are a lot of couples out there who would love to adopt a baby. If there is anything I can do for you..." she said.

"I know you are just trying to help, Marcia, but maybe you need to just stay home with Danny and the twins a little more," I said. The look on her face was priceless, and I knew I had hit a nerve.

The thought of being a single mother did not excite me, but I knew I could do it. I was all I had to depend on, and I discovered long ago, I was a survivor. I didn't need or want anybody.

I named the baby Billy Jo, knowing full well it was going to be a boy. Nobody would ever know who the real Father was.

That afternoon I was in my office doing some paperwork when someone knocked at the door. There stood Garret, holding a dozen red roses and a box of candy. I invited him in, and he handed me the roses and candy. After finding a vase, I arranged the roses and set them on the table.

"I came over to see if you would like to go out for some dinner," he asked shyly.

"Garrett—" I started.

"I know you are going to have a baby, Bobbie. Marcia told me," he said. "But that doesn't mean I want to stop seeing you. I had a great time at the fireworks show, and I thought you did too. If you just don't want to see me anymore, then just say so."

"Garrett, I did have a great time, but I didn't think you would want to date a pregnant woman," I told him.

"What difference does it make? Instead of three hot dogs, I will have to buy four," he mused.

I laughed at his silly joke, and he said, "This new Japanese place is supposed to be excellent. Why don't you get dressed, and we'll go on over and try it out ourselves."

He helped me off the couch, and I took a shower and dressed in some warm wool pants. He opened the truck door for me, and I hopped in.

Chapter Twenty-three

Garrett was right. The Japanese place was excellent, and it was very popular too. We had to wait in line for a half hour before we even got in the door. Garrett held me tightly in his arms so I wouldn't get cold. Finally, the waitress showed us to our table and took our drink orders, and we were on our way to a dinner filled with, well, I really don't know the name of half the things I ate, but man were they good.

Garrett beat me back to the table, and his plate was layered three times high. I laughed at him and told him he was going to look like the pregnant one.

"I am eating for two. What is your excuse?" I laughed.

"Hungry. Me big man with big appetite," he said, trying to sound like Tonto.

The place was too noisy for much talking, so after we ate, he paid the bill and helped me with my coat.

"Would you like to take a walk?" he asked. "Looks like the wind has calmed down."

"I'd love to," I said and put my hand in his big calloused one.

It was a beautiful evening, so he took my hand. As we walked, he started telling me things about himself.

"It really tore me up when Phyllis left me after high school. For the longest time, I didn't think I would date again, and then, when I finally got over her, there wasn't anybody around worth dating. When I heard about your divorce, I wondered if you would want anything to do with me. I have wanted to date you since high school."

"I didn't know that," I said, surprised at his words.

"Nobody knew but Mom. I used to tell her everything. We had a special bond, and she knew how much Phyllis meant to me too," he said. "Thank you for tearing down a couple of bricks from that wall you have built around you so no one else will hurt you."

"Nobody is supposed to know about that," I said.

"I know about it because I have one too. Did you enjoy the restaurant?" he added quickly.

"The food was great, but it was way too noisy," I told him.

We walked a little farther, and then he stopped and turned me around to face him. Slowly, he bent his head to kiss me. "Can I, like, be a regular date?"

"What exactly is a regular date?" I asked.

"It means that we date each other and no one else. That is regular dating," he explained.

"Oh, I see. You mean like going steady?" I teased.

"Yeah. Something like that," he said.

"I'm not sure, Garrett. I'm not sure I am ready for any kind of commitment right now. That doesn't mean I don't want to see you though, okay?" I said hurriedly.

"Okay." He bent over and kissed me again.

I enjoyed being with Garrett. He was quiet and honest. *Honest. Now that is a quality I have not found in a man since Father. I know quite a lot of men who need that virtue.*

On Valentine's Day, Garrett brought a dozen red roses to my house, and we went out to a beautiful restaurant in Columbus. He wore a black suit with a white shirt and black tie, and I, of course, wore my long-sleeved black dress with a set of pearl earrings to match my necklace.

We ate T-bone steak and gnawed at the bones like a couple of hillbillies. We laughed, and when the band played a slow song, we danced.

"This was a wonderful evening, Garrett. Thanks!" I told him.

"How about I fix you a big dinner tomorrow after church? I can fry some mean chicken," he said.

"That would be nice. Is it okay if I bring Butch? He has been feeling rather neglected lately," I said.

"Sure. No problem. I'll pick you up at nine a.m. for Sunday school," he offered.

"I'll just drive over to your house when you get home from church if you don't mind," I suggested.

"That will be okay," he said.

"Do you want me to bring anything?" I offered.

"I thought you were bringing Butch." He laughed.

"You are really funny, Mr. James." I smacked him on the head.

The evening ended too soon, and I hated to see him go. As I watched him walk to his old truck, I wondered what kind of a husband and father he would be. We were getting close, and I was scared to death. I wasn't ready for another trip down the aisle, but I had to think of Billy Jo.

"Billy Jo," I said as I rubbed my protruding belly. I was starting to show already. "What kind of a life can I give you? Maybe Mother is right, and I should give you to a family with a father and mother to raise you." The thought made me cry. I knew I could never give up that precious life. He was mine. It didn't matter who the father was. He was mine.

At about noon the next day, Butch and I drove over to Garrett's house. He was in the kitchen, cooking and singing hymns, when I arrived. I knocked on the door several times and finally walked in.

The house was old but spacious. The front door opened to a huge front room, and the kitchen came off it with a dining room in between. The furniture was old and worn, and he had laid blankets over top of them. There were pictures of his parents on top of the

TV and pictures of landscapes on the walls. When I looked at them more closely, they had initials GJ in the corner.

Garrett welcomed me and took my coat. "Did you paint these?" I asked as I pointed to the pictures. "They are beautiful."

"I did that a long time ago. I seem to only have time to paint houses and cars now. Hey, Butch," he said as he gave him a treat and pet him.

He guided me to the dining room, where a big table was set for two. There were plates of chicken, corn on the cob, green beans, and mashed potatoes, and he brought in a basket filled with biscuits.

"Are you expecting someone else?" I asked, wondering why he had prepared so much food.

"No. Just you and me and, of course, Butch." He bent down to pet him again before sitting in his chair. He reached for my hand and bowed his head.

"Lord, I just want to thank you for all this food you continue to bless me with and for bringing this lovely woman into my life. May your will be done. Amen."

The food was better than any restaurant, and we ate until no more room was available. I helped him clear the table and do the dishes, and we had a water fight when I kept flicking dishwater on him. We laughed so hard that tears came to my eyes. Finally, he took my hand, and we went outside to see his porch he was building.

"It doesn't look like much now, but it's going to go from here," he said as he pointed to beyond the front door, "to here." The porch was going around the corner so he could enter the kitchen also. "As soon as warm weather comes, I am going to get it finished."

We went inside and sat on the couch, and he wrapped his arm around me.

"Thank you for coming, Bobbie. I really enjoy being with you. I hope the food was edible."

"I think it was great. Where did you learn to cook like that?" I asked.

He told me, "Mom was a great cook. Living by myself, I learned if I didn't cook I would starve. I'm building this house for my wife. I don't know who she is yet, but I've been praying for one, and I know God is going to answer that prayer. I met a girl last year, and I thought she was the one, but I learned that the devil always tries to imitate God, and what he gives is not worth having."

"How are you going to know when that right girl comes along?" I asked.

"I'll just know," he said. "God will tell me."

At 7:00 p.m., I told him I needed to get home because I had to work in the morning. I thanked him for a great meal, and he asked when he could see me again.

"Would you like to go to a movie next Saturday?" he asked.

"I don't know, Garrett. I would like to just take this slow and easy. I have a lot of things to think about." I tried to be honest with him.

"I'll wait, Bobbie. Time is all I have, and we are not promised that."

He walked me to my truck and kissed me good-bye. I saw him wave until I turned the first corner. Garrett was a very nice man, and I was so afraid of him; not that he would ever hurt me, but that I would end up hurting him.

After work, I started taking walks at sunset. Not many people were out and about then. Butch came with me, and we would walk to the park, and I would get on the swings and swing until my muscles ached. Around the park we would walk for a couple of hours and then go home.

Occasionally, Oscar Studds would be there at the lake, fishing, and I would sit with him. Oscar was the neighborhood drunk. No one knew how old he was, but his hair was gray and long, and he kept it back in a ponytail. He never bothered anybody, but he did drink quite a lot and fished. He loved to fish. When I saw him, I gave him a bottle of wine, and he would drink and tell me fish stories.

"Bobbie, did I ever tell you about Big Cat? He is the biggest catfish I have ever seen. He watches everything that goes on in this lake. I almost caught him once, but while I was pulling him in, he jumped nearly ten feet in the air and I swear that fish winked at me and shook the hook right out of his mouth."

Oscar always had a treat for Butch, and I enjoyed listening to his tall tales. Nobody wanted anything to do with Oscar, and I can remember Mother telling me to always stay away from him because he was a bad man. He didn't go to church. I figured I must be a bad woman then, because I no longer went to church either.

Chapter Twenty-four

At six months, I decided to get some stuff for the baby. I didn't have anything. Frances told me of a hand-me-down shop in Columbus, so I headed up there and finally found the place. They had cribs, high chairs, changing tables, bottles, clothes, and everything else a baby would need. They even had a section for mothers.

I bought a crib complete with mattress, mattress cover, and cute little sheets with farm animals. I was going to try to nurse him, so I only bought a few bottles. The high chair would have to wait.

The clothes were so cute I just couldn't resist. I bought lots of diapers, onesies, T-shirts, and blue jeans. They even had a pair of cowboy boots. I knew it would be awhile before he could fit into them, but I just had to have them. I took everything to the cashier, and she rang it up and bagged it.

Loaded down with my packages, I didn't see the man walking toward me until I bumped into him. "I am so sorry," I began and then recognized Garrett. "What are you doing here?"

"I needed to buy some supplies for the porch. It looks like you have been shopping. Here. Let me help you. Where is your truck?" He took the packages out of my hands and took my arm. When we found the truck, he unlocked it and put my packages on the front seat.

"I have sure been missing you, Bobbie. Would you like to come over and see how much I have done to the porch? It should be finished by the time Billy Jo is born. I thought maybe you would like swinging him on the porch swing I put up," he said.

"That sounds great, Garrett. When can I see it?" I asked.

"Why don't you follow me home? Let me go get that crib you bought first and throw it in the back of the truck," he said, heading back to the store.

The porch was almost done, and hanging right in front was the swing. I sat down and started pushing it. As I held my belly, Billy Jo started kicking.

"I think he likes it already."

Garrett sat down and started to put his hand on my belly but then stopped and looked at me. I nodded and smiled and took his hand and placed it where Billy Jo was kicking. He laughed and felt it and laughed some more.

"I have never felt a baby kick like that before. Does that mean he is going to be strong?" he asked, still holding his hand in place.

"He is going to be very strong. I'm sure he will be able to help you with your next project in a few years," I told him.

Garrett's eyes became watery, and he looked away. He took his hand from my belly and asked if I would like some iced tea.

"Garrett, is something wrong?" I asked.

"No. Let me get you some tea." He hurried inside.

He came back a few minutes later carrying two glasses filled with tea, and it tasted so good. Spring had come in hot and dry, but I preferred it over winter. The snow was pretty, but I didn't like the cold.

"Bobbie, I have been thinking about us, you and me, and, well, I think we need to do something about it," he said quietly.

"What exactly do you want to do, Garrett?" I was scared to death and held my breath until he answered.

"Well, I was talking to Nat Apecs," he began.

"Nat! Garrett, what is going on?" I could feel my anger getting the best of me.

"Now, wait a minute, Bobbie. I talk to him too. We all live here in Fairville together, and he brings his car to my shop. I didn't do anything wrong," he said quickly.

Apologizing, I said, "I'm sorry, Garrett."

"Well, going on with my story, I asked him if a woman has a baby and she is not married then what would that baby's last name be. Well, he said it would be the woman's last name," he said, looking at his glass of tea.

I was waiting for the punch line, so I sat quietly.

"Well," he continued after seeing I was not going to say anything, "it seems to me that Billy Jo needs a name. I mean, it would be okay if his name was Patterson, but that is your father's name, and it just doesn't seem right to me."

"What are you getting at, Garrett?" I pushed right on in there. I didn't like surprises.

"I want you to marry me, Bobbie," he said quickly. "I know you have just gone through a big mess in your life, but I promise I will take care of you and Billy Jo."

I didn't say anything for a few minutes, and he didn't either. I was mulling this all over in my head, and I had no idea how to answer him. He was a wonderful man and would make a good husband and father, but I didn't want to make the same mistake. The longer I sat there, the more confused I became. I just didn't know.

He knew I was uncertain, so he added, "It's okay. You don't have to answer me now. I just wanted to do what was right for the two of you. I love you, Bobbie Jo, and I always will."

***

For the next several days, all I could think about was Garrett and his proposal. Mother came to see me and declared how big I was getting, and I reminded her I was almost seven months.

"Well, Mother, I am due in only a couple of months," I told her.

"Have you decided if you are going to keep the baby?" she asked. "There is a wonderful young couple who just joined our church, and they have been trying to adopt but have been turned down three times now."

"Mother, I am keeping the baby. He is my baby, and I am keeping him," I told her angrily.

"You can't raise a baby by yourself, Bobbie Jo. You need to stop acting so foolishly and start thinking right. That baby will be born out of wedlock. You said so yourself," she told me pointedly.

"Are you calling my baby a bastard? Let me tell you something. This front door swings both ways, and don't let it hit you in the rear end as you leave." I opened the door wide, and she started to protest.

"Bobbie, I am only thinking about you—" she began.

"Good-bye." I then slammed the door behind her.

I lay on the couch crying until someone knocked on the door. "Go away." I yelled.

The knocking continued, and I opened the door, and there was Frances. "I am so sorry."

"Bobbie, are you okay? I noticed that your mother left in quite a hurry. Is something wrong?" she asked.

"No. Nothing is wrong," I said.

"Oh, look at the beautiful crib," she exclaimed.

"Yes. I bought it at the hand-me-down store in Columbus you told me about. Look at these cowboy boots. I know it will be awhile before he can wear them, but aren't they precious?" I exclaimed, showing her the brown leather shoes.

"Only a couple more months, Bobbie," she said. "Have you planned anything as to how you are going to get to the hospital when the time comes? I think you had better plan ahead of time. If I am here, I would be more than happy to assist."

"Gosh, Frances. I just figured I would drive there. I didn't know I needed an emergency plan. Some women pack a bag too. I guess I need to do all of this. Next week, I am going to start going to some natural birthing classes. I don't want to have any pain medicine unless there are complications. Can you think of anything else I will need?" I hadn't given it a thought.

"Just remember that I am here if you need me. I am excited about having a little one around. You must let me babysit or just come and hold him," she said cheerfully.

"Of course. Anytime. I look forward to all the help you can give me."

When the birthing classes started, I felt very out of place. The room was full, but they were all couples. I was the only single. The teacher, Ms. Pierce, said, "The only way this works, Bobbie, is for you to have a helper; someone who can help you through the pain by talking to you and assisting you with the breathing and pushing. Isn't there anyone you could call on?"

I told her Wednesday that I would have a partner, although I didn't know who it would be. I had kicked my mother out of the house, and I had no best friend. The only one I could think of was Garrett, so on my way home, I stopped by the shop. He was talking with a couple men when I entered, but they excused themselves after saying, "Hi, Bobbie."

"Hi. Is something wrong?" he asked.

"Nothing is really wrong. I just need to ask a big favor," I said.

"Okay. Ask," he said, standing there, patiently waiting.

"It isn't that easy." I swallowed, trying to find the right words.

"If it is just a big favor, Bobbie, ask. You know I would do anything for you." He looked at me with those big, pleading eyes.

"Even be my helper for birthing classes?" I blurted out.

"Of course, I would love to. When do we start?" His eyes sparkled with excitement.

"I started tonight, but I really don't have anybody else to ask," I pleaded.

"I already said yes. Stop worrying. Everything will be fine," he encouraged me.

Chapter Twenty-five

The birthing classes were fun, and Garrett was a big help. I learned to listen to his voice and obey it, and he learned how to help me breathe and what was going to actually happen when the baby was born. Three days a week, we went to the classes; and then, on Saturdays, I went to the nursing classes. I was determined to raise a healthy baby.

The nurses surprised me with a baby shower one day at work. I had no idea as they led me to the conference room. Linda said Mrs. Boyer fell in the lobby and they carried her to the conference room. While I was walking, I kept wondering who Mrs. Boyer was and found the answer when I opened the door.

Frances had made the cake, and it said, "Welcome to our world, Billy Jo." There was a table overflowing with gifts of the cutest baby clothes I had ever seen. Even Mr. Greenfield had a package for me. It was a savings bond from the board of directors for $1,000.

We ate cake and drank punch, and some of the more ambulatory residents also came with various gifts. I cried with each gift I opened, and Frances made sure she wrote each gift down and who it was from.

After work, she helped me load it in the truck, and when I brought it in the house, I couldn't believe how many gifts there were. As I put them away, I thought of what Billy Jo was going to look like. He was going to look just like me, I decided.

On August 1, I went to Michael's grave with Butch and set up the lawn chair I kept in the back of the truck since I couldn't sit on the ground any longer. As I sat there, talking to Michael, I felt a little twinge of pain in my back. Thinking it was just the way I was sitting, I rearranged myself and started again telling Michael about what was new with Billy Jo and the new things I had bought him.

Suddenly, I was bent over with pain. It caught me so off guard that I nearly fell out of the chair. When the pain stopped, I threw the chair back in the truck and called Butch. Another pain shot through me as I put him in the truck, and I had to wait until it was finished before I could climb in.

I grabbed my purse and tried to find my cell phone, but I must have left it at home. I drove to the gate of the cemetery, and another pain pierced through me, so I pulled over and lay on the seat. I thought about how messed up my truck was going to be if I had Billy Jo there on the front seat.

I tried to sit up, but the pains brought a wave of nausea, and I opened the door to vomit. I lay back down on the front seat, and the glove box flew open. There was my cell phone. I dialed and had to stop as the nausea came again. Once the next pain stopped, I could dial, and I heard it ringing.

Garrett answered on the fifth ring. "Hello."

"Garrett, help…" I couldn't say any more. Another pain shot through me. My stomach was as hard as a rock.

I could hear Garrett saying, "Bobbie! Bobbie where are you?"

"Michael's…"

The next thing I remember, Garrett opened the truck door and scooted in beside me. I laid my head on his lap, and every time the pain would come, he would sing to me. It was such a beautiful song, and he would sing it loud enough for me to hear him over the truck noise. The pain was still intense, but I concentrated on his singing.

Finally, we were at the hospital. I felt him pick me up and carry me in. A stretcher was brought, and he laid me on it. The nurse told him he had to stay and give her my information while they took me back.

He told them, "The information can wait. Can't you see we are having a baby?"

They wheeled me down a long hallway, and Garrett stayed right by my side, holding my hand. They stopped at a big room and lifted me onto a bed. The next pain was more intense than the last. Garrett stayed right by my side, singing to me. He would not allow them to make him leave. He was determined that his place was with me.

Dr. Hansen walked in the room, and the intern handed her the report. "Well, Bobbie, it seems Mr. Billy Jo is trying to come into this world backward. We will have to turn him around if possible and hope he doesn't get tangled in the umbilical cord. Glad to have you with us, Garrett."

Garrett just nodded his head and smiled. I kept my eyes on Garrett each time a pain attacked me. He sang and brushed the hair from my face.

"You look so beautiful, Bobbie. Your baby is going to be beautiful too because he is a part of you."

Beautiful. He said I was beautiful. Who is he trying to kid? I am having a baby, for Pete's sake, and I hurt like heck. I have been screaming and saying words that would make my mother blush, and he is sitting here, telling me how beautiful I am. I really am going to have to marry this guy. They just don't make them like this anymore.

"Yes!" I told him.

Garrett looked at me with a questioning look on his face. "Yes what, Bobbie?"

"Yes, I will marry you, Garrett. I want to do it right now so the baby's name will be Billy Jo James. Dr. Hansen, did you hear that?"

"Bobbie, I really don't think this is the time or the place for a wedding. Are you sure you want to do this?" she questioned.

"Yes. More sure than I have been about anything in a long time," I said reassuringly.

While Dr Hansen worked on Billy Jo, someone ran to get the chaplain. Finally, Chaplain Johns came to the room with a marriage license. He was also a notary public. Garrett gave him ten dollars, and he proceeded with the wedding, stopping as each wave of nausea hit and each pain would make it impossible to go on. When Garrett said, "I do," then I said, "I do." We kissed, and I pushed. The next thing I heard was a baby squealing.

I was crying, and Reverend Johns was crying, and so was everybody in the room. Dr. Hansen placed Billy Jo in my arms before he was cleaned up, and he was the most precious thing I had ever seen.

"Here, Billy Jo. I want you to meet your daddy, Garrett James."

The nurse took him and cleaned him up. Garrett kissed me and went out in the hall to make some phone calls so I could get cleaned up a little bit. By the time he came back in, Billy Jo was all cleaned up and trying to nurse.

"I'm sorry, Bobbie. I will wait outside," he said, blushing and turning around.

"You are my husband now, Garrett. Come here and see your new family. Do you know what you just got yourself into?" I asked.

"Yeah. Isn't it great?" he said, looking at me with loving eyes.

"Here. Take him. He is your son now." I handed him the tiny bundle.

He weighed five pounds two ounces and was twenty-one inches long with lots of coal-black hair.

Garrett took Billy Jo and was scared to death of dropping him, but he held him and walked around the room and sang to him. Billy Jo went right to sleep. The door opened, and Frances and all the unit managers, along with Mr. Greenfield, came in. Garrett showed them Billy Jo, and they were so excited.

Next came Ms. Joyce, and she just stood there, looking at the baby, and cried. We finally got her to hold him, and she didn't want to let him go. When everybody left, Garrett handed him back to me. He was fussy, and we changed his first diaper. It wasn't a very good fit, but it would do. It wasn't like he was going dancing or anything. I held him up to my breast, and he latched right on. Garrett just stared at him and had a smile from ear to ear.

Marcia and Danny came the next day. I had just finished taking a shower, and Garrett was holding Billy Jo. He had stayed the night in the room with us and even snuck in Butch so I could make sure he was okay.

Marcia held the baby, and Danny kind of stayed in the background but congratulated us. When we told them we got married, Marcia was astounded.

"That was kind of sudden, wasn't it?"

"Are you kidding? I have wanted to marry this beautiful woman since high school," Garrett said as he took the baby from Marcia because he was getting fussy. He held him tight and sang to him.

"Congratulations, Bobbie, and I do mean it. I hope we can all be friends and maybe have dinner sometime. Melodie and Harmony have been asking me about you, and when they find out you had a baby, oh my goodness. Please come over so I can keep my sanity," Marcia pleaded.

"That would be nice, Marcia. Thanks." I hoped that came out right.

Danny took one look at Billy Jo, and he knew.

Garrett was terrific with Billy Jo, and on the day of our departure, he was the one who carried him out. He must have been the happiest man in the world because he was always smiling, especially when he had Billy Jo cradled in his arms.

Garrett passed my place, and I said, "Garrett, I need to get all my stuff."

"Yeah. I know. I did all that while you were still in the hospital. Wait and see. If you don't like it, I will arrange it any way you want. Bobbie?" he said.

"Huh?" I answered.

"Are you sorry you married me?" he asked.

"Not yet. Just don't do anything stupid." I laughed.

"I'll certainly try not to. I love you, Bobbie Jo, and I love Billy Jo too. I promise I will be a good husband and father," he said.

"I know you will, Garrett. I know you will."

At the house, a lot of people had gathered to have a party. There were two banners strung across the front of the house. One said, "Congratulations! It's a boy!" and the other one said, "Just Married."

Preacher Carr and Sandy were there and invited me to church on Sunday. I told them I would think about it, and Oscar was there. I was so glad to see him. He looked at the baby wrapped up in the soft blanket, and I handed it to him. I heard the crowd go, "What?" as his arms went out to hold Billy Jo.

He held him close to him and then closed his eyes and prayed this prayer: "My most precious heavenly Father, I thank Thee that Thou hast hid these things from the wise and prudent and hast revealed them unto babes. Even so, Father, for so it seemed good in thy sight. Use this family for your glory to further your kingdom."

He then handed Billy Jo back to me, kissed me on the cheek, and bowed to the crowd before turning and walking back to the lake.

The people were shocked that I had let a nasty old man like Oscar hold my baby.

"Why, who knows where those hands have been?"

"God knows," I said, and I even shocked myself.

Chapter Twenty-six

Billy Jo was such a good baby. Only once or twice did he wake us at night, but I was up every three to four hours just to look at him and make sure he was real. Some nights, I would find Garrett in his room, brushing his rough hand against his soft baby face and singing to him. Billy Jo slept soundly, and Garrett would sneak back to bed, where I pretended to be asleep.

I took six weeks off from work, and Frances came to the house every morning and evening. "I have to pass this way anyhow. I might as well bring you the paperwork. Besides, I get to see my little man too. Did you see that? He winked at me! Imagine that!"

The real estate agent called to tell me someone had put a bid on my house, and several weeks later it was sold. The dog days of summer kept me in the house, but in the cool of the evenings, when Garrett came home, we could be found on the porch swing. Billy Jo loved to swing. If I got up before he was asleep, he would let me know. Garrett loved to hold him and even helped with the diaper changes. He was a great father, just like I knew he would be.

Garrett brought home a stroller one of the ladies at church gave him, and I would lay Billy Jo in it and walk all over the yard. We lived about five miles from town, and our nearest neighbor, which was Frances, was two miles down the street. Sometimes I would walk to her house, and we would visit for a while and then walk back home.

I was a size four before I got pregnant, and after Billy Jo was born, I put on my pants, and they fit perfectly, a little snugger, but not so much I couldn't breathe. Garrett told me over and over how much he loved me and how beautiful I was. I just couldn't get over how lucky I was.

After my six weeks was up, it was time to get back to work.

Garrett fussed about it. "Where is he going to stay? Are all those other children healthy? I don't want them giving Billy Jo some kind of disease. How are you going to know when he is hungry? Bobbie, is he going to be okay? I feel like I am letting him go out to the big, cruel world all alone."

"Garret, he'll be fine. You know Mary. She loves each and every one of those kids as if they were her own. She is so thrilled about getting to care for Billy Jo. I promise he will be fine. Why don't you come over when you take lunch, and we will eat together," I suggested.

"I'll sure try. Judd Carr is bringing that white limo in for servicing today, and as a matter of fact, I had better get going. I'll see you tonight. I miss you both already," he said as he hurried out the door.

Mary met us at the door and took Billy Jo from me. I told her what times he nursed and that I thought I had brought plenty of diapers for him. I handed her a list of everything I had just told her, and she put it in her pocket.

"He'll be fine. You'll know what time to come down and feed him. Stop fretting. It will put wrinkles on your face," she said, laughing at me.

Mary was right. Two hours later, my breasts were so full they hurt. I went downstairs and heard him fussing. Mary was changing him and telling him, "Your momma will be here soon. See. There she is right there. Over here is our nursing room. A couple of the girls are already in there."

Deanna and Jeannie were just starting, and I sat down on one of the rockers with Billy Jo. He took the breast immediately, and the milk was coming out fast, but he drank every bit of it. I loved nursing. It gave me a chance to be close to him and hold him tight and tell him I loved him.

Deanna asked me how I was doing with nursing. "He has taught me. He just latched on the first time and hasn't let up since," I told her.

"My little Sarah did not like the breast at first. The doctor said it is easier to drink from a bottle, but I was determined, and when she got hungry enough, she nursed. Now look how big she is," she said, holding up a chubby little Sarah.

After Billy Jo was full, I burped him and rocked him to sleep. Handing him back to Mary, she changed him and laid him down for a nap. I hated to leave him, but I had work to do.

At noon, Garrett came for lunch. I was so excited that he had remembered. We walked hand in hand to the nursery, and Mary greeted us and handed Billy Jo to Garrett, who kissed him over and over and told him how much he missed him. We went up to my office, and I told Frances I didn't want to be bothered.

We sat on the floor and ate sandwiches that Garrett had made, along with some iced tea. Billy Jo was nursing and making funny noises like he was trying to sing, so Garrett sang with him. I enjoyed our lunches together. Garrett made it a point to come every day and have lunch with us. He would hold Billy Jo after he'd eaten and even change his diapers. He loved him so much.

At night, he would bathe him while I did the dishes after supper, and then he would put him to bed after he ate. What a happy, content life I was leading. I had everything I had ever wanted. Garrett was the most wonderful husband in the world, and Billy Jo was the perfect baby. We were the perfect family.

Chapter Twenty-seven

One night after work, I stopped by the grocery store and picked up a few things when I noticed they had my favorite wine, Rose Petals, on sale. I picked up a couple of bottles and put them in my cart. Garrett was already home and carried in the groceries while I put Billie Jo in his crib.

"What is this?" Garrett asked, holding up the two bottles of wine.

"They were on special, so I bought two bottles. I haven't had any since before I was pregnant, and Dr. Hansen said it would be fine."

"I didn't know you drank," Garrett continued.

"You make me sound like an alcoholic or something," I replied. "I just like a glass of wine sometimes at night to help me relax."

"I really don't want you to be drinking," he said pointedly.

"Garrett, you're being silly. There is nothing wrong with having a glass of wine at night," I said.

He opened both bottles and poured them down the kitchen sink while I stood there with my mouth open.

"What in the world has gotten into you? It's just wine," I told him, shocked at his reaction.

"I don't want that stuff in this house. It doesn't look right," he argued.

After he said that, he went outside without kissing me. I couldn't see the big deal about having a glass of wine at night, but obviously, he did.

Okay. I will not drink here at the house, or at least not so he will know.

Billy Jo was growing up so fast, and every day, I saw Danny in him even more. Garrett adored him and spent as much time with him as he could.

"You are getting right big, boy. I guess we will have to be teaching you some carpentry and how to fix a car real soon," he told him.

"Yeah. Maybe he will be able to fix that old truck of yours," I teased.

"Now don't you be picking on my old truck. It gets me where I need to go." He laughed.

Mother was on my mind a lot those days. Not once had she bothered to come see her grandson, so one night, I decided to call her and invite her for Thanksgiving dinner. The phone rang and rang, and no one answered. Being concerned, I asked Garrett if we could drive over and see what was going on. We loaded up Butch and Billy Jo and headed over there.

When we got to the house, all the lights were on, so I knocked at the front door. Garrett was behind me with Billy Jo and Butch right on my heels. Mother answered the door and looked shocked to see us.

"Bobbie, I wasn't expecting you. Garrett, please come in," she said as she opened the door wider for us to enter. "Can I see the baby?"

She took him from Garrett and cooed and talked to him. He responded by laughing at her.

I took it all in and smiled. *Maybe we can at least be civil to each other.*

"What did you say his name is?" she asked.

"Billy Jo," came the reply in unison from Garrett and I.

"I don't recall anybody in the family by that name, but it's your baby," she said and handed him back to me.

"I tried to call you, but you didn't answer the phone." I said.

"I was out back, sitting. It is warm for November, and I decided to enjoy it. I didn't hear the phone ring, and I didn't think to take it outside with me," she explained.

"I just wanted to make sure you were all right," I told her.

"Why, Bobbie? You haven't made sure I was all right for several months now. Why start now?" She laughed.

"Mother, please. Why can't you just try to get along with me?" I begged.

"What have I done wrong, Bobbie, pray tell?" she asked, looking all innocent.

Garrett interrupted. "Mrs. Patterson, we actually came to invite you for Thanksgiving dinner. I will come pick you up if you would like."

"Thank you, Garrett, but I will be going to Tony and Ashley's for Thanksgiving," she said, looking me straight in the eye.

I picked up the baby and bundled him up. "Come on, Butch. I'll meet you in the truck, Garrett."

Several minutes later, Garrett got in the truck, and we drove back home. I was fuming mad, but I didn't say anything and neither did Garrett.

When I put Billy Jo in his crib, Garrett asked," Why do you give your Mother such a hard time? She loves you very much, and if Tony asked her to dinner first, what is the big deal?"

"The big deal is that he is my ex-husband. She spends more time with him than she does with me. She never did believe me when I told her about finding him and Ashley in his office that night, and they weren't playing doctor either. So now you are going to stick up for him too?"

"I'm not sticking up for anybody. I'm just asking," he said quietly.

I went in the kitchen and found my bottle of wine I had hidden and took a long sip. I missed swirling it and inhaling all the fragrance, but here lately, I just needed the effects of it. I took another long swig and then put it back in its hiding place as I heard Garrett come down the steps. I grabbed a little candy bar from the fridge and was munching on it when he asked if I was ready for bed. That night, we slept on opposite sides of the bed, and I cried into my pillow.

———————————

On Thanksgiving Day, it was Garrett, me, Billy Jo, and Frances. She had jumped at the chance of not being by herself on a holiday. We ate all we could possibly eat, and then the men went to watch football while Frances and I cleaned up.

"He is a wonderful father to Billy Jo, Bobbie. I hope someday to find one of them. I keep looking. I met a new guy last week at the mall. You have been so busy that I keep forgetting to tell you about him. His name is Brett Nivy. He is a CPA and has his own business. He is kind of short and chunky, but he has such a wonderful personality. Why don't we all get together Saturday and go out to eat?"

"That sounds like fun, Frances. I'll see what Garrett says about it."

We finished dishes and joined the men watching TV.

"Garrett," I began when the commercial came on, "Frances would like for us to meet her new beau. She has invited us to go out with them Saturday night."

"Well, Frances, I'm glad you have met someone, but why don't you bring him here? We can cook up something or get a pizza," he said.

"Garrett, we haven't been out on the town since Billy Jo was born. It will be fun to get away for a change," I told him.

"I don't want to take Billy Jo to a big restaurant where there will be a lot people," he explained.

"Then we will get a babysitter," I pled along with Frances.

"Maybe some other time, Frances. I think I am going to change him and put him to bed," he said and then picked Billy Jo up and headed upstairs.

The next day, I stayed home from work to spend some time with Billy Jo. It was kind of chilly, so I bundled him up warmly when I put him in his stroller. We walked all over the yard, and Butch followed right behind us. When we got back to the house, we sat on the swing, and Billy Jo fell right to sleep. I took him upstairs and changed him after nursing him and then laid him down as I went downstairs to prepare supper.

After supper, I asked Garrett," Why don't you ever want to go out and have fun? You used to take me out before we got married," I said.

"That was different," he said. "We have a baby now, and I want to raise him right. Parents aren't supposed to run around, going out to eat. They are supposed to stay home and take care of their children."

On Sunday morning, bright and early, Garrett got up and dressed and bathed Billy Jo, and then brought him to me in bed to nurse while he fixed breakfast. He then brought me breakfast in bed, kissed me good-bye, and he and Billy Jo went to church. I really did not like the arrangement, but for some reason, my opinion didn't seem to count in the marriage. Garrett was going to have to lighten up a little bit.

I had Sunday dinner all ready when they arrived, and I took Billy Jo upstairs to change and nurse him, laying him down for a nap while we ate.

"Preacher Carr and Sandy are coming next Sunday for dinner. I think you need to start coming to church with me, Bobbie Jo. It is right embarrassing to be married and my wife not there at church with me," he said.

"We have had this discussion before, and I don't want to talk about it now," I said.

"We need to talk, Bobbie. You just seem to be getting farther and farther away from me. I love you, Bobbie Jo. That hasn't changed. I am trying to do what I think is right," he explained.

Chapter Twenty-eight

Garrett pointed to the sofa, and I sat down like an obedient child. I was fuming. I wasn't sure if I should just shut up and let him say his piece and be done or if I should let him know how I feel.

"Bobbie," he began with his hands together like he was praying, "we are married now, and Billy Jo doesn't deserve to be left with a babysitter just so we can go out partying with friends. He is a big responsibility, and he already doesn't get to see us all day because he is in that day care center at work. He thinks Mary is his mother."

He continued, "There is no reason to be getting all upset over this. What is wrong with Frances bringing her gentleman friend over here for pizza? I think it would be nice."

I didn't say anything. I was afraid of what was going to come out. I couldn't believe what I was hearing.

Where was I when this rule book came to live in this house? I must have missed that day.

"Bobbie, another thing, I really think you need to quit your job—"

That was it. I couldn't be still any longer. "Quit my job? Are you going to quit yours too? Why do I need to quit my job?" I asked him sternly.

In the same monotone voice, he said, "I make enough money to get by. We have everything we need, and I think Billy Jo needs to be raised by his mother, not by some woman named Mary."

"I am doing a fine job raising my son, Mr. James. How dare you accuse me of being a bad Mother just because I work and send my baby to day care! It happens every day of the year to all kinds of babies, and they grow up to be just fine."

Garrett continued, "I didn't say you were a bad mother. I simply stated it would be better if you were at home to raise him properly and watch over him better."

"I think I have heard enough of this conversation. You are dead wrong, Mr. James. I do take care of my son, and you have nothing for which to accuse me. Who put these filthy thoughts into your head? Preacher Carr or Marcia? You tell them to keep their noses out of my business. Do you hear me?"

Garrett got up and walked out the door. The rest of my sentence was lost in the air behind him. He got in the truck and drove off. I went upstairs and found my bottle of vodka. I didn't like it as well as wine, but it hit home a lot faster, and Garrett couldn't smell it on me. I took the first of it fast, and it burned all the way down, which made me even madder. The second one I sipped and walked into Billy Jo's room.

He was lying there so sweetly, and I gently brushed the hair out of his face. "I love you, little one, and I am going to take care of you," I whispered to him. "Sleep tight."

I finished my drink and went to get another one but heard Garrett come in the front door, so I hid my glass and hurriedly changed my clothes and climbed into bed. I heard him come up the steps and go to Billy Jo's room, and I thought I heard him singing to him. The next thing I knew, the alarm clock went off.

When I turned around, Garrett was gone. The clock said 6:00 a.m., so I got up and went to check on Billy Jo. He was not in his crib, so I figured Garrett had gotten him and taken him downstairs. I took my shower and dressed for work.

In the kitchen, Garrett was sitting at the table with a half-empty bottle of vodka sitting in front of him. This was not going to be good.

"Nipping a little before dawn?" I asked jokingly as I grabbed a cup and poured some coffee. "Where is Billy Jo?"

"Billy Jo is at Marcia's house."

"Why is Billy Jo at Marcia's house? I don't want him at Marcia's house?" I told him.

"You were drunk last night when I got home. The baby was screaming, and you didn't even move. He was stuck between the mattress and the crib. He could have been seriously hurt. You were too drunk to take care of him. I took him over to Marcia's so we could talk. You have got to stop drinking, Bobbie. You are going to end up not only hurting yourself but Billy Jo and me. Is that what you want?" he accused.

"I really don't like being cornered like this, Garrett. I am not an alcoholic, and I do not appreciate you treating me like one. I suppose the whole town knows I like a sip once in a while because now you have made us the laughingstock of Fairville. Marcia does not miss an opportunity to make a fool out of me, and you have put yourself right in the middle of it. Now, go get my baby." I pointed at the door.

"Bobbie, I did not tell Marcia anything. I just asked her if she could watch him for a couple of hours and said that we had something to do. Marcia is a good Christian woman, and she loves you. You need to start looking around you instead of being so selfish all the time. There are a lot of people who love you and care about you, and you just keep pushing us away."

"Garrett, I have done absolutely nothing wrong. I had a couple of drinks before I went to bed. Big deal! I am over twenty-one, and that is legal drinking age. Since we have been married, you've become my dad, and I don't need a dad. I need a husband who is going to love me and take care of me and Billy Jo. You've made up so many rules around here for me to live by that you can't even keep them straight," I said.

He got up and went to the sink, pouring out the rest of the contents of the bottle. He looked at me and said, "This will not be brought in my house again. I'm going back to work. Marcia is going to bring Billy Jo back at noon."

With that, he walked out of the door. I was so mad I could have spit nails. *How dare he treat me this way?* I decided to get Billy Jo, pack my things, and get out of there. I was not going to spend the rest of my life having someone look over my shoulder and accuse me of being an alcoholic. I went to the kitchen and started throwing plates and cups and whatever else I could catch hold of.

Garrett must have heard the noise because I felt his big hands close around my arms and pull me up to his face. He was breathing hard, and his face was red. The words came out slow and deliberate.

"Now, Bobbie Jo, you can clean this place up before Marcia sees it. Tomorrow, I am going to take you to the doctor and see about making you better. I think you're going crazy in your head."

"I am not crazy. What's wrong with you? You are crazy. There is absolutely nothing wrong with having a couple of drinks before bedtime. Do you hear me?" I spit in his face, and when I looked at him, there were tears rolling down his cheeks.

"Okay, Bobbie. You do whatever you wish, but you are not going to put Billy Jo in jeopardy like you did last night. I don't care what I have to do to protect him, but I will," he said, and his words sent a chill down my spine.

I heard a car pull up in the driveway, and I tried to get loose from his grasp. He held on tighter than ever.

"I mean it, Bobbie. I'll do everything in my power to protect him. Everything," he said in a low, deep, threatening voice.

He let go of my wrists, and I heard the doorbell. Garrett walked over and opened it so Marcia and Danny could come in. They didn't say much, but they knew something was going on. Garrett still had tear-stains down his face, and I was just standing back by the kitchen door.

Marcia handed the baby to Garrett, and he turned to me and said, "He needs to be changed and fed. Why don't you take him upstairs?"

Obediently, I picked Billy Jo up and hugged him to me and slowly went upstairs. I changed his diaper and cleaned him up and then sat in the rocking chair and nursed him. He was so hungry he couldn't get a good grip on my breast, so I finally had to force him to hold his head still so he could feed. I was laughing at him wriggling around so much, trying to find the nipple, until Garrett walked in the door.

"Marcia said good-bye and to call her if there was anything she could do to help. She said the twins really enjoyed having Billy Jo over this morning. They had a good time playing with him. Are you going to be okay?" he asked.

I didn't answer him. I just hugged Billy Jo and nursed him, and then I held him up and burped him. It scared me that he had gotten hurt last night. I only drank two glasses, or so I thought.

"I love you, Billy Jo. You are all I have, and now Garrett is threatening to take you away, and I won't let him do it. I just can't. I promise I will take better care of you. I am so sorry."

I sat there all day, holding him. That night, I found some blankets and made a pallet on the floor. I lay on the blankets and put him right beside me. We fell asleep together on the floor, and I held him all night. I didn't remember when or if Garrett came home, and I didn't really care.

Chapter Twenty-nine

We barely spoke to each other except when necessary. I slept on the floor in Billy Jo's room every night. I was afraid to leave him alone. I was so afraid Garrett was going to take him from me. I couldn't eat or sleep, and I was becoming haggard looking. I must admit that my drinking was getting worse. The need for it consumed me, and I had to find more places to hide it not only from Garrett but from everyone.

I was so paranoid, thinking that everybody was watching me. I started lying about my drinking and sneaking around to different towns to buy it. Garrett just kept watching me. I had to figure out how to get away from him and take Billy Jo someplace safe. I had never told Garrett about the safe deposit box, so I had money to run away with.

On Christmas Day, Garrett cut down a small tree and decorated it. There were two gifts under it: one for me and one for Billy Jo. Garrett handed them to us, and I laid mine aside to watch Billy Jo. He played with the package for a while, and then I helped him open it. It was an old-fashioned jack-in-the-box, and every time Jack would jump out of the box, Billy Jo would smile.

"Open your package, Bobbie. I hope you like it," Garrett said.

"I don't want anything from you, Garrett."

He got up and went in the kitchen while I played with Billy Jo. It had started snowing, so we dressed in our warm clothes, coats and hats, and went outside. Garrett decided to carry in some wood for the stove as I held the door open for him.

I carried Billy Jo all around the yard, talking to him and telling him about the snow. His eyes were as wide as saucers, and he was taking it all in. My bottle of liquor was in my pocket, so I made sure Garrett was gone in the house, and I took a long taste and appreciated the burning as it numbed my senses.

Garrett cooked dinner with a ham, mashed potatoes, corn, green beans, and biscuits. I held Billy Jo on my lap while I ate. I moved the food around on my plate so it looked like I was eating. Butch got most of it, as I dropped pieces to him.

"Why don't you let me change him for you while you finish eating?" Garrett offered.

"I'm through eating. I'll take care of him." I pushed away from the table, and I heard the doorbell ring. I looked at Garrett and said, "Looks like some of your friends are here."

I could hear him talking as I climbed the steps. When I looked out the window, I saw Marcia, Danny, and the twins. Billy Jo was hungry and trying to find my breast, so I sat on the rocker and helped him.

"I love you, Billy Jo, and I am not going to let Garrett and Marcia take you away from me." I heard somebody behind me, and I just figured it was Garrett, so I didn't bother turning around.

Marcia came around to face me.

"Bobbie, Merry Christmas. Garrett said you weren't feeling well. Is there anything I can do?"

"I think you have done enough, Marcia. You have helped turn everybody against me, and I will not let you take my baby. Now, leave me alone."

As she walked out of the room, I heard her say, "Jesus loves you, Bobbie."

When we finally came back downstairs, I found the jack-in-the-box and could relate to him. It seemed like somebody was always trying to get me to pop up and do what they wanted me to do. I felt trapped, and suddenly, I couldn't breathe. I grabbed a blanket for Billy Jo and ran out on the porch.

The snow was still coming down, and it looked like a white blanket that came down to cover the earth. We sat on the swing, and I held him and talked to him. Garrett came up to the porch and sat on one of the chairs, watching me.

"Bobbie, I love you, and I just want to help you. I don't know where you got the notion I was going to take Billy Jo away from you. We can have a good life again if you want to," he begged.

The swing was squeaking with each movement, and as I listened to it, I thought it sounded like it was singing a song to me.

> Run, Bobbie! Run, run far away!
> Billy Jo is with you and,
> So is the end of this day.

Garrett said something and then got in his truck and left. The snow was falling, and the song was more intense than ever.

> Run, Bobbie! Run, run far away!
> Billy Jo is with you and,
> So is the end of this day.

I took another couple of drinks and then went inside. The stove needed some more wood, so I opened the door and put a couple logs in the best I could. The door wouldn't shut, so I figured they would burn down. I didn't notice the flue was wide open and how quickly the fire was consuming the logs.

Billy Jo was fast asleep, and I laid him in his crib and came downstairs to fill my bottle. Suddenly, I felt so tired. I lay on the couch and fell fast asleep. I was dreaming of Michael when I heard Garrett call my name. I didn't want to talk to him, so I rolled over, and I felt him pick me up and carry me outside. I tried to hit him with my fists, but I couldn't. I was too weak.

When I opened my eyes, there were people standing around everywhere. I heard people yelling, and I didn't know what was going on. I sat up and looked at the house, and it was on fire. The fire was coming out of the windows, and the firemen were pouring water on it.

Immediately, I jumped up and ran to the house. "Billy Jo! Billy Jo! Where is my baby?"

An arm grabbed me and held me tightly.

I was kicking and hitting with all my strength. "Billy Jo, where is my baby?"

The arm belonged to David Stone, one of the firefighters. "Bobbie, where is your baby? What room is he in?"

"He is in his crib," I said, shaking my head, trying to remember. "Please, please get him." I could hear Billy Jo crying, and I couldn't go to him. David wouldn't let me go, so I begged him, "Please, please get my baby!"

While we were watching the house burn, the roof collapsed and David grabbed me and we ran away as the fire spread to the trees and engulfed everything around it. The men ran to get water on it as fast as they could. No one could get close enough to it. It was out of control. I finally broke free from his grasp and ran to house and up on the porch. My clothes caught on fire immediately, and someone grabbed me, threw me to the ground, and wrapped me in a blanket.

When I opened my eyes, I was in the hospital. My body felt like it was on fire, and there were tubes everywhere. I couldn't move because my hands were tied down. I was so weak I just closed my eyes and hoped I would just die. When my clothes had caught on fire, they burned my arms and part of my back.

Dr. Nathan New was the burn specialist at the hospital, and he introduced himself when I woke up. "How are you feeling today, Mrs. James?"

"Bobbie," I tried to say, but it wouldn't come out. My mouth was as dry as a popcorn fart, or so Father would say.

He was tall and broad shouldered. He talked with the nurse, Doris, who was assisting him in taking off my bandages.

"I know this is very painful, Mrs. James, but Doris is going to give you some morphine in your IV, so you shouldn't feel too much. I will be as gentle as possible."

I felt a pleasant warm sensation as the morphine coursed through my veins. I fell asleep instantly and dreamed of Michael running in the field, and then there was Billy Jo, and they were holding hands, but then there was a fire; and I tried to run to them to get them away from it, but they were running too fast, and I couldn't move. My hands were tied down, and I couldn't run. My body was thrashing as I tried to get to them, and I felt a strong arm across my chest and a voice calling my name.

"Bobbie. Bobbie, wake up." A pleasant soft voice was calling me, but I couldn't wake up. "Bobbie, open your eyes," it said. "I have your breakfast for you."

Doris brought a big tray with a bowl of oatmeal and a cup of coffee. I half opened my eyes and tried to tell her to go away, but the words would not come out. She pushed the button on the side of the bed, and the head of my bed went up. Straightening my pillow, she carefully helped me sit up to eat.

The food smelled awful, and I started gagging. She ran for the emesis basin, and I vomited. She wet a couple wash clothes for me and wiped my face and laid them on my forehead, and I laid back and went back to sleep.

The same dream came back to me. That time, Garrett had Billy Jo, and Michael was running after him, and they were going into a house that was burning. I tried to yell to him, but he turned around and laughed and walked into the fire before I could stop them. I screamed and cried and tried to run, but I was still tied down.

Dr. New woke me the next time and looked into my eyes with a bright light. Once again, I felt the comfort the morphine created in my body and welcomed it.

The next time I was awake, I asked Dr. New where I was and where Billy Jo was. I had to find out so I could go to him and nurse him. My breasts were engorged, and I needed to feed him.

"There is someone outside who will answer all those questions for you," he said as he checked my IV and my bandages.

"Hi, Bobbie." I turned to see Preacher Carr and Sandy walk in the room. "How are you doing?"

Thinking that was a dumb question, I asked him where Billy Jo was. He looked at me and didn't have to say a word. I knew he was dead. Everything came flooding back to me: the fire and the roof collapsing.

I shut my eyes and screamed, "No!"

Preacher Carr took my hand and held it and said, "Dear Lord, take care of this child of yours. Only you can take the pain away and turn her life around to be pleasing to you."

When he left, I cried. The nurse tried to wipe my face with a wet cloth, but I continued to cry. My heart was broken clean in two, and I just wanted to die. I wanted to be with Michael and Billy Jo.

Why? Why did he have to die? Why?

Chapter Thirty

The nurses were very patient and kind, but I didn't want to get better. I wanted to die, and every moment of the day, I wished for death to come and relieve me of the heartache I carried.

Marcia came to see me, and when she walked in the room, I turned away from her. She told me how sorry she was about Billy Jo and said that Garrett was doing fine.

"He is trying to build another house right beside the old one, so that is keeping him busy."

"Go away, Marcia. Go away and leave me alone. I don't care about Garrett or anything else. I guess you and he got your wish. I don't have my baby anymore," I told her viciously.

When I looked at her, she had tears in her eyes; and as she walked out of the room, she told me, "Jesus loves you, Bobbie."

My cough was getting worse, and sometimes I started coughing until I coughed up blood. Dr. New came in the room a few minutes later to check me. He brought another doctor in my room with him and introduced her as Dr. Levter.

"She is a respiratory specialist. We are going to be taking you downstairs to x-ray as soon as she is finished."

"Hi, Bobbie. The nurse told me that you have been coughing quite a lot. This is quite common in burn patients. I hear you inhaled a lot of smoke before they brought you out of the house. We took x-rays when you first arrived, but we want to do another set to compare them and see how well you are doing with the treatment. First,

I just want to listen to your lungs. Now, take a big deep breath. That's good. And let it out."

She did this for a long time, it seemed, making me breathe in and out, and she put her stethoscope in various places on my chest and back. The funny thing was, no matter how many times she moved it, it was always cold.

The x-ray tech's name was Michael, and I told him about my Michael. He was very nice and talked to me through the whole procedure. Once again in my room, the nurse brought me a meal tray, but I refused it.

I asked if I could get up in a wheelchair for a while, and two nurses came in to assist me. With my Foley catheter and all the IV tubes, it took a while to situate everything. They pushed me up to the window so I could look out.

The whole city of Columbus lay before me. It was a sunny day, and the sun glistened off the windows of all the tall buildings. I saw people and cars passing below, and they seemed so small and so far away. Maybe it was just me who was so small and so far away.

Frances came to visit me and was pleased that I was sitting up. She asked if there was anything she could help me with, and I asked her if she would stay with me for a few minutes.

"What is the date? What day is today? I have lost all track of time."

"It's Valentine's Day, Bobbie. February fourteenth."

I had been in the hospital for a month and a half. It seemed like only yesterday that the fire burned down the house and took my life away from me.

"Frances, tell me about the fire. Tell me about Billy Jo."

"You mean nobody has told you?" she asked.

"I know Billy Jo is dead, but that is all. What did he look like at the funeral? Did he have a nice outfit on?" I asked.

"Bobbie, the casket was closed. The body was almost completely destroyed by the fire. Garrett buried him and Butch out in the back of the old house. The firemen did not know where they were. They said they could hear Butch barking but couldn't get to him before the roof collapsed."

Butch. Oh, Butch. I completely forgot about him. I've been so heartbroken over Billy Jo that I completely forgot about him.

My mind went back to that night, but all I could remember was someone calling me and carrying me out of the house and the roof falling. I couldn't remember anything else no matter how hard I tried.

"The fire inspectors said that the cause of the fire was from the woodstove," she said. "Evidently, it was not closed and the flue was left open. Garrett told them he knew the door was broken but just never got around to fixing it."

When Frances left, the nurse helped me back to bed, and I fell into a fitful sleep, having the same dream of Garrett taking Michael, Billy Jo, and Butch away from me. No matter how hard I tried, I could not reach him to stop him. When I awoke, I was still in the hospital, and I felt so empty inside. I had no home, no baby, and no husband. I had no one.

Dr. Levter told me I had pneumonia in both lung bases and started me on antibiotics. When the nurses gave me my medications, I would cheek them and pretend to swallow them. Working in a nursing home was quite beneficial when one becomes the patient.

After another chest x-ray, it was determined my pneumonia was not any better, so they started giving me antibiotic injections. They stung like bees when they gave them, and I had to have them twice a day for ten days.

When I was released from the hospital, the nurse rolled a wheelchair into my room. I got in it and she rolled me down the hall. I remembered the last time I was in a wheelchair leaving the hospital when Billy Jo was born, and the tears flooded my eyes.

No one was there when I was discharged. I had no ride, and the only clothes I had were the blue jeans one of the nurses gave me from the lost and found room along with a scrub top and footies. The nurse stopped the wheelchair, and I stood up and was a little dizzy at first, but then I was okay.

"Where is your ride?" she asked.

"I don't have one. I guess I'll have to walk. Thank you for being so kind to me. I really appreciate it," I told her.

When I started walking down the road, I heard the nurse calling me. I turned around, and she came running up to me and handed me $20.

"This will get you a taxi. God bless you!"

I thanked her and started walking.

Columbus is a very big town, and I had no idea where I was, so I went into a little store and asked where the pay phone was. The little man behind the counter pointed to the back wall near the bathrooms. I thanked him and called for a taxi. Several minutes later, it pulled up in front of the store. When I climbed in the backseat, I asked him if I could get to Fairville on $20. He told me I could get close enough.

He stopped about five miles outside of Fairville, and I gave him the money, told him thanks, and headed down the road. I was going to go to the bank first and get some money.

The bank was busy that day with long lines at the cashier's windows. When I walked in, I could have heard a pin drop. Everybody turned and stared at me, watching as I knocked on Mr. Apsun's, the bank president, door. When he finally answered the door, he hurriedly ushered me inside.

"What do you want?" he said rudely.

"I need some money. I want—"

"You don't have any money here. Garrett took it all out to build another house since you burned the first one down and killed your baby."

"How dare you," I started.

"Go away, Bobbie. I don't ever want to see you in this bank again." He then got up to open the door.

"I want my money. Garrett couldn't take all the money because it was in CDs in my name," I said, trying not to yell.

"I said you don't have any money here." He opened the door, but I refused to leave. "If you don't leave, I will call the police."

"I don't care who you call. I want my money. Give me the key to the lockbox so I can get it," I insisted.

He walked over to his desk and hit a button, and suddenly, Charles Leisl, the security guard came in the office. He looked at Mr. Apsun and then at me.

"It looks like Bobbie Jo has forgotten where the front door is, Charles. Would you be kind enough to show her?" he told him.

"Mr. Apsun, please. Look at me! I need my money. Garrett could not have taken it. It was in my name. Please!" I yelled at him.

Charles took me by my burned arm, and I screamed with pain, but he continued to hold it and took me to the front door. The people in the bank watched all of it, but no one came to help me.

I sat on the curb of the road and put my head in my hands. *Why wouldn't Mr. Apsun give me my money?* I turned around and looked toward the bank, and Charles was still standing guard at the door.

It started sprinkling, and I wondered, *What else can go wrong?* I got up and walked down the street.

A police car pulled up, and I saw Melvin and Tom coming toward me. "What are you doing here, Bobbie Jo? You need to go back where you came from. You are not welcome in this town. Garrett might have saved your neck, but I wouldn't have. You are nothing but a drunk and a murderer. Now get on down the road before I put you in jail."

The words hit me like a block of ice. I watched them drive away, but I couldn't move. *This whole town thinks I killed Billy Jo. Why would they think that?* No matter how hard I tried, I could not remember what happened that night. I remembered the roof falling, and I could still hear Billy Jo crying. That was the worst part of it. He was still crying, and I couldn't shake the sound from my head. I couldn't get to him, and the sound echoed off each cell in my brain.

Lightning flashed and lit up the whole sky, and I thought, *Yes.* *Maybe it will hit me and take away this misery and pain inside of me.* The thunder sounded a few seconds later, and as I walked, I welcomed death. I craved death. Hearing Billy Jo cry every day, every moment of the day was devouring me.

Chapter Thirty-one

Garrett was on a ladder, working in the rain when I walked up. The house had been totally destroyed. It was as if it never existed. The only thing there was a blackened burned area.

When he saw me, he came walking across the yard, and before I could react, he back handed me across the face with all his strength and I fell in the mud. Blood gushed out of my nose, and I couldn't move. When I looked at him, he kicked me in the ribs and then turned and walked away.

I was so mad at him for stopping. I wanted him to hit me again and again until it came. Death, I longed for it. The pain and grief was intolerable, and I got up and ran toward him, hitting him on the back. He turned around and hit me again, this time with his fist in my stomach. I laid on the ground, gasping for air, and I choked on my vomit.

When I could finally breathe, I got up and walked over to him. "Go away, Bobbie Jo," he said. "Just go away. I am not going to kill you, if that's what you want. Death would be too good for you. I want you to be tortured the rest of your life with the thought of murdering your own son. I want you to hear his screams and have them torment you as long as you live, and I pray to God that will be a long time. Don't ever come around here again. If you do, I will have you thrown in jail, and believe me, the whole town would love to do that. I have saved your neck for the last time." He spit the words at me.

The rain was coming down harder as I turned and started down the driveway. I had nowhere to go, so I headed for Frances's house.

It was such a long way, and it was late, so I lay down in a ditch and slept.

When I woke up, I was laying on an army cot. I had no idea where I was, and I hurt all over. I looked around to see a small room. I didn't see or hear anyone, so I tried to sit up, but a pain shot through my side.

I screamed and held my side, and I heard someone say, "Don't try to move. Here. Drink this."

A bottle was placed up to my mouth, and the golden liquid satisfied me as it seared my brain. I welcomed its relief and asked for more. The liquid was once again offered, and I took it in as fast as I could before choking on it.

Sleep came easily after that, and my same dream came back to haunt me: Garrett, Michael, and Billy Jo walking into a burning house. I screamed and tried to stop them, but they didn't even look back.

"Bobbie, it's okay." I heard a voice say. "Wake up. It's just a dream."

When I opened my eyes, I saw Oscar Studds leaning over me.

"Here. Let me help you sit up. You have been sleeping for quite a long time."

"Oh, Oscar, it's so nice to see a friendly face." I cried into his shoulder as he held me. "The whole town hates me. I can't get my money out of the bank. Garrett hates me, and I tried to get him to finish me off, but he wouldn't."

"It's okay. Here. I made you some eggs and coffee. I hope you like it black."

He handed me a plate filled with scrambled eggs and a couple pieces of toast and a large cup of coffee.

The coffee was hot and bitter, and it warmed up my cold body. I was naked, sitting there with only a blanket wrapped around me.

"You were soaking wet and bleeding when I found you. I washed your clothes. I had to get them off of you because you needed to get warm."

"Thank you, Oscar," I said as I enjoyed the coffee. I tried to eat some of the eggs, but I couldn't. I did take a few bites of the toast. "How long have I been here?'

"A couple of days. I was driving home and saw something in the ditch. I thought it was a deer that had gotten hit by a car, so I stopped to investigate. Imagine my surprise when I saw you laying there. I didn't know what happened to you after the fire. You just disappeared. No one would give me any information, and the talk of the town was that you started the fire and killed your baby."

"Oh, Oscar, Billy Jo is dead, and I killed him. Oh, Oscar, I honestly don't know what happened that night. All I remember is Billy Jo crying upstairs, and then the roof collapsed." I cried into his shoulder.

"Garrett told the investigators the wood stove door had been broken for a long time, but he never got around to fixing it, and you probably thought it was closed," he told me.

Then I understood what Garrett was talking about when he said, "I have saved your neck for the last time." The tears came, and there was no stopping them. It was like a dam had broken. Oscar put his arms around me and tried to comfort me, but they still came.

I killed Billy Jo. I killed my baby.

The next day, Oscar drove me to Beautiful Gardens. When I walked in, the place became deathly silent. Mr. Greenfield was in his office with Jeb Hardy. When he saw me, he excused himself and came out.

"Bobbie, what can I do for you?" he asked impatiently.

"I need to know if I still have a job. I have no money and nowhere to go. Please give me a job. It doesn't have to be the D.O.N. position. I will mop floors if you need me to," I pleaded with him.

"Your position has already been filled, and we aren't hiring at this time. I do believe Frances has your last paycheck. Now, if you would be so kind as to leave this facility and not return. We do not want bad publicity around here."

He turned and walked back into his office, slamming the door in my face as I tried to follow him. Frances was sitting at her desk, and when she saw me, she got up and hugged me.

"How are you? I wondered what happened to you. I came to the hospital to see you again, but you were asleep."

"Frances, Mr. Greenfield said you had my last paycheck. I really need it. I have no money, and Mr. Apsun will not let me have my money from the bank. If I sign this, will you cash it for me? He said he would throw me in jail if I go in there again," I said.

"It's time for my lunch, so come on. We can go there now."

I waited in the car until Frances came back out with my money. I thanked her and got out of the car.

"Bobbie, if there is anything I can do, please call me," she said.

I thanked her again and headed down the road when Oscar pulled up beside me, and I hopped into his truck. I handed him the money to buy groceries, but he told me that he didn't need my money and for me to keep it.

"Keep your money. It ain't no good here," he said. "You are welcome to stay as long as you want. I could use some company."

Oscar told me I could stay with him until I could figure out what to do. He taught me how to fish, and every night, we would share a bottle of whiskey. My dreams haunted me, and sometimes they weren't just at night. They would stop me in my tracks and paralyze me each time they came.

One morning, I went to the lake alone before sunrise and watched as the ducks landed in the water. It was so hot and humid. I brought some bread crumbs, and as I threw them in the water, the ducks would swim over and eat them.

I lay back on the grass and watched as the sun peeked over the horizon. The sky turned red and yellow, and it was magnificent to look at. I watched as the sun came up in its full glory and was amazed at how beautiful it was.

Suddenly, a scrawny black puppy came out of nowhere and started licking my face. I jumped up and looked at him. His legs were long, and he was completely black. He walked unbalanced, and I laughed when he tried to follow me and kept falling over.

I looked around for the owner, but there was no one around, so I got up to look further. The puppy kept following me and trying to nip my heels. I finally picked him up and took him home. Oscar laughed when he saw him and asked where I had found such a mongrel.

"What in the world is that?" he asked.

"Oscar, you are going to hurt his feelings. What do you think we should name him?" I asked.

"We? Do you have a mouse in your pocket? We are not going to name him anything. What in the world are we going to do with a dog? They are nothing but trouble," he said.

I took the puppy's head and made him look all sad, and I stuck out my lower lip, trying to get him to change his mind. He laughed, and I started laughing with him. It felt good to laugh again. It had been entirely too long.

"Okay. I guess we will call him Mongrel. That is a perfect name for him. "Look," he said as Mongrel came to him. "He knows his name already. He is not as dumb as he looks."

Mongrel was a very smart dog, and he made me laugh. He gave me a reason to live. I took him out every day and trained him. He was very smart, and I never had to leash him because he stayed at my heels all the time. He would only chase the squirrels and rabbits when he was told to.

One day we were at the lake, and Mongrel was lying under a tree beside us. A squirrel came down and walked right up to him. Mongrel laid there, watching it until I clapped my hands and said, "Get him." I had never in my life seen a dog move as fast as he did that day. The squirrel was between his teeth faster than lightning. The funny thing was he never hurt it. When he dropped it, the squirrel took off as fast as his legs would carry him.

Chapter Thirty-two

Sleep was impossible mostly due to the dreams. They wouldn't stop. Sometimes I would wake up screaming, and Oscar would have to hold me until I calmed down. When Oscar fell asleep, I would usually get up and sit outside with Mongrel. I tried to decide what in the world to do with my life, but I just didn't know.

As I was sitting there, I heard Oscar start coughing. He was coughing more frequently, especially at night. He tried to hide it from me, but I heard him. Sometimes, he would get up and come outside to vomit. He never talked about it, but I knew something was wrong.

"Oscar, are you all right?" I asked, feeling his forehead for fever.

"I'm fine, Bobbie. I am just so cold. Will you lay down with me for a while and warm me up?" he asked.

I pulled the blankets back and slid in beside him on the pallet he had made. He was burning up with fever. I hugged him close to me, and he cried in my hair until he finally went to sleep. When daylight came, I was all alone on the floor. I jumped up and saw that Mongrel was not there either. I walked down to the lake, and Mongrel came running toward me. I saw Oscar sitting on the picnic table.

"How are you feeling today?" I asked as I sat down beside him. "You were pretty sick last night."

"I'm not pretty sick, Bobbie," he started. "I'm dying. I have lung cancer, and it has now moved to my liver and my stomach. I was diagnosed a couple of years ago."

"Oh, Oscar," I said, taking his hand in mine. "What can I do to help?"

"There's nothing you can do." He looked at me sincerely. "I really like having you here. Thanks for staying with me. I know the good Lord is going to take me home when it is time, but I'm glad you will be with me while I am still here."

"I promise, Oscar. I promise," I said, hugging him.

His cough was getting worse, and what he was coughing up had a foul odor. He was having difficulty breathing, so I had to keep him propped at night. He seemed to be fine in the daytime, and we would spend most of our days at the lake, feeding the ducks and the fish.

Mongrel was getting bigger and he was very protective of me. No one could get close to me or he would growl. I had to tell him no, and then he would calm down as soon as he felt like I was in no danger.

One day, Oscar went fishing while I dug for some worms by the house. It had rained the night before, and the night crawlers were everywhere. I took a coffee can with me and started piling them in. I heard someone come up behind me.

"Did you drown all the—?" I asked as I turned around.

He hit me before I could get the rest of the sentence out of my mouth. There were two of them, and one of them grabbed me and started taking my clothes off. Suddenly, I heard a gunshot and saw Oscar pointing a double-barreled shotgun at the man.

"I think you two have overstayed your welcome. If you come back here, I will kill you." He fired the gun again. This time, it barely missed his groin area. "Don't think I missed. I hit exactly where I was aiming."

The two men ran as fast as they could, jumped in their truck, and spun tires trying to get out of there before Oscar shot them. I pulled my jeans back on, and Oscar walked over to me.

"Are you all right?" he asked.

"Yeah. Just scared to death. My heart is beating a mile a minute. Who were those guys, and what did they want?" I asked.

"I think they were here to hurt you. Maybe you should take Mr. Apsun's advice and move to another state," he suggested.

"Who would take care of you then?" I asked.

"I took care of myself long before you came along," he said.

"Does that mean you don't want me here anymore?" I asked.

"No. Of course not. I'm sorry. I didn't mean for it to sound like that. I'm so glad you are here. Forgive me. I didn't mean to sound so heartless." He held me close to him, and I felt safer than I had for a long time.

"Maybe we should move to Texas. I don't want to go anywhere without you," I suggested.

As the months went by, Oscar got sicker and sicker. He was too sick to get out of bed, and I bathed him daily and gave him whiskey for his pain. He reached in his pocket and pulled out some sort of legal paper and handed it to me. It was my divorce papers from Garrett. I didn't know anything about it. I hadn't given it a second thought.

"Now that you are legally divorced, I want you to marry me. I am going to die real soon, Bobbie, and I want to make sure you are taken care of. I have some money in a lock box at Sam Ross's house. I want you to go get him now. He will know what to do. I hope you will do this."

"Yes, Oscar. Whatever you want me to do," I said as I kissed his forehead and drove to Sam's house.

When Sam opened the door, he knew exactly what to do. He got all his papers and his wife, Chris, and we drove as fast as I could back home.

Oscar was having a hard time breathing, but he said, "Sam, I want you to marry Bobbie Jo and me. I want you to make sure she is taken good care of after I die. You know what to do."

Sam told me to stand by Oscar and hold his hand, and the wedding ceremony began. After the pronouncement of husband and wife, Oscar kissed my hand and said, "Thank-you, Mrs. Studds."

I laughed at him and signed our marriage license and certificate. Oscar finally went to sleep after I gave him a couple swigs of whiskey, and I walked Sam and his wife to the car.

"Bobbie, Oscar is a very rich man. He has over two million dollars' worth of assets that now belong to you, or they will after his death. He chose to live like this after he found out about his cancer. He has two sons, but they have not spoken to him for years. Oscar was a heavy drinker back then, and his wife took his kids and left him. I'm sure they will contest the will and your marriage, but I will do all I can to help you. I am also Oscar's attorney. Not many people know about that. Oscar put me through law school and paid for my bar exams and got me started, but with Nat Apecs in town, I became a justice of the peace, and Chris and I have been very happy. Here is my card. Call me if you need anything."

Chapter Thirty-three

Mongrel and I were out drowning worms, for the fish weren't biting, and the ducks had flown south for the winter, but I sat there until it started snowing. It came down in big flakes, and I tried to catch them on my tongue. Mongrel was running around, trying to catch birds; and finally, I told him, "Come on, you silly dog. Let's go home."

When we drove up to the house, I noticed that Oscar was not outside as usual. I walked in the house and proclaimed, "Oscar, I didn't catch a thing. I think the fish went south with the—" I stopped and looked at him, and he wasn't breathing. His face was white, and I yelled, "Oscar! Oscar!"

He was on a chair, and I threw him to the floor and tried to remember my CPR training. My heart was beating hard and fast. I put my face down to his mouth and did not feel any air, and I didn't see his chest rising either. I tilted his head back and blew two breaths and watched as his chest rose and fell, so I knew they went in. Then I traced my fingers to the exact spot and started chest compressions. I did three rounds, and he still was not responding. He lay limp in my arms.

Finally, I told Mongrel to stay and I ran to the truck and drove to town.

Juxton Medical Clinic was busy, but I ran to the desk and demanded to see Tony. "I need to see Tony now!" They looked at me like I was crazy, and the people in the lobby stopped talking to look at me.

"Don't just sit there! Tell Tony I need him now!"

I finally ran through the door that led to the back of the clinic, and I saw him enter his office. I ran in, and he looked at me. My heart was pounding, and I was out of breath.

"What's wrong, Bobbie? It must be important or you would never come here," Tony said.

"Oscar. It's Oscar. He is not breathing. Please, Tony. Please come with me," I said, trying to catch my breath.

He grabbed his black bag and told his nurse he would be back as soon as possible. I drove like a maniac trying to get back home. Tony jumped out of the truck and ran in. Mongrel growled at him, and I told him no, and he lay back down.

Tony took his stethoscope out of his black bag and listened. He put his ear close to his mouth and felt for a breath. He finally looked at me and said, "Bobbie, Oscar is dead. I'm sorry." He then took a blanket that was lying beside him and covered his face and called the funeral home.

"No, Tony! No! Please, Tony! No!"

Tony held me in his arms, and I cried. My body shook with the sobs.

As I sat on the cot, I watched Theodore Austin, the funeral director, pick Oscar's body up and place him in a black bag, zip it up, and wheel him outside to the hearse. Tony signed the death certificate, and they took him away. The house seemed so empty without him. He was my only friend besides Mongrel.

Tony asked, "Are you going to be okay?"

"Yes. Thank you for coming. I really appreciate it." I didn't look at him. I watched as they took Oscar away, and I felt my heart rip in two.

Tony got in the hearse, and they drove him back to the clinic. I was all alone again. It seemed to be my lot in life. I couldn't die. I had already tried that, so I lived, and I guess *existed* would be a better term for it.

They buried Oscar at the same graveyard Michael was in, and nobody came to the funeral but me and Mongrel. It was so sad that such a wonderful man had no one to grieve for him, and I felt privileged to have gotten to know him. Preacher Carr read the Twenty-Third Psalm and then put his arm around me and walked me to the truck while they lowered the casket into the ground.

"Bobbie, I'm sorry about Oscar. What are you going to do now? Believe it or not, you are looking for the same thing Jesus wants to give you: love. He loves you, Bobbie. And each of these things happens in your life to bring you to Him," he told me.

"That's nice, Preacher Carr, but I just don't think your Jesus would want much to do with me, so thanks but no thanks," I told him casually.

When I got home, there was a package waiting for me on the steps. It was the jack-in-the-box Garrett had bought Billy Jo for Christmas. It was black from the fire, but when I turned the handle, he still popped up.

I placed the toy on the shelf, wondering why Garrett would bring it there. *He hates me that much to make me look at that toy for the rest of my life.* I never knew that kind of hate was real.

The next day, I drove into town to see Sam Ross. Chris answered the door and led me to his office in the basement. There were two men sitting in front of the desk when I walked in, and I excused myself, saying, "I'm sorry, Sam. I will come back later."

Sam rose from his chair and said, "No, Mrs. Studds. Please come in and join us. These are Oscar's boys, Leon and Marshall. They are here for the reading of the will, as you are."

Chris brought a chair in for me and sat down beside me.

Sam began reading, "I, Oscar Riley Studds, do hereby declare…"

None of it made sense to me, but I tried to understand, especially when he mentioned a wife. He handed the marriage license to the boys, and the look they gave me could have melted steel. They wanted to kill me right then and there.

Chris then handed the boys an envelope each, and they opened them and counted $1,000 in each. They began to call Sam names, and then they started in on me. I didn't move, but Mongrel's hair rose on his back, and he gave them a deep, guttural growl. Chris reached behind her and pulled out a .44 and pointed it at them. Slowly, they sat down.

Sam said, "Thank you, honey. I think you can put it away now. These boys are going to cooperate and be nice now. Right, boys?"

They both nodded their heads in unison, and they looked like bobbing dolls on the dashboard of a car. They sat quietly until Sam finished reading the will. Getting up, they turned and said, "You have not heard the last of us."

After they were gone, Sam gave me a locked box and key and told me, "This is why Oscar wanted to marry you. He has had these stocks for years and some gold blocks you will have to go to the bank to cash in. I will go with you."

"I think I will find another bank. Thanks. What do I need to do, Sam?" I asked.

"We need to figure out exactly how much is here and how much Uncle Sam wants. My fee has already been paid a long time ago. Oscar takes care of those people who took care of him. That is a good motto to live by."

"Will you take care of all this for me and be my financial man? I don't know what they are called, but I figure if Oscar trusted you, I should too," I told him.

My life didn't change much except the hurt was deeper inside. I had a big, dark void that I didn't know how to fill. It was with me all the time. I don't even remember what I did during those days after I buried Oscar. Mongrel and I would go to the graveyard every day and sit for hours, talking to him. I missed him so much. He was my whole life, and now he was gone, gone just like Michael and Billy Jo. Gone.

Tony brought Mother to the house one evening. I was cooking some fish, and I heard Mongrel growl. I opened the door, and Mother gasped at the sight of me. I had lost a lot of weight, and my hair was down to my derriere. I usually kept it in a pony tail and then wrapped it around on my head, but I hadn't had time to mess with it.

"Are you coming in or not? I am busy and don't have much time, so say your derogatory remarks and then be gone," I said, turning my back on her.

Tony helped Mother in the house, and she sat on one of the milk carton chairs.

"Bobbie, she needs to talk to you."

"I told her to go ahead," I told him.

"Bobbie, please," Mother began. "I need your help."

"Well, imagine that. You need my help. Well, Mother dear, I needed yours too. And did I get it? No. You threw everything ugly you could at me until I finally decided I would just hate you and get it over with."

I stopped dead in my tracks. Just a few days before, I was thinking about Garrett and how much he hated me, and that was exactly what I have done with her. What kind of a monster had I become?

"Bobbie, I'm sorry about everything," she said.

"Me too, Mother," I said, and then went back to my supper.

Tony came out and stood beside me. "Look at her, Bobbie. She is getting too old to take care of the house, and she wants to move into an independent living facility. It is a great place. Judd Carr built them a couple of years ago. They are all three-bedroom apartments, and they have some luxurious dining rooms, and they stay busy with activities."

"So what do you want from me?" I asked without turning to look at him.

"She needs to sell the house and use the money to pay for the apartment. Your father made provisions for her as long as she lives in the house, but it has gotten too much for her to handle," he said.

"I don't want to sell the house, Mother. It is the only thing from my childhood that I have left. Go see Sam Ross, and he will give you the money you need for the apartment. Let me know when you have moved, and I will move to the house. It isn't very safe out here by myself," I told her. "Here." I sat and wrote on a piece of paper and handed it to Tony. "Give this to Sam, and he will take care of it."

Mother got up to hug me, and I went back to my cooking. I heard the door shut as they left, and it echoed from wall to wall. I threw my food across the floor and hit the door. I lay on the cot and cried until I finally fell asleep.

Chapter Thirty-four

When I woke, I heard a noise, and I saw him before he saw me. I picked up a big stick and hit him square between the eyes, that was enough to stun him, and I ran outside. There, another man grabbed me and threw me on the ground. Mongrel growled and jumped on the man, knocking him to the ground. Mongrel bit his face, and the man grabbed him and threw him.

"Let's get out of here," one said, but the other one wouldn't go.

"You have no old man to help you this time," the other man said as he fought to pull my blue jeans off.

I hit, kicked, and scratched when the first man grabbed his arm and said, "Let's get out of here."

They dropped me on the ground, and I had a clear shot, so I kicked him with all my might right between the legs.

"You little—," he yelled as he bent over in pain. "Kill her."

A horn blared from somewhere, and they both took off running. It was dark, and my body ached. I tried to get up but I couldn't, and then I remembered Mongrel.

He was lying by the tree where the man had thrown him. I crawled over to him, and he tried to lift his head but couldn't. He wagged his tail, and I hugged him to me. I cried in his fur until I heard somebody call my name.

"Bobbie! Bobbie, are you all right?" I heard Chris hollering.

Sam was calling me too. I opened my eyes and started crying. I was so thankful to see them. He helped me inside the house, and I lay on the cot. Then he carried Mongrel in and put him on Oscar's pallet.

"Is Mongrel okay?" I asked.

Chris answered, "Yes. I think he will be fine."

"What happened?" they asked.

"Two men. They are the same ones Oscar shot at last time," I explained. "He told me they were here to hurt me. They were not from Fairville. Do you think Garrett would hire someone to hurt me? I know he hates me, but…" I stopped, afraid of the answer.

"Why don't you come back to town with us, and maybe Tony will check you out," they offered.

"No thanks. I am going to be fine. A good dip in the lake will clean me up," I said, standing up.

"It's November, Bobbie. The water will be like ice," Chris reminded me.

"Yeah. I know. I like it like that. It helps clear my head," I told him.

"Bobbie, the reason we came out here so late was that Tony and your Mother came to the office and gave me this paper, saying it was from you. I didn't want to do anything without asking you face to face," he told me.

"Mother wants to sell the house, but I don't want to. Oscar has enough money to pay for the apartment, so just give her the money," I told them.

"I will definitely check into it. Instead of giving Tony or your Mother the money though, I will talk to Judd Carr," he assured me.

"Thanks, Sam. I really appreciate it," I told him.

"Are you going to be okay here?" Chris asked.

"I'll be fine. Thanks. I think as soon as Mother moves out of the house, I will move in. I can't stay here anymore."

Again, the sound of the closing door echoed through the quiet little house. I used to feel so safe there with Oscar, but I was afraid to stay there. I hated leaving that place, but I had to.

In the morning, I carried Mongrel to the lake and washed all the dried blood from his fur. I checked to see if he had any internal damage, and I hoped I was right. The cold water invigorated both of us, and we swam for a while before walking back to the house.

That night, I turned off all the lights and slept in the kitchen with a big knife. I figured they would not expect me to be behind them when they entered the door, and I was hoping to draw first blood.

———

Thanksgiving, Christmas Day, and New Year's Day came and went. There was no reason to celebrate, but I did tell Mongrel Happy New Year's.

My thoughts went back to that fatal Christmas Day and the fire. The dreams were still there. Every night, when I shut my eyes, the fire became real again, and I could hear Billy Jo crying and Butch barking.

One night in my dreams, I saw a man by the wood stove. I was turning around, and there he was, just standing there. It was not Garrett or anybody else I knew. When I awoke, the man's face stayed with me. I had seen him before, but I couldn't remember where.

———

In May, I moved into the house. Mother had moved the last of her stuff out, and all I had were the clothes on my back. I was still wearing the blue jeans and scrub top they gave me at the hospital. I didn't have any shoes, as I went barefoot all the time. I would have to get some because it was too far to walk to the lake now. I had Oscar's old truck, and it got me where I needed to go. It wasn't as nice as Father's old truck, but it had been destroyed in the fire.

The house seemed so empty as I walked from room to room. Memories of my childhood invaded my thoughts, and I let them pour over me. It had been a long time since I was a child growing up there, and I longed to turn the clock back.

I could just picture Father sitting in his chair, looking over the paper to talk to me and Mother in the kitchen, of course, singing and cooking.

Upstairs, I opened each door, mostly to make sure I was alone. When I opened the door to my old room, I was so amazed at what I saw.

Mother had kept my room exactly the way it was. The bed was made, and my little stuffed pig was sitting on the pillow, where he always was. Most of my clothes were gone, but a few were still in the back of the closet. The dresser drawers had various articles of clothing, bras, and underwear.

As I walked to my bathroom, there was a note stuck on the mirror. It was in Mother's handwriting.

> Dear Bobbie, I love you dearly, and I wish I could make you understand that. I'm sorry if I have done anything to hurt you. It was done unintentionally. I am so glad you have moved back home. Love, Mother.

I went through Oscar's house with a fine-toothed comb. Hidden in a compartment he had made under the sink was a roll of money. I always wondered how he had money but never went to the bank. I discovered another compartment under the bathroom sink. It too had a roll of money. When I counted it, I was holding over $10,000.

I poured gasoline all through the house and all along the outside wall. As the match went flying, I told Oscar thanks. The house went up in flames and was burned to the ground in about five minutes. When the fire department showed up, they asked me what happened.

While standing there with a can of gasoline in the back of Oscar's truck and a book of matches in my hands, I said, "Must have been a short in the wiring." I then put Mongrel in the truck and drove to our new home.

Mongrel loved the backyard. Father had fenced it years ago, and the fence was still in good shape. He ran around trying to catch the birds, and one day, he actually caught one, and I think it scared him. He gently put the bird on the ground, and it didn't move. Mongrel tried to scoot him with his nose, but it still didn't move. When he turned to walk in, the bird took off and soared in the air.

"You are a sucker, Mr. Mongrel." I laughed at him

The days turned into weeks and then months. They went by slowly, and I wished for something to do. I had no job, and all Mongrel and I did all day was play, fish, and swim. Not that there was anything wrong with doing all of that, but I just felt like my life was slipping away, and I was not doing anything with any purpose.

Chapter Thirty-five

Slowly, he made his way around the headstones until he came to a small purple one, and there he knelt down. Quietly, he sat there, and I watched him for a while and then went back to planting my petunias on Michael and Oscar's graves.

It was cloudy and had been threatening rain all week, but so far, the rain gauges remained empty. The grass was growing thicker, and the weeds always managed to survive. I fussed with each one I tried to pull out. I figured the roots went all the way down to hell and the devil himself had a hold on them. I called it devil grass.

Walking back to the truck for my little shovel, I noticed that the man was still sitting in front of the tombstone. I thought maybe I would ask him if he would like to plant some of my petunias on the grave but decided that he looked like he would rather be alone.

I didn't hear him walk up behind me, but Mongrel gave one of his low, guttural growls.

"If you don't want your arm ripped off, I suggest you don't come any closer," I said without even looking around.

"I promise I will stay right here," he said quietly.

I put my hand on Mongrel and stood up. When I turned around, there stood the most handsome man I think I had ever seen. He was maybe six feet tall and had a stocky build. His face was as smooth as a baby's behind. He had brown hair mixed with a little gray, especially at the temples, and beautiful brown eyes that twinkled.

"What do you want?" I asked, wishing I hadn't been so gruff sounding. He looked like a nice enough man.

"My name is Zachary Huntington. I am new in the area and just thought I would come over and introduce myself," he said, smiling.

"Okay. Zachary Huntington, just what made you think I would want to know who you are?" I asked him, half amused.

"I noticed you over here planting flowers on these two graves, and I thought maybe we had something in common. I'm sorry if I am disturbing you. Would you rather be alone?" he asked suddenly.

He turned to walk away, and something got a hold of me, and I said, "Wait a minute. I didn't say that." Why I was talking to that man, I had no idea. I didn't want to be left alone. I was tired of being alone.

"Please have a seat," I said, pointing to a grassy spot where he could sit without getting too much dirt on his blue suit. "My name is Bobbie. This," I said, patting Mongrel on the head, "is Mongrel."

He looked from Mongrel to me and said, "Bobbie and Mongrel. Two very unusual names. Is Mongrel friendly?"

"Mongrel is, but Bobbie usually isn't." I laughed.

Mongrel took that as his cue and walked over to the man and put his head on his lap. Zachary pet him from head to toe, and Mongrel rolled over so his belly wouldn't be missed.

Zachary laughed, and it sounded so sweet. There was something peculiar about the man, but I wasn't sure what it was. He was not one to fear, but a little caution is always a good thing.

"My wife is buried over there. She died five years ago from cancer. It was a long, hard battle, but it finally won," he explained.

"I'm sorry to hear that," I said, and I really was. He seemed lonely, and I could feel his pain. "This is my son Michael's grave here." I pointed to the headstone in front of me. "My husband Oscar is buried over there." Once again, I pointed in that direction.

"So you too are alone now in this world? It is not much fun being alone, but I try to stay busy," he said.

"No matter how busy you are, you are still alone, and it nags at your very being," I said, not knowing I had grown so philosophical.

"That is very true, Ms. Bobbie." He said my name in such a way as to make it sound important, not like I was a piece of trash that needed to be tossed away.

"Well now, Zachary, can I call you Zach for short?" I hinted.

"By all means," he laughed. "My mother was fond of long, important names, she called them. My full name is Zachary Arthur Huntington."

I said smiling, "Well, Zachary Arthur Huntington, that is really a mouthful. Zach, would you like to go get something to eat? I know a great place for a good steak, and since you are all dressed up and all." I stopped and thought about what I had just said, but it was too late. He stood up and wiped his pants off and then put his hand out to help me up.

"Do you need to go home and freshen up?" he asked.

"No. They know what I look like."

He helped me gather my hand tools, and then we hopped in my old truck with Mongrel in the middle.

"What is the name of this great place for a good steak?"

He laughed, and once again, I was caught up in the moment. He was so genuine and at peace with things.

"It is called the Hole in the Wall, or the Hole for short," I told him. "Pete and Gloria are the owners, and Pete makes a mean steak."

The Hole was quiet, and I looked at my watch and saw that it was only two o'clock. No one was usually there at that time. We sat in a booth against the back wall. I scooted in, and he sat across from me. Pete brought the menus, and I told him to give me the regular and the same for Zach.

Pete pushed his glasses down his nose and looked over them at Zach and said, "She can be a little pushy sometimes. Is this order okay with you?"

Zach laughed and said, "Yes. That will be perfect. Thank you for asking."

Pete then turned to me with his glasses still pushed down his nose and said, "Where is he?"

"I left him in the truck." Pete and Mongrel were best friends since we frequented the restaurant so often. "Don't spoil him too much," I added.

Zachary was looking around, so I decided to tell him the history of the Hole. "Pete and Gloria were taking a walk one day," I began, and when he looked at me, he was hanging on to every word I said. Suddenly, I felt important, as if what I had to say was important.

"They passed an old cement block wall with a hole in it and came up with the idea of this place. Pete framed in the hole with railroad ties and used it as the front door. This place is a popular hangout on weekends."

The Hole was actually a large room with booths placed all along the wall. A huge mahogany bar was on the back wall, and in the center of the room was an enormous jukebox. It was Pete's baby. He found it at an antique store and refurbished it. In the evenings and on weekends, it played constantly. Now, being two o'clock in the afternoon, it sat, silently waiting for the next quarter to be inserted.

"This is a rather unique place. Do you come here often?" Zach asked.

"Quite often. I usually sit at the bar. I don't think I can ever recall sitting in a booth," I said, feeling very awkward.

Pete brought our dinners, and the steaks were cooked just right. They were identifiable and did not moo when you stuck the fork in. When Zach tasted the first piece, his face said it all.

"Mmm!" That was all he could say. He kissed his fingertips and threw it at Pete and said, "This is the best steak I have ever had the pleasure of eating. It melts in your mouth."

We sat in silence as we ate, except every once in a while, we would ask each other how the other's dinner was. Afterward, Pete came over to the booth with Mongrel and gave him the bones. I ordered a glass of Rose Petals, and Zach ordered a glass of water.

"That was wonderful, Ms. Bobbie. Thank you very much." He looked at me and then shyly asked, "Will you tell me who Bobbie is?"

I looked at him, and he was genuinely asking. He didn't look like the type who was going to make fun of me or shame me.

"Bobbie is a very lonely woman who just buried her husband, Oscar. I live in my old family home and play with Mongrel every day unless I am at the graveyard talking with Michael or Oscar."

He looked at me, and I did not see pity in his eyes but interest. He seemed to actually care about me. I started talking and couldn't stop. I told him about how I grew up and my parents and Tony and Michael and Garrett and Oscar. I even told him about Billy Jo. When I finished, he kindly reached across the table and placed his hand on mine. It was not a gesture of, "Come to bed with me." It was an "I understand because I have been there" kind of touch.

Zach paid the tab, and Mongrel and I walked out to the truck. The rain had finally started falling, so I just stood in it and let it soak me through and through. It was a warm summer rain, and I loved it. It felt like not only my dirt was washing away but a little bit of guilt and sorrow too.

Zach hurried out the door to the truck and then saw me standing in the rain, enjoying it. He stopped and walked over to me and took off his suit coat and loosened his tie. The rain started pouring down harder, and he started singing and took me in his arms, and we started dancing. Around and around we went with no particular care in the world. It was as if we were the only people in the whole world.

I started laughing and threw my head back. My clip came out of my hair, and it fell down my back. I didn't care. I felt free, free of life right at that moment, and I didn't want it to end.

Suddenly, a flash of lightning brightened the whole sky, and a thunder bolt was right behind. He took my hand, and we ran for the truck. Mongrel was sitting on the seat, looking at us like we were crazy for being out in such a storm.

As we drove back to the graveyard for Zach's car, he asked me if he could see me again.

"Would you like to go swimming tomorrow? I have a special spot on the lake that Oscar gave me. I will pick you up here at noon."

"Swimming at noon? Sounds great. Why don't you pick me up at my apartment? I am renting a place behind Ms. Joyce's house. Do you know where that is?"

"I am familiar with it. I'll pick you up there at noon. Thanks for dinner," I said as he hopped out of the truck. I pulled off before he could respond, and I saw him wave at me from the rearview mirror. What kind of man was Zachary Arthur Huntington? He was so different.

Chapter Thirty-six

The water was warm from the storm and muddy. Mongrel was first out of the truck and jumped into the lake. Zach was right behind him, and I was next. The storm had lasted all night, and it gave us some much-needed water. The sun was shining with all its glory, and it was hot and muggy, just like I loved it.

When Zach jumped in the water, he went down deep, and I was kind of worried about him. It took him a long time to surface, and he came up laughing. He looked so funny with a piece of old bark caught in his hair. I reached over to try to brush it out, and I could feel the heat between us, and our eyes met until I turned away.

"Don't be afraid of me, Bobbie. I will not hurt you," he said, pulling me near him.

I couldn't resist for some reason.

"You are a very beautiful woman, and I am a very lonely man, but I will never take advantage of you."

Mongrel swam in between us, and we laughed at him. I found a big stick and threw it for him. He swam out to fetch it and brought it back. Zach laughed as we watched him try to fetch the stick and go after the ducks at the same time. He couldn't figure out which one was more important. Finally, he brought the stick back to me and went after the ducks.

As we came back on shore, Zach and I leaned against the old log and dried off. The sun was warm on my body, and I noticed that

Zach had a nice tan also. His chest was broad, and the hairs were turning gray. I reached over and pulled one, and he jumped.

"Hey," he said, laughing. "That's not fair."

"What's not fair? I just wanted to see if it was attached," I said, laughing back at him. I pulled another one, and he took my hand and rolled over on top of me.

My body ached to be kissed and caressed. He looked at me and stood up, pulling me with him.

"Bobbie, you are just too tantalizing. It's not that I don't want you. I just can't have you."

I felt rejected and stupid. I called Mongrel and put him in the truck. "Are you coming?" I asked Zach rudely.

At Ms. Joyce's house, he turned to me and said, "Bobbie, don't be upset with me for withholding pleasure of you. It is actually a compliment. I don't have sex with just anybody. It is something to be shared with someone special. I would really enjoy getting to know you better if you will allow me to and not shut yourself off to me."

At home, I poured myself a drink and sat on the back steps, watching Mongrel chase the birds. My mind kept going back to what Zach had said: "It's not that I don't want you. I just can't have you." I couldn't figure out what that meant, and it fascinated me. This man was so different. He seemed to be so at ease with everything, and nothing seemed to bother him. His eyes were gentle and kind, and he talked with me, not to me, trying to be more than what he was.

That is the question. What is he? Who is he? All I know about him was his name and his dead wife's name. He really hasn't told me anything. I was so ashamed for opening up my life to him. I wondered what he thought of me or if he did think of me. *I wonder what he is doing right now. Is he sitting on his back steps with a good drink in his hand, thinking about me?*

Saturday was my birthday, so I bought a cake and headed to the graveyard to have a party with Michael and Oscar. It was a beautiful day, and the graveyard was empty. I was actually hoping Zach would be there. I parked my truck, and Mongrel and I got out and walked to the grave.

Somebody had put a beautiful vase of flowers on Michael's grave, and a note was attached. It read:

Bobbie,
I waited every day for you to show up, but alas you did not come,
I have no way of calling, for you weren't forthright with your whereabouts.
I hope you find these flowers before they get too old.
They are beautiful flowers for a beautiful lady.
Zachary

He brought me flowers. He brought me flowers. Wow! I just can't believe he brought me flowers. I hugged them to my breast and cried and showed Michael and Oscar and Mongrel. I danced around the tombstones and held on to the flowers.

"He brought me flowers!" I yelled as I danced by myself.

Suddenly, I stopped and was aware that someone was watching me. When I turned, there stood Zach in a pair of blue jeans and a cotton button-down shirt. I felt foolish, and I started crying. I handed him the flowers and started dancing again. He must have thought I was crazy.

"You brought me flowers," I told him.

"Yes. I brought you flowers. I will buy you flowers every day if that is what makes you happy," he said.

I laughed and danced and twirled myself around and round until I was so dizzy I fell on the ground. Zach sat down beside me and held me in his arms, and the tears flowed like rain. They were happy tears though.

Somebody actually cares for me? Somebody actually cares for me! "You brought me flowers," I cried to him. "You brought me flowers."

We must have sat there like that for a long time because when I could finally compose myself, it was getting dark.

"Are you okay?" he asked worriedly. "I hope all those tears were tears of joy. I wanted to make you happy."

I sat up but stayed close to him and looked in his eyes. He gently touched my cheek with his rough hand, and I kissed his hand. He had tears in his eyes, and I gently touched his soft cheek. He took my hand and kissed it.

"What do you want from me, Zach? I don't have anything to give a man. Are you looking for a one-night stand or a long-time commitment? I'm not sure of either one of them."

"Then we'll just take this one day at a time. How does that sound?" he asked with a smile that wiped away all my tears. "Let's get to know each other. Okay?"

"Okay." That was all I could say.

"Today is my birthday. Will you share my cake with me?" I asked.

"That would be great, but we have nothing to eat it with." He looked around for a knife or fork.

I started laughing. I hadn't thought about bringing silverware or plates. I took my finger and removed a piece of the cake and offered it to him. He took it and then did the same for me. It was so much fun. We nearly ate half the cake, and then I took a big piece and smeared it all over his face. He looked at me and then started laughing as he wiped it off his face and ate it. He took what was left of the cake and smeared it on my face. I started laughing and wiped the cake off with my finger and ate it.

I leaned over and licked a big hunk of cake from off his face. He turned and met my mouth with his and kissed me passionately, his breathing quickening. When he pulled back, he got up and walked to his car, and I thought he was leaving. He came back a minute later with a roll of paper towels and wiped our faces off.

He looked at his watch and said that he needed to go and would not be able to see me the next day but hopefully Monday afternoon maybe we could get together.

"I have other engagements tomorrow, but what about Monday? Do you think we could get together then?" he asked. "I would like to take you to a special place I know. Can I pick you up at your place at noon?" he asked slyly.

"My place, huh? And just where is my place?" I asked, teasing him.

"I don't know, but I certainly hope you will let me know so I can pick you up there Monday at noon." He laughed.

"Thirteen Three Forty-One Pine Road. You can't miss it. Where are we going so I will know what to wear?" I asked.

"Do you have a pretty dress?" he asked.

"Yes," I said, hoping there was something in my closet. I hadn't worn a dress in years.

"Good. I will see you at noon on Monday." He then lowered his head and kissed me on the forehead. "You be careful driving home."

"You too," I said.

Chapter Thirty-seven

Monday could not get there soon enough. Sunday dragged by, and every time I heard a car, I jumped up to see if it was Zach. I wondered why he couldn't see me that day, and I was worried that he didn't want to see me anymore. Maybe he was married or maybe… The list went on and on. Maybe this and maybe that. I was driving myself nuts.

On Monday morning, I looked in my closet and found a yellow sundress I had bought years before. I hoped it would be appropriate. After my shower, I looked at myself in the mirror and found a pair of scissors and started cutting my hair. I must have cut two feet off. Finally, I got it exactly right, and it fell down past my shoulder blades. I finished dressing just in time as the doorbell rang.

I was so excited, and I took a big deep breath before opening the door. When I did, there was Zach, holding out a fistful of dandelions for me. I found a cup to put them in and filled it with water.

"Thanks. I love dandelions, especially when a field is full of them. They look like a blanket covering the field," I explained.

"I saw them along the side of the road, and I thought about how happy the flowers made you on Saturday, so I picked them." He looked like a little boy, and his face was so loving and kind. "You look great. If I thought you were beautiful before, you are stunning now. I will be the envy of every man there. If you are ready, your chariot awaits. I thought I would drive today. I suppose Mongrel will have to stay here. I hope he won't be too lonesome. I did bring him something though."

He leaned over and pet Mongrel and then stepped outside. When he returned, he was holding a big ham bone.

"Ms. Joyce said to tell you hi, and after dinner last night, I asked for the ham bone for Mongrel. She was so happy you had another dog and said, 'Of course he can have the ham bone.'"

As we drove to Columbus in Zach's big car, I wondered where we were going. He was not saying anything and would not even give me a hint even though I kept asking him.

"You will just have to be patient, Bobbie."

"Patience is not one of my virtues, Zach. If you hang around long enough, you will find that out."

"I am going to hang around." He then reached over and held my hand.

I felt so safe with him and maybe a little content too. It was a strange feeling, and it scared me because I wasn't good at depending on people. I couldn't trust too many of them. They either up and died, cheated on me, or just ended up hating me.

We stopped in front of an old movie house, and Zach found a parking place not too far away. He held my hand as we walked to the movie, and I found myself getting very excited. I wondered what was playing. I was transported back to my childhood, and I wanted to skip and twirl.

He bought our tickets, and inside, we were handed a pair of special 3-D glasses each. We bought popcorn and chocolate-covered raisins and two large drinks. We found a place close to the front and watched as the theater packed up.

─────────────

As the movie started, Zach moved closer to me and put his arm around me. I snuggled in to him and looked at him. He smiled down at me with one of those perfect smiles that said that everything was fine.

My feelings for him were growing stronger, and even though we decided to take it slowly, I wasn't sure how to act. He was so handsome and strong and intelligent. He always greeted everybody we passed on the street and tried to assist everyone. A lady with a baby stroller was having a hard time trying to hold her packages and hold onto the stroller, and Zach carried her packages for her across the street to her car.

This man was genuine, sweet. No imitation or fake stuff in him. I was so afraid of holding on to him, but I was even more afraid of losing him.

After the show, we walked down the street hand in hand. We laughed and talked, and I felt like a little girl again. We stopped at all of the little shops along the way, and when we passed an ice cream shop, we went in. We took our purchases outside on a picnic table and sat down. The ice cream melted as we sat in the sun, but it was so beautiful.

A lady with a baby boy sat down across from us, and I thought of Billy Jo and Michael and had to turn away. Zach saw me turn away and asked if I was all right.

"Someday, I would like to have a baby again. I have buried two of them. And maybe if I had a third one, he would live."

"Oh, Bobbie. I am so sorry," he said.

"Do you have any children?" I asked.

"No. Peggy couldn't have children. And when we tried to adopt, one thing or another would stop it. I too would like to have children someday. A whole house full would be nice. Can't you just see Mongrel with a whole house full of children?"

"That would be funny." I laughed.

"Let's take a walk. The sun is shining, and it is a beautiful day. Are you up for it?" he asked.

"I'm ready," I said, wiping off my mouth on a napkin.

He put his finger on my chin and lifted it up to face him. Slowly, he bent down to gently kiss me on the lips. It was so soft and sweet.

"Come on. I think it's time we headed on home."

At the house, he walked me to the door and asked if I would like to play tennis the next Saturday morning.

"How about it? Are you up to it?" he asked, snickering.

"I've never played tennis before."

"Good. Maybe I will have a chance at winning. I will see you Saturday then. Let's say nine o'clock."

I wanted to stop him and say, "Hey, wait a minute. What about tomorrow or the next day or the next day? Why do I have to wait until Saturday?" but he walked to his car and drove off, honking the horn and waving at me.

On Wednesday, Marcia came over to the house. Cautiously, I opened the door, and she followed me to the back steps, where we watched Mongrel playing.

"How are you doing, Bobbie? I sure miss you," she began. "I just had to come tell you my exciting news. It's not much fun not having a best friend. I am going to have a baby," she shouted. "I am eight weeks now. The twins are so excited and are hoping for more twins. Danny was a little fearful at first, but I think he will be fine."

"Congratulations. I hope you have twins too, one for Melodie and one for Harmony. You could name them Tune and Song." I started laughing, and Marcia put her hands on her hips and then started laughing too.

"I do wish you could be as happy as we are, Bobbie. I love you so much. The girls ask about you all the time. Why don't you come over for dinner Saturday night? We have a few other people coming, but I promise it will be fun."

"Sure. I would like that. I would like to see the twins again. I have missed them. Do you want me to bring anything?" I asked.

"No. Just yourself. Danny is grilling steaks, hot dogs, and hamburgers, and I am fixing potato salad, beans, and a fruit salad. Do you think that will be enough?"

"It sounds great. Thanks for the invite." I wanted so much to have a best friend again. I was so lonesome.

"I have to get going. The twins are at swimming lessons, and we need to stop at the store to pick up a few things. Oh, by the way, four o'clock will be fine. Sorry. I hope you don't change your mind because I am going to tell the twins you are coming."

I walked her to her car, and she looked at me and said, "You are looking good, Bobbie. I like your hair cut like that. You are still as pretty as ever."

I waved good-bye and watched as she drove away. *I wonder if Zachary would like to come Saturday night. It would be kind of fun to bring a date and introduce him to Marcia. I wonder what she would think of him.*

Chapter Thirty-eight

The week crawled by. I decided I was going to get a telephone so I could at least call Zach. He never once came by the house to see me, and the longer it was before I saw him the more doubts started trickling into my mind. I figured the guy was either married or he was also seeing somebody else. There had to be some reason why he never came by.

On Friday evening, it was hotter than a firecracker, so I took a glass of iced tea and sat on the porch swing. Mongrel lay in the shade, panting, so I brought a big bowl of water out for him. A car stopped out front, and Zach got out. My heart skipped a beat, and it took everything I had to not go running to him and wrap my arms around him. I was so glad to see him.

As he walked up the steps, he said, "That iced tea sure looks good."

"It tastes good too," I said as I took a long swig.

"I'm glad you haven't changed any since Monday. I'm sorry. I just couldn't wait any longer to see you. I tried to wait until Saturday, but it was just too much burden to bear," he said, eyeing my glass of tea.

He sat beside me on the swing and took my iced tea glass out of my hand, pulled me toward him, and kissed me fervently on the lips. He then looked at me and told me again how much he had missed me. I cuddled up close to him, and he wrapped himself around me.

"You are all I have been thinking about all week. I can't work, or write, or even think about anything but you. You have taken complete control of my thoughts. I just had to come here and see if you were real," he said, holding me tighter.

"I'm not going anywhere," I said, wondering if I should ask the questions that had been bothering me.

"Zach," I began as I sat up on the porch swing and looked him straight in the eye, "are you married?"

"Bobbie, of course not. I told you my wife died five years ago. No. Please believe me. I am not married, and I am not seeing anybody else either. I am seeing you, and I hope you will allow me to continue seeing you. I enjoy every minute we have spent together," he assured me.

My mind felt satisfied, but my heart still had questions. I was afraid to ask any more. I leaned back into him, and he wrapped himself back around me. He started singing to me, and I recognized it as an old hymn we used to sing in church. It was so peaceful and calm sounding, and his voice was so pure.

"Are we still on for tomorrow morning?" he asked.

"I hope so. I'm going to beat the pants off you." We started laughing.

"Then I guess I'll have to wear two pair of pants then," he said as he continued to laugh. "Now, can I have some of that iced tea or not?"

"I'm sorry. I forgot all about it. I'll get it for you."

"Would you like something to eat?" I asked.

"No. I just ate. It sure is pretty today. Why don't we go swimming? I have my shorts in the car."

"We are always ready for swimming. Let me go change," I told him.

The water was warm, and the ducks were everywhere. I brought some bread along to feed them, but Mongrel kept scaring them off. Finally, I just threw the whole thing in, and Mongrel jumped in and ate every bit of it.

Zach held my hand, and we jumped in, going way down to the bottom. We were still holding hands when we came up. He pulled me near him and smiled. I let go of his hand and went down under the water, swimming as fast as I could to get around behind him. Quietly, I came up and pushed his head under. When he came up he was right under my legs, and I went up in the air and dove in the water.

We were exhausted as we dragged ourselves on shore and leaned against the old log. The sun was hot on my skin, and I turned over on my belly on the grass. Zach lay down beside me on his side, propping his head up with his arm. He looked at me, and I turned toward him on my side and started tracing my finger across his chest. He pulled me toward him and rolled over on his back, pulling me on top of him.

I lay down on his chest, and he wrapped his arms around me. He rolled us over to our sides and wrapped his legs around me also. He made me feel so comfortable, and the longer I lay there, the longer I wanted to stay right where I was.

Mongrel came out of the lake and walked over to us and started shaking, spraying water all over us. We jumped up and started laughing, chasing him around. He thought it was a game, so he would run away and then run back to us. Finally, he lay down beside us.

"What do you like to do, Bobbie?" Zach asked.

"I like to swim and fish. What about you?" I answered.

"I like to hold you tight against me. No. I take that back. I love to hold you tight against me," he said.

I turned and looked at him and said, "I like that too."

The evening came before I wanted it to, and we drove back to the house. He said good-bye and told me I had better be ready at nine o'clock.

"Don't forget now, I am going to win every game tomorrow, so you'd better prepare your losing speech." He laughed and pulled me close.

"I think you had better prepare yours, Mr. Huntington," I said.

Tennis was not an easy game, and the harder I tried the worse I got. That little yellow ball needed to be bigger. It was fun though. By noon, we were exhausted. I think I must have hit that ball at least two times. The rest of the time was spent running after it. Zach was great though and gave me a few pointers, and we made reservations for the next weekend.

As we sat on the picnic table, watching the others play tennis, we drank some lemonade and held hands. It was such a beautiful day.

"Zach, a friend of mine asked me to dinner tonight. Would you like to come with me?"

"Oh, Bobbie," he said hesitantly. "I would love to, but someone has already asked me to a barbeque tonight, and I was going to ask if you would like to go with me."

"I can't, Zach," I explained. "My friend would really be hurt if I didn't come after I promised her I would."

"I'm sorry. I don't want to hurt this couple's feelings either," he said honestly. "Do you want anything else to eat or drink?"

"No. This is fine."

We sat for a few more minutes, and I wondered how he really felt about me. He was so loving yet withdrawn. He had never made an attempt to be anything but a gentleman.

"You are thinking deep thoughts, Bobbie. Should I hope they are about me?" he asked.

"You can hope if you would like," I teased.

"Come on. I had better get you home. We will both be late for our dinner invitations. It is going to be hard to concentrate on the barbeque when all I will be thinking about is you."

"That is exactly what I was thinking," I said.

He kissed me good-bye at my door and drove off. A huge void formed inside of me every time he left, but when we were together, it was as if I was made whole again, free again somehow, free to be myself and free to love again. I felt like someone was actually giving me permission to love again. That was such a wonderful thought, but it also scared me. I wasn't sure I was ready to get married again, but I wanted to have children so badly. "A whole houseful of them." That was what Zach said. I liked that idea.

Chapter Thirty-nine

Mongrel jumped in the truck, and we headed over to Marcia's house. I hoped this evening was not going to be too boring. I had a flask in my pocketbook just in case. I wasn't drinking as much those days, but once in a while, I just needed a bit to get by.

I stopped at the store and bought the twins each a pair of earrings and a matching necklace. They cost a hundred dollars apiece, but what good was the money if I didn't spend it? I sure didn't use it for anything else, and Sam was constantly sending me statements informing me how much was in the bank.

When I arrived, I parked down the street in case I needed to make a fast exit. After I jumped out of the truck, Mongrel came down and we walked to the door and knocked.

Marcia answered it and hugged me and said, "Come in. Come in. Since when do friends knock?" she chastised me.

"I brought something for the twins," I said.

Melodie and Harmony came down the steps and stood to either side of me. Both of them were going to be tall, and they laughed and enjoyed calling me Shorty. I handed them each their present, and they kissed me and hugged me before opening them.

We sat down on the couch, and slowly, they opened the gifts. They squealed with delight when they saw the jewelry, and I got kisses and hugs again. They showed Marcia and then ran out to show Danny. Mongrel was right on their heels. The doorbell rang, so I went out to speak to Danny and watch the girls while Marcia answered it.

Danny was making a big fuss over the jewelry and trying to put the necklaces on with his big hands, so I pushed him aside and put the necklaces on, telling them how beautiful they looked.

Danny started to say something, but I heard Marcia say, "Bobbie, this is our interim preacher, Preacher Huntington." When I turned around, there stood Zach. I almost fainted. I know my face turned white, and so did Zach's.

"Preacher?" I asked as I walked by him and out the front door. He followed me, and I heard him tell Marcia he would be right back.

"Bobbie, wait," he yelled after me.

I turned and angrily confronted him. "And when were you going to throw this little surprise at me, preacher man? Do you think this is funny? Was all of this planned to make a fool out of me? It all makes sense now, not wanting to make love to me because you are a goody two-shoes preacher man. Well, I don't want nor need anything you are peddling, so just stay away from me."

I opened the truck door, and Mongrel jumped in. I couldn't get the key in the ignition, so Zach walked up to the window. I was crying, and I was mad. It was not the time for me not to be able to start my truck.

"Bobbie, please. I did not know you knew these people. I was not trying to hide anything from you. I just wanted to get to know you—"

"Get to know the poor little rich girl who can't keep a husband and killed her baby in a fire?" I spit the words at him. "Is that what you wanted to do? Huh? Maybe you can save me. Go away, preacher man. I don't want you in my life."

Finally, I started the truck and peeled rubber heading home. I didn't want to go home though. I went to the graveyard. I had to talk to someone. Oscar and Michael were there, and they were great listeners. They weren't much on advice, but they never got up and left in the middle of one of my talks.

I sat on Michael's grave and cried. I was so hurt and so empty. *How could I have been such a fool? A preacher, for Pete's sake! I fell for a preacher man. Well, the whole church can get a good laugh out of that. Oh, Michael, Oscar, I wish you two were still with me.* I lay down on the grass beside the tombstone and cried myself to sleep. Mongrel lay beside me, and I wrapped my arms around him.

━━━━━━━━━━━━

The sun was rising when I woke, so we got in the truck and drove to the lake. Somebody was there, but I couldn't tell who it was until I walked up on him. Lying in the grass, fast asleep, was Zachary Arthur Huntington. I quietly walked to the lake and filled an old bottle full of water and then walked back over and poured it all over his face. He jumped up and looked around, and when he saw me, tears came to his eyes.

"Oh, Bobbie, I have been waiting for you to come back. Where have you been? I have been so worried about you. I was so afraid something had happened to you." He started walking toward me, but Mongrel growled and he stopped.

"Go away, preacher man. Just go away." I then took off my clothes right in front of him and jumped in the water. Mongrel was right behind. We swam for a long way down the beach until I heard his car start up and leave. I felt empty. I wanted him to stay and hold me again. *Why did he have to deceive me?*

Saturday morning in November, I opened my truck to find a beautiful vase of flowers on the seat. The note said:

> Bobbie,
>
> I'm sorry I was not honest with you. I never meant to hurt you. I was going to tell you, but I just wasn't sure how.
>
> I knew you weren't fond of church and preaching, so that made it easier not to tell you.
>
> I cherish the times we did get to spend together, and I hope you can find it in your heart to forgive me and give me another chance. Preacher man.
>
> Zachary.

When I turned around, Zach was standing behind me with tears streaming down his face. He reached his hand out to me. I took it, and he pulled me to him, holding me tightly. We both cried, and he led me into the house.

We sat on the floor, and I looked at him and said, "I can't do this, Zach. I can't be with a preacher man. I am nothing. You will be the laughingstock of Fairville. It would be better if we had never met."

"Don't ever say that, Bobbie. I enjoy being with you, and I think I am a much better person for knowing you. Please don't ever take off again. I was afraid you weren't coming back. I need you, Bobbie. I need you. Let's try it. That's all I'm asking. Just try it."

"I'll try, preacher man, but I'm not promising anything."

My heart was beating so hard I thought it was coming out of my chest. How in the world was Bobbie Jo Patterson-Juxton-James-Studds going to be anything to a preacher?

Chapter Forty

And try I did. I actually started going to church again and being just like everyone else, or so I told myself. That first day I walked into church, I could have heard the church mouse singing a hymn. Everybody was deathly silent as Zach escorted me to the front of the church. During the service, I was so nervous. I knew every eye was on me. Zach said the preacher's girl always sat in front to give him moral support.

Zach was a pretty good preacher. He sure knew his Bible, or so it seemed. Each sermon was different, and it was more like a Bible study than a preaching service. He bought me my own Bible and had my name engraved on the front of it. I carried it with me each Sunday.

During the week, I would try to read it but couldn't make heads or tails out of it, so I just kind of pretended to read it. Zach started quizzing me, so I tried again to read it, and he would help me understand it.

The church folk were not overly fond of their interim preacher dating a "whore and a baby killer." Yes, I could hear their whispers, but I kept my head high and acted like it didn't bother me. At home, when Zach dropped me off, I would change my clothes and pour myself a drink. It was a lot easier to tolerate hatred with a little bit of whiskey in me.

Marcia came over to the house, and when I opened the door, she hugged me and then started laughing.

"I can't believe you, Bobbie Jo. I just can't believe you are dating the preacher. Wherever did you meet him? Come on. Tell me all about it."

I told her about meeting Zach in the graveyard and how we just hit it off.

"Did you really not know he was a preacher? The look on your face when I introduced you was priceless. I am so sorry. I didn't realize what was going on. Where did you take off to? Zach was beside himself with worry."

"No, Marcia, I really did not know he was a preacher," I said. "It all seems funny now, but not at the time."

"Well, I think you are going to get your fresh start with Zachary Huntington. He just adores you," she said. "Your mother was quite shocked too. She told me she was going to try to come over today."

I thought of Mother. I hadn't seen her since before I moved into the house. She would probably have something to say that will probably make me mad and tell her to leave.

"I'm going to get on home. I need to rest. I have not been getting enough, according to Dr. Hansen," she said, patting her belly.

"I just hope it is a healthy boy," I said, hoping my envy did not come through.

"Dr. Hansen doesn't know. It will never be still enough when she has the monitors on. Anyway, Bobbie, how would you and Zach like to go out Saturday evening? There is a new restaurant in Honston, and I hear they have great Italian food," she said.

"I will have to run it by him, and I will let you know. By the way, I now have a cell phone." I ran to get the phone and wrote the number down on a piece of paper for her.

"Okay. Great. Now I can keep track of you," she said, smiling.

Marcia was right. Mother came calling the same day. A man named Cecil was with her, and I was so happy that Mother had found somebody to share her life with. When they came in, I took them in to the front room and told them to have a seat. Of course, I still had not purchased any furniture. I poured some tea, and we went out on the front porch to visit.

Mother and Cecil sat on the swing, and I noticed that as soon as they sat down, Cecil reached for her hand.

"Bobbie, I know that there are a few folks who are not too delighted by the fact that you and Preacher Zach are dating," she began, and I held my breath. "But I just wanted to let you know that I'm so happy for you."

She could have knocked me down with a feather. I was totally shocked, and I must have looked it too, because she continued.

"Preacher Zach is a very nice man, and now maybe you can straighten out your life. I would like it very much if you would sit with Cecil and me in church. I understand Preacher Zach likes you sitting in the front, so we would like permission to come up front and sit with you and be a family again."

Permission to sit by me? Never would I have thought my mother would need permission for anything. She had always been so strong and forceful, and now she was humbling herself and asking me for permission, and for what, but to sit with me and be a family again?

I walked over and hugged her and told her I would love to have her and Cecil sit with me in the pew.

"I would love to have you and Cecil sit with me in church," I said. "Maybe I won't be so nervous then."

After they left, I thought about Mother and how old she was getting. Cecil was good for her and to her from what I saw. They seemed to be so in love, and I hoped the best for them.

The phone rang, and it was Zach, asking if I wanted him to stop and get a pizza and bring it over. I told him that would be fine, and I anxiously waited for him.

When he finally arrived, I met him at the door and found some paper towels and poured some tea. We sat on the front room floor with our backs against the wall. The pizza tasted great, and I remembered I hadn't eaten all day.

"How was your day? I have missed being with you today. I did get a good start on my sermon," he said.

"My day has been full of visitors. Marcia stopped by and wants to know if we want to go to a new Italian restaurant with her and Danny Saturday night," I told him.

"That sounds like fun. What do you think about it?"

I couldn't believe he was actually asking my opinion instead of just making a decision. "I think it will be a lot of fun too," I said. "Marcia and I used to be best friends."

"And hopefully you will be again," he said hurriedly.

"Mother came over with her new friend, Cecil. They seem to be very happy. She asked my permission to sit in the front pew with me," I told him.

"Your mother is a sweet lady, and she is trying her best to reconcile herself to you," he said. "I hope you will allow her to be a part of your life, our life."

He left at about 9:00 p.m., saying he did not want anyone to think bad things about us. "We mustn't do anything that would start any rumors. I want people to know you are a respectable lady," he said.

Before he left, he held me tightly and ran his fingers through my hair and kissed me over and over.

"I am in love with you, Bobbie. I am crazy in love with you!" he proclaimed, grinning from ear to ear.

On Saturday, Danny and Marcia picked us up at 5:00 p.m., and we drove to Barryville together. Danny and Zach sat in front and talked man talk while Marcia and I talked about pregnancy and babies.

"Have you thought of any names yet?" I asked.

"Tune and Song," she said, laughing. "Dr. Hansen confirmed it yesterday. Just one baby. Melodie and Harmony are just so pleased. They had me buy a baby name book for each of them, and they have been pouring over the names. They both think I am having another girl."

"That is exciting, Marcia." I didn't say anything else because we had arrived at the restaurant.

Zach held my hand and told me how beautiful I looked. I had found a little black dress in the back of the closet. It hung just above my knees and showed a little cleavage, but Zach liked it.

The restaurant was filled, and we had to wait for a half hour. Marcia and I went to the little girl's room, and while I was in the stall, I heard a conversation at the sink.

"I can't believe she has the gall to be dating a preacher man. She has already had her share of husbands. She can't keep the ones she does get," the voice said. "And did you get a look at the new preacher? He is a hunk. I'd like a chance at him."

"Yes. Me too," the other agreed.

I then heard Marcia flush the toilet and walk out to where the conversation was taking place. Instantly, the conversation changed.

"How are you girls doing this evening?" Marcia asked.

"Fine. We are doing fine," I heard them say in unison.

"You never know who is behind those doors, do you?" Marcia insisted. I took this to be my cue, so I flushed the toilet, straightened myself up, and came out of the stall.

The girls ran out of the bathroom so fast I think their hair dye stayed in there. Marcia looked at me and said she was sorry.

"I'm sorry, Bobbie," she said. "Just remember that not everybody is like that."

"It's not your fault. It is something I just have to get used to. Go on out, and I will be in shortly." After she left, I took a big swig of vodka to help me make it through the rest of the evening that had just begun.

When I caught up with Zach, Marcia had already told him about the conversation, and he was quite upset.

"Everything is fine, Zach. Marcia took care of it. Let's just forget it and enjoy our meal," I said, but not before seeing the look in his eyes.

We followed Danny and Marcia behind the maître d', and she led us to a big, quiet table in the back of the restaurant. She handed us each a menu, and we discussed what would be good and what to order. Finally, the waitress came and took our orders. Marcia and I ordered lasagna, and Danny and Zach both ordered spaghetti.

Zach reached for my hand under the table, and it felt so good to be so close to him. I felt like every eye in the restaurant was on me. When our food came, my stomach was so upset I couldn't eat but just a little bit. Zach put the rest in a doggie bag for Mongrel.

The evening was fun, and it was as if time had been turned back, and Marcia and I were best friends again. Danny never said anything to me, so I just obliged him.

The evening ended way too soon, and when they dropped us off, we made plans to get together again. Zach kissed me good-bye and then left also. The house was empty again, and I sat in the dark, sipping my drink as Mongrel ran around in the backyard.

I had a wonderful time tonight, but it was all just pretend. I am trying to be something I am not.

I was in love with Zachary Huntington, but Preacher Huntington scared me to death.

━━━━━━━━━━

Marcia went into labor, and Danny called as he pulled into the hospital parking lot.

"I'm on my way there now." I could hear Marcia in the background puffing. "I should be there in about ten minutes."

"We're on our way," I assured him.

Marcia had an eight-pound-six-ounce baby boy, and she named him Danny Jo. I almost cried when she told me. I held Danny Jo close to my heart. I wanted a baby so badly. Finally, I gave him back to Marcia, and I kissed them good-bye. The tears were streaming down my face when I left the room.

"Everything is going to be all right, my love. You need to stop this fretting," he said, and it made me laugh when I saw the face he made.

Chapter Forty-one

Christmas Eve services were held with candlelight, and we sang songs and prayed. Zach spoke about loving one another. Mother and Cecil were with me on the pew when suddenly, a light shone on me, and when I looked up, Zach was right in front of me. He bowed on one knee and looked me straight in the eye and in front of the whole church.

"Bobbie, would you be my wife?" he asked earnestly. "I love you, and before God and all these people"—he swept his hand in the air—"I am asking you to marry me."

I was so touched and embarrassed. Mother prodded me with her elbow, and the church was silent. That church mouse was singing a hymn again, and I heard it as clear as day.

"Yes," I said quietly.

I didn't want anybody to hear except Zach, but he would not let it be silent.

"What is it you said, Bobbie?" he prompted me.

"Yes!" I shouted out.

He picked me up and swung me around, and the congregation rose to their feet and started clapping. My mind was racing a mile a minute.

I am going to be a preacher's wife. I am going to be a preacher's wife. Oh my. What have I done now?

After the service, we stood in front of the church, and the congregation passed by, congratulating us with hugs and kisses. Marcia was ecstatic. It was so nice to be in her good graces again, and Mother too was pleased.

When the church was empty, Zach ushered me back to the office and once more kneeled before me. He pulled out a box from his pocket and opened it up. It was exquisite. When the light caught it, the sparkles were so intense. He slipped it on my finger, and it fit perfectly.

"Do you really want to be my wife, Bobbie, or was that yes just for the crowd?" he asked.

"I really do want to be your wife, Zach. I love you. You are a good man. It is the preacher's wife thing that scares me to death."

"I know, but you will be perfect. Let's go over to your house, and we will talk. Do you want to stop by and grab a sandwich or anything?"

"No. My stomach is a little queasy," I said.

We planned our wedding for when Preacher Carr would be back in town. That only left us six months to plan, but Mother and Marcia helped with the arrangements, and I asked Marcia to be my matron of honor. Mother was to walk me down the aisle, and she was so excited. She tried to lower her voice and sound like Father, and we laughed.

I felt young and alive again, but all through the planning and fun came this little nagging feeling that I should get Mongrel and go as far away as possible. I was so scared, but I wasn't quite sure why.

I tried to express this feeling to Zach, but, of course, he just told me it was called cold feet. He was so reassuring that I tried to put the nagging feeling away; and most of the time, I could, but sometimes it would come out and haunt me. Try as I might, a preacher's wife was not in this five-foot-two-inch, hundred-pound body.

The winter came hard and cold that year, but Mongrel and I, and sometimes Zach, would still go to the lake, fishing and swimming.

The water stayed fairly cool until the end of January, when we had a big freeze for about a week and it froze over. Mongrel could not understand where the water went. He tried to walk on the ice, but his feet kept sliding out from under him. He was hilarious.

We built a bonfire and roasted hot dogs and marshmallows, and Danny and Marcia brought the twins out to try to ice skate while Grandma kept the baby. They stayed up pretty good, and then they tried holding on to Mongrel and skate, and he kept falling. It was a good time.

"Bobbie, would you like to go to Columbus next week and hunt for a wedding dress?" Marcia asked.

"Gosh, Marcia. I never even thought about a dress." I turned to Zach. "What do you think? I can't actually wear white. I know! I will wear black." I started laughing until I looked at Zach, noticing he was not laughing.

"That is unacceptable," he said.

I looked at Marcia, and we both started laughing.

"What is so funny?" Zach asked.

"That is Marcia's famous line. 'That is unacceptable.'"

"Well, now, I don't want you wearing a black dress down the aisle. People will think it's a funeral."

"We will go next Saturday and look around," I assured him. "I'm sure we can find the perfect dress."

That next Saturday Marcia picked me up at 9:00 a.m., and we drove to Columbus, stopping first at a little restaurant for some coffee and bagels and to feed Danny Jo.

"Are you excited about the wedding, Bobbie?" she asked.

"Yes, but scared too. I don't know anything about being a preacher's wife. What if I do something wrong? Those people are vicious," I told her.

Marcia laughed and said, "Yes, there are a few people in church who have an uncontrollable tongue, but don't let those few ruin the whole crowd. Our church has some pretty terrific people in it, and they care about you."

———

At the house, we talked about where we were going to live. "Preacher Carr will be back in May, and he has offered me the position of assistant pastor. I will fill in for him whenever he is gone and be in charge of the youth groups. It is a step down from being the pastor, but I am not sure if I want to be a full-time pastor anymore. How do you feel about that?"

I felt relieved. Being an assistant pastor's wife was sure to be easier than a real pastor's wife. My heart slowed down a little, and I breathed a sigh of relief.

"If that is what you want to do, Zach, it is fine with me," I told him.

"I will be traveling more, taking other speaking engagements. Do you like to travel?" he asked.

"By the way, where do you want to go for a honeymoon? I am not a very rich man, and I don't even have a house to offer you," he said sadly.

"Zach, I have a house, and I have money. If that is all I needed, I would not be marrying you. I need you and the love you have for me," I told him.

"We need to go furniture shopping if we are to stay here. People frown on having to sit on the floor." He laughed, and I loved to hear it.

"I noticed that. What kind of furniture do you want to get? Let's go shopping tomorrow and see what we can find," I suggested.

"It's a date." He looked at his watch and said, "I'm late for a meeting. The deacons needed to speak to me before Preacher Carr returned. I will see you later. I love you."

He kissed me, and then he was gone.

One Sunday after church, I was standing by myself in the vestibule when Garrett came in the door. He stopped and looked at me.

"I see you landed a big one this time, Bobbie," he said just loud enough for me to hear him. "I hope you don't blow it, but you will, because you are living a lie just like you did with me."

When he left, I felt a cold draft go all the way to my bone marrow. *How could he know? I have cleaned up and go to church now, and we even entertain church folk every now and then. I know deep inside that it is all a lie, but how does Garrett know, and who else knows?*

Marcia arranged a bridal shower for me the first of May, and we received a lot of beautiful gifts. She kept track of the gifts and from whom they were given. I would have to buy some thank-you cards to send to everyone.

We got a camera, blenders, toasters, sheets, quilts, kitchen stuff, blankets, pillows, clocks, etc. It was a never-ending array of gifts. My heart was touched by their generosity. When Zach came over that night, I showed him all the gifts, and he just couldn't believe it.

When Preacher Carr came back to town, he and Sandy came to the house for a visit. I poured some iced tea for them, and then Preacher Carr cleared his throat. I was prepared for the worst. He knew me from the time I was born, and I knew he knew.

"Well, Bobbie, congratulations. I am happy to be the one to have the privilege of marrying you and Zach. He is a fine man, and you have done wonders for him since his wife died. It looks like he has done wonders for you too," he said heartily.

I released the air that I had caught up in my lungs, waiting for the blast of condemnation that I had expected from him.

"Thank you, Preacher Carr. Zach is a wonderful man, and I know we will be happy together. I am so glad you were able to make it back in time to do the ceremony." I chose my words well and thought about each of them before I allowed them to escape.

I was so relieved when they finally left. I poured myself a drink and sat on the back steps, watching Mongrel. The drink burned my senses, and I felt the immediate release of cares drift away from me.

Chapter Forty-two

Two weeks before the wedding, Zach became deathly ill. His fever continued to rise, and I was frantic. He had some kind of an infection. I called Tony, and he immediately came to the house to see him.

After examining him, he decided that Zach needed to be in the hospital. "He has pneumonia, Bobbie. It sounds like double pneumonia, but it is hard to tell without an x-ray. Go ahead and drive him to the hospital, and I will send some orders with you."

I drove like a maniac all the way to the hospital, and while he was being x-rayed, poked, and prodded, I was walking the hallways.

Marcia drove up as soon as she heard, and she sat with me.

"I'm fine, Marcia. Why don't you go home and take care of your family?" I told her.

"You are my family, Bobbie. Danny can take care of things. I need to stay with you," she persisted.

Once he was admitted into room 406, we were allowed in to see him. He looked so pale and thin. I kissed him on the forehead, and he was still hot. He opened his eyes and smiled.

"This is not cold feet. I promise you. I do want to marry you."

"You silly goose, nobody is getting married if you don't get well," I told him.

I stayed with him the whole time he was in the hospital, leaving only to get something to eat and go home to check on Mongrel. Five days later, he was released and very weak, so I took him to my house and put him in my bed. He was worried about what people were going to think about his staying here with me, but for Pete's sake, we couldn't have done anything if we had wanted to. He was so weak.

Two days before the wedding, Zach was feeling a whole lot better. He went back to his apartment, but Ms. Joyce kept a good eye on him. They would not allow us to see each other before the wedding, and no phone calls either. The only contact we had with each other was from friends. Marcia kept me updated on his physical condition.

On our wedding day, I woke up, and it was pouring down rain. I wondered if this was a sign to call off the wedding, as was the pneumonia. It probably was, but I didn't know how to stop it. The funny thing is, when you wear an engagement ring and plan a wedding, people expect to you to get married.

Marcia came over early, looking spectacular. Her dress was simple and red. Everything was in place but the groom. He had not shown up yet, and I was a nervous wreck. I couldn't sit down because I didn't want to wrinkle my gown, so I paced, nervously paced back and forth until I could see the wear on the carpet.

Marcia brushed my hair up and swept it on top of my head, fastening a beautiful rhinestone comb in it to hold it in place. I wore the necklace and earrings Zach had given me for Valentine's Day, and Mother gave me a special dainty cotton hankie my great grandmother wore when she was married. I kissed her and told her I loved her.

Finally, I heard the wedding march as Lois started playing the organ. The twins checked their hair and dresses one more time in the mirror and then, in unison, said, "We love you, Bobbie."

I watched through the crack in the door as they walked slowly down the aisle, strewing tiny flowers along the way.

I looked up at the front of the church and saw Zach. Oh, he was so handsome in his beige suit and red shirt. Danny was the best man, and he was standing right behind him.

Marcia kissed me on the cheek and then followed the twins down the aisle. The music became louder, and Mother kissed me and told me she loved me. I held on to her arm tightly, and she told me that everything was going to finally be okay. I wished I believed that. The whole thing was wrong, and I didn't know what to do, so I did what was expected of me. I became Mrs. Zachary Arthur Huntington.

We spent the night at our house, and as Mother would say, the feathers were flying. The next day, we packed the car and headed south to Mississippi with Mongrel in the backseat.

We unpacked, and Mongrel was just dying to go outside, so we put our swimsuits on and ran down the beach to the ocean. It was a beautiful day, and it had been such a long ride. Zach and I lay in the sand on an old blanket I found, and Mongrel headed to the water. I fell asleep immediately until Mongrel came over and shook water all over me. I got up and chased him around the beach and then followed him into the water.

We stayed for two weeks, and it was so nice to just be Zach and me. No one called, and no one came to the house, and Zach wasn't locked up in his study all day. It was great. The two weeks went entirely too fast though, and before I wanted to, we were heading back up the highway after saying our farewells to all our friends.

Well, there I was, the assistant preacher's wife. Well, I was supposed to be. I had no idea what an assistant preacher's wife was supposed to do, so I just did what I normally did except I had to be quiet because Zach was usually upstairs in his office, preparing a sermon for the youth group. The next week, he had a speaking engagement in Columbus, and then, after that one, in North Carolina.

I accompanied him to each of these meetings and met quite a few new people. They were always pleasant around me, and most of the pastor's wives escorted me to the different functions and introduced me.

At about the middle of August, I woke up nauseated and ran to the bathroom to vomit in the toilet.

What in the world could I have eaten last night to have made me so sick? I wondered.

Zach knocked at the door and said, "Honey, are you all right? Can I get you anything?"

"No. I am fine. I must have eaten something last night that did not agree with me," I said, trying to stand up.

"I'm going downstairs to make some coffee," he said.

"Okay. I think I am going back to bed," I said so quietly that he probably didn't even hear me.

A couple of hours later, I woke up and the house was empty. Zach had left a note on the table stating:

> Honey,
> You were resting so well that I didn't want to wake you, so I decided to go on to the meeting by myself.
> I will see you in a couple of days.
> I love you. I hope you get to feeling better fast.
> Love,
> Zach

I noticed a vase of flowers sitting on the kitchen counter, and I hugged them and twirled around in circles and then ran to the bathroom again. After a couple more times hugging the toilet, I finally decided to check my calendar. I hadn't really been keeping track of my periods for a long time. As far as I could figure up, I hadn't had a period for awhile. I was pregnant.

I was pregnant. I jumped for joy, and then I sat and cried as I thought of Michael and Billy Jo. I picked up the phone to call Marcia and had to hang up to rush again to the bathroom.

Marcia came over a couple hours later with three pregnancy tests. I was so sick I couldn't even do them myself. She got some rubber gloves I had and held the stick while I tried to void. We did all three sticks, and all three turned blue for positive. I was pregnant.

I waited until Zach came home before I told him, and it was so hard to wait. He called me two and three times a day, asking if I was okay, and I assured him I was.

When he pulled into the drive, I just couldn't wait any longer. I opened the door and ran out to greet him, and the only thing I could say was, "I'm pregnant."

He looked at me, stunned, and then his face broke into the biggest, most wonderful smile. His whole body smiled. He picked me up and kissed me and twirled me around and then put me down hurriedly so he wouldn't hurt me.

"Have you told anybody?" he asked.

"Marcia brought me three pregnancy tests over, and all three were positive. I have an appointment with Dr. Hansen on Monday."

"Oh, Bobbie, I have wanted children for as long as I know you have also. What shall we name him? He is going to be beautiful like you, with dark hair and your beautiful face."

He just went on and on, and the tears poured down his cheeks. He was so happy. His happiness made waiting to tell him even better.

In the months that followed, he went to every doctor appointment with me, and we poured over baby books and discussed names. I wanted his name to be Zachary Henry Huntington, after his father and my father. Zach loved the idea of his son being named after him.

Girls' names were never even mentioned because, for some reason, we knew it was a boy, and the day Dr. Hansen proved it, Zach just smiled his all-knowing smile.

Thanksgiving Day we spent with Ms. Joyce. She was so precious and excited about the baby. She gave him his first baby gift: a beautiful baby book with places in it for pictures. She had his name imprinted on the top of it in big, gold letters.

On Christmas Day, we spent the morning by ourselves. I bought Zach a new suit with a shirt and tie to match. He was so excited and wore it the rest of the day. Zach's gift to me was a set of books about Christian women. I thanked him and picked them up, scanning through them.

We were invited to Mother's house for dinner, so I dressed and we drove on over. The snow had been falling all night, so Zach drove the truck and we had no trouble. Cecil and Mother announced that they were getting married, and Mother showed off her ring. It was humongous. She was like a teenage girl. I loved watching her, and I told her how happy I was for them. The wedding was set for February 14, Valentine's Day.

Chapter Forty-three

Mother's wedding was beautiful with just a few friends and family. She wanted Zach to do the wedding for her, and he was more than honored. The reception was at our house, and it was a busy afternoon. Marcia came over to help with everything, and some of the ladies from the church also pitched in, telling me to go enjoy this day with my mother.

I was so relieved when everyone left. I was exhausted. The baby was kicking hard, and I just needed to rest for a while. Zach covered me up on the bed, and I kissed him and told him I loved him.

I woke up with a sharp pain in my lower back, and then it went to my abdomen. The baby was cramped up inside of me, and I rolled over to wake up Zach.

"Zach, I think it's time," I told him gently.

"Time for what, honey?" he asked, not even knowing who he was talking to.

"Time to go to the hospital." Another contraction hit, and I was doubled over with pain.

"Zach, please wake up!" I yelled.

He jumped out of bed and tried dressing, but he couldn't figure out how to get his pants on, so he fell across the bed. If I weren't in so much pain, I would have thought it comical.

The contractions were coming too close, and if I stood up, the baby was coming out. I needed to push, but I resisted with all my might.

"Go get Tony, Zach. Go get Tony," I told him.

He ran out the door, and I heard the car start up. I hoped he had remembered to grab his shirt on the way out, but I didn't think he did. It was still hanging on the back of the chair.

"Okay, little one. You are very impatient. I wish you would wait for Tony, but I guess you are not going to," I said.

With that, I gave one small push, and, *whoosh*, I had a baby boy. He was squealing, so I tried to reach down for him, but I had to push the afterbirth out. Little Zach was still squealing, so I finally picked him up and held him tightly. I wasn't sure whether to cut the cord or not, so I just held him.

When Tony and Zach finally arrived, I was sitting in a bloody mess, holding my precious little Zach. Zach was so excited, but Tony told him to wait while he examined me and the baby and then allowed Zach to cut the cord. He was shaking so badly that Tony had to help him hold the scissors.

Tony examined me and told me that he called 911 so the ambulance could take me to the hospital. He didn't think Zach was in any shape to be driving. I looked at Zach, and he was holding the baby and singing to him. I didn't think I could recall a happier moment in my life.

We stayed in the hospital overnight, and when we arrived home, Marcia was there, waiting for us. She had cleaned up the house and gotten the baby's room ready. I went upstairs and changed him and fed him. Zach bought a rocker for the nursery, and it had a big red bow on it. I was sitting in it, feeding the baby, when he came upstairs.

"Oh, Bobbie, you have made me the happiest man in the world." He cried and sat down on the floor in front of me. He gently touched the baby and started crying even more.

Mother stayed with us for a week, saying that she needed to show me how to bathe him and take care of him. I think it was actually so she could hold her grandson. She cried when she left, but I assured her that he would be right there whenever she wanted to come over.

I was very cautious with little Zach. I was so afraid of losing him. I became too cautious I guess. I put his cradle in our room, and with each sound he made, I would pick him up to make sure he was okay. Zach didn't seem to mind. He was in his own little world. He would pick little Zach up and carry him all over the house, telling him Bible stories of Adam and David. He would repeat them over and over, and I told him he was going to say, "David," before he said, "Daddy."

When Mary was born, the snow had been coming down all night, and Zach had to drive the truck to the hospital. I bundled little Zach up and held him as he went back to sleep. It was 2:00 a.m. when we finally made it to the hospital, and she wasn't born until 9:00 p.m. that night.

I was exhausted. When they brought her to me, I could hardly stay awake. Zach stayed with me the entire time I was in the hospital, which was three days. Marcia kept little Zach, and I missed him terribly.

Little Zach and Mongrel both ran to see me when I got home, and neither one of them could figure out what I was holding. Mongrel kept sniffing at her, and little Zach kept saying, "Mary." Well, at least that was what it was supposed to be.

I laid Mary on the carpet, and both of them went up to her. Mongrel sniffed at her, and when she moved, he jumped back and started barking at her. Little Zach held her hand and touched her face and kept saying, "Mary," over and over.

Mother and Marcia were terrific. I was so tired. I couldn't seem to get over it. I would nurse the baby and go right back to sleep. When little Zach wanted to read a book, I would fall asleep in the middle of it. I even fell asleep in church.

Finally, Zach took me to Tony's clinic to see what was wrong. He poked and prodded and made me breathe and took blood and urine.

"It's funny how I have been fighting you all these years, and now you are my doctor," I said as he examined me.

"Bobbie, I have never had a chance to apologize to you either. I really blew it with you, and I am truly sorry. I am glad you finally have the life you wanted," he said.

"Well," he began as we sat in his office. "The only thing I could find was that you are a little anemic. You lost an awful lot of blood after both of the children, and I think a shot of Vitamin B-12 each month is the answer. I am going to write you a prescription for it and for the syringes. You can give your own injection, and that way it will not cost you an office visit."

The B-12 shots did help, but it was more than that. I wasn't sure what was wrong, but I wasn't enjoying anything anymore. I remembered what Tony had said: "I am glad you have finally got the life you wanted." *Did I? Am I leading the life I wanted?* I couldn't answer that question, and I had no one to talk to. I was not happy inside. I did everything that was expected of me. I took care of the house, my husband, and my two children, but something deep inside of me was still missing. There was a deep, black hole inside.

The children were growing. Little Zach was five years old, and Mary was three years old. I visited sick folks in the hospital and helped Zach prepare for his meetings. Each time I asked to go with him, he told me, "No, you now have children to care for."

I cleaned house every day and took care of the children. Bobbie Jo no longer existed. I was now Mrs. Zachary Huntington, preacher's wife and mother of two. I felt it a duty instead of an honor to be a mother. I loved my children, but I felt stuck. I felt like I was not allowed to be me anymore. Zach was traveling a lot more at speaking engagements, but I had to stay home. I took care of the children, but it was because I had to, not because I wanted to.

I looked at myself in the mirror and saw an old lady with a husband who was never home and two children. I had lost Bobbie Jo. I didn't know where she went, but I had to find her.

I started drinking again, just a little nip at night to help me sleep, especially when Zach was away. I kept a good eye on the children, and we didn't have a wood stove.

The fighting began when Zach discovered my whiskey bottle. I had forgotten to put it away after I filled my flask, and he found it sitting on the kitchen table when he walked in after one of his travels. He came upstairs to our room and woke me up.

"What is this?" he asked, trying to control his temper.

"It looks like a whiskey bottle to me," I answered and then rolled over again.

"Bobbie, you are my wife and the mother of our children. You can't be drinking. We have a reputation to uphold," he said.

"No, Zach. You have a reputation to uphold," I told him.

———

After that, I hid my drinking better, or so I thought. I found new places to hide my bottles anyhow, so Zach would not find them. The children were fine, and his precious reputation was not going to be tarnished.

Each time he would leave on his speaking engagements, I would drink more. I made sure the children were okay before I took a drink, but sometimes I would get just a little carried away and stumble around. When I woke up in the mornings, I usually had a horrible headache, and I found that a little nip in the mornings would help with that too.

One day, Zach came home early and found me passed out on the couch. The children were running around with food all over them and had not been bathed except for what little Zach had done for

Mary. It seemed that when I was passed out, he became the mother, and he took care of Mary.

Zach was furious and jerked me up off the couch, threw me over his shoulder, and carried me upstairs.

"Get dressed. We are going to see a counselor," he said and then went back downstairs to bathe the children. He called Marcia, and I could overhear what he was saying to her. He told her I was drinking heavily and that he was going to take me someplace where I could get cleaned up.

I ran down the steps and grabbed the phone out of his hand and threw it across the floor. "How dare you tell people I am a drunk and need to be cleaned up!" I yelled at him. "Just who do you think you are? You go off to your big, fancy meetings and get to talk to people and leave me stuck here day after day. I don't need to be cleaned up. You do."

With that, I went to the kitchen and poured another drink. Zach came into the kitchen, quietly closing the door behind him so the children could not hear us.

"Bobbie, I love you so much. What can I do to help you? Look at you. You have turned into somebody I don't even know," he said.

"No, preacher man. I am turning into who I am, who you never bothered to get to know because you wanted me to be another Peggy, your perfect little wife."

When I looked at him, big tears were running down his face, but I didn't care. I had to get out of there. The walls were closing in on me, and I couldn't breathe.

I then turned and walked out of the kitchen and upstairs to the bedroom, locking the door behind me. I had a flask hidden in my bedside table, and when I found it, I quickly unscrewed the cap and poured the golden poison down my throat, enjoying the burning as it seared my brain and energized my body.

Zach knocked at the door, but I didn't open it. Finally, he stopped and, I heard the doorbell ring. I ran to the window to see him hand my children over to Marcia. That was the last time I saw my children.

Chapter Forty-four

I pulled on a pair of blue jeans and grabbed a few things, throwing them in my suitcase. He had just taken my children away from me.

Zach jumped out of the way as I bolted my way through the door and down the steps. Mongrel was waiting for me at the door. I don't know how he knew we were leaving, but he did. He jumped in the truck, and Zach tried to grab my arm to prevent me from leaving, but Mongrel growled deeply and he let go.

"Bobbie, I love you. Please, Bobbie. What about the children?" he begged.

"What about the children, Zach? You just gave them away. I now have four children that are gone. I can't believe you took my children away from me. I hate you! I hate you!" I spit the words at him.

He stepped back from the truck as I threw it in reverse and headed out of the driveway. I didn't know where I was going, but I knew it was not going to be there. I put the truck in gear and burned rubber all the way down the street. I wasn't thinking very clearly, but I kept the truck on the road. I drove until I ran out of gas. I didn't know where I was, but it was dark, so I fell asleep on the front seat.

It was pouring down rain when I woke up, and I sat up to see I was at the Hole in the Wall. I laughed to think the truck had taken me there by itself. I walked inside, and Pete was sweeping the floor.

"Hey, Bobbie," he said. "I didn't think we would ever see you in here again. I thought you got religion when you married that preacher."

"I need a place to stay," I said, opening up my purse. Since Oscar died I always kept cash on me and in my truck. I handed Pete all the cash I had, and he pointed to the steps.

"You planning on staying for awhile?" he asked, counting the money.

"Maybe," I said, and I grabbed a bottle of whiskey as I headed up the steps.

The room was small but clean with a fold-out couch and coffee table. The kitchen and front room were one, and there was a tiny fridge and one burner stove on the counter. One small window was in the kitchen, and it was covered over by a curtain with big sunflowers on it, as if it had been taken from my house.

I walked in and closed the door behind me, pushing the bolt lock closed. My hands were shaking, and I slid down the door. The whiskey knocked off the edge, and I drank until I passed out.

In the morning I heard someone beating at the door but I didn't answer it. It was Zach, and he was the last person I wanted to talk to.

"Bobbie, I am sorry. The children are here with me," he said. "Please, Bobbie, please come home so we can be a family again."

"Mommy, please come home," I heard my precious Mary cry, and my heart was ripped open. "Please come and be my mommy again."

I could hear little Zach crying, and then he said "I hate you, Mommy. I hate you."

I couldn't stand it. I went to the sink and ran water, hoping to drown out their pleas. Finally they left, and I watched them get into Zach's big car and drive off.

That night, my dream came back. The house was on fire, and I saw Michael and Billy Jo walking into it. The man was there again, standing by the woodstove. He was just standing there, looking at me and calling the children.

When I woke up, my clothes were wet with sweat. The sun was just starting to peep through, and I was so cold. My bottle was empty so I crawled downstairs for another.

Gloria was there serving drinks. She didn't say anything to me when I grabbed another bottle and went back upstairs, but I heard her talking to Pete.

"How long is she staying?" she asked. "I don't like that preacher and her kids coming in here."

"She paid me cash. I figure a month will probably be enough," Pete told her.

Chapter Forty-five

December came in snowy and colder than I could ever remember. I was stumbling downstairs for another drink one day. Zach knocked softly on the door. When I didn't answer, he started beating on it.

"Bobbie, are you there?" he asked. "I really need to speak to you. Mary is sick. I had to take her to the hospital last night. Bobbie, do you hear me?"

I opened the door and stared at him through my foggy eyes, holding onto the doorframe for support.

"And just exactly what do you want me to do about it?" I over-pronounced each word so they would come out right. "They are your children, Zach. I don't have any. Don't you remember? You gave my children away to Marcia. Now go away and leave me alone." I slammed the door and bolted it tight before he could push it open. It was a solid oak door, so I knew he couldn't break it down.

As he was leaving I heard him talking to Pete. "Do you have a key to that room?" he asked.

"She has paid for that room, and I am not going to go barging in there," he said. "She is a paying customer."

I passed out in the shower trying to drown out the voices in my head. They were so loud, and I tried to put my hands over my ears, but nothing would help. The shower was cold when I woke up, and it was dark outside. The bar downstairs was quiet, so it must have been past two in the morning.

I got dressed and went out to my truck. Mongrel was still there waiting for me. Pete had been taking care of him. He was so happy to see me he licked me and wagged his tail. I found a full gas can behind the building, so I poured it in, priming the carburetor, and finally Oscar's truck roared to life.

At the hospital I asked which room Mary Huntington was in, and an elderly lady with a name badge that read Thelma smiled and told me, "Three seventeen."

"Just follow this hallway to the elevators," she said, pointing me in the right direction.

When I stepped off the elevator, nobody was around, so I quietly walked down the hall toward room 317. I couldn't enter the room, for there in a big huge bed lay my Mary with tubes coming out from everywhere. The monitors were beeping, and a machine was squawking, and she lay there with her eyes closed, not moving.

Zach was asleep in the chair beside her, and he did not wake when I walked over to her.

"Oh, Mary," I cried softly. "I love you. I wish I could be your mommy again. I love you."

Mary opened her eyes, and I saw a tear run down her face. I kissed my thumb and touched her lips with it. She smiled up at me and held her tiny little arms up for me to hold her, but I couldn't. I wanted to so badly, but I couldn't. She was not mine anymore. God had taken all of my children away from me.

I turned around for one last look and blew her a kiss. I watched as she caught it and put it in her pocket. I mouthed "I love you" before I left. Nobody saw me leave except Thelma, and she wished me a good night. I cried all the way back to the bar, and Mongrel snuggled close to me.

In the morning I gave Pete some more cash, and I took two bottles up to the room with me.

One night at the Hole, I met a guy named Keith. He sauntered over to me and bought me a drink, so I took him home with me. He was about my age with blonde hair and blue eyes. He worked at the paper mill during the day and drank all night. He had a horrible temper, and when I did something he didn't like, which was most of the time, my face felt the sting of the back of his hand.

I never ducked or tried to protect myself. I just stood my ground and let him hit me. What did it matter? I was just a piece of trash that everybody had discarded.

On Christmas Eve, I heard the children outside, singing carols. I peeked out the window and watched as they went from door to door, stopping at each one to sing. They walked right past, not even look-ing at it. I closed the curtain and wiped the tears from my eyes. The emptiness and loneliness screamed at me, and the whiskey wasn't hiding my pain anymore.

I drew a Christmas tree on the wall with a black marking pen and drew presents under it. I pretended I had a husband and children and I was handing them their presents. They would slowly unwrap each gift so as not to tear the paper, and then they would squeal with joy as they held the colorful paper up for examination. I laughed and pretended it was my turn, and I held my present in my hand, trying to find where the tape began.

My daydream was interrupted when Keith and his friend came barreling in. I could tell they had been drinking by the way Keith slurred all his words.

"Hey, get me a beer!" he yelled at me when he saw me in the front room. "Now! And get Joe one too."

I just stood there, staring at him. He looked at me and said again, "What is wrong with you, you piece of trash? I said get me a beer."

Once again, I just stood there, not moving. It was like I was frozen in place. I don't think I could have moved if I wanted to. He was furious and grabbed my hair, dragging me out to the kitchen with him. He opened the fridge door and threw me down in front of it.

"I said get me a beer."

He was yelling as loud as he could, and I sat on the floor and watched him as he reached in the fridge and got two beers out and returned to the front room.

I got up off the floor and took a big, long swig of whiskey from the bottle. It tasted just as good as it did from a glass, and I didn't have to waste the time pouring it. I noticed that it had started snowing again. They were just fine, white flakes floating down to the ground. The ground was already covered with several layers.

I heard Keith and his friend in the front room, talking and laughing, and then once more, I heard him holler for another round. I watched as the snowflakes twirled and fluttered and spun around before they hit the ground, and I thought, *How free they are, but then they are gone.*

Keith came in the kitchen and saw me standing at the window. He grabbed my hair and said, "I need another beer. What is your problem tonight? Get me a beer." His face was so close to mine that our noses touched.

He opened the door and again threw me down. I fell to the floor, and he was infuriated. He picked me up by my hair and slapped me across the face. I fell to the floor, and he started kicking me with his pointed boots.

I heard his friend come in the kitchen and say, "Hey, man, if you are going to kill your old lady, I am out of here."

Keith said, "She ain't worth killing. Wait up. Let me get my stuff. I'm tired of this piece of trash anyhow." He walked over to the trashcan and dumped all its contents over me. "That is what you are a piece of trash."

I heard them get in his truck and peel out of the parking lot. I don't know how long I lay there. I kept going in and out of consciousness and imagining things, seeing and hearing things. Marcia and Danny with the twins. They were walking away from me with Mary and Little Zach. Oscar was running around in a field of grass, chasing Mongrel. Tony and Ashley, Garrett, and Oscar were all running around and around me as I lay there. They were all laughing at me.

Then the mysterious man in my dreams appeared and told me to get up. "Get up and come with me," he said softly. I slowly got up off the floor, holding onto the table, and went outside.

The snow was coming down in big flakes. I turned my face up to soothe the burning. The blood from my nose had matted in my hair, and my whole body throbbed with pain with each step I took down the dark street. No one was around. It was hard for me to go very fast. My breathing was labored. I knew one of my ribs was fractured, but I kept going, just putting one foot in front of another.

I imagined Mary holding my hands and helping me keep my balance. Little Zach, Billy Jo, and Michael were playing in the snow and having a snowball fight. Father was waiting for me on the street corner, but for some reason, I couldn't go to him. He kept calling me, but my body would not turn that way. I just kept walking down the road.

Garrett was working on his truck, and Michael was there with him, and in my mind, Billy Jo was there too. They were laughing and playing. Oscar too was at the lake, and he was throwing sticks to Mongrel, who was jumping and running and barking. They called me to play for a while, but I couldn't go to them either. I just kept walking.

The church was empty. Christmas Eve services were over, and the people had gone home to their families and friends. I walked slowly down the aisle, still lit from the candles at the altar.

I remembered coming there as a little girl, and Momma would tie a hankie on my wrist with my offering money so I wouldn't lose it. I remembered Father singing in his deep bass voice.

Sweet memories flooded over me as I sat there, crying at the remembrance of some of them. Oh how I missed those days when I was so carefree and life was fun and easy. Where had it all changed? Why did it go bad?

I picked up a bulletin and noticed the picture of a woman with long, dark hair on the front of it. She was standing beside a well, her hair covering her face as if she were hiding. She was all alone, just like me. As I thought about the woman, I heard the back doors open, and I sat quietly in the pew, hoping whoever it was would not see me.

"I have been looking for you." It was Zach. "I wanted to give you a Christmas present."

When I didn't say anything, I heard him walk down the aisle toward me. He stood beside me and kneeled on the floor. Slowly, he took the bulletin from my hand.

"Do you know who she is?" he asked me.

"No," I answered quietly.

"She is you, Bobbie. She too was looking for someone to love her, and the funny thing is, he was hunting for her the whole time too."

I looked at Zach and frowned at his words. *How could this be a picture of me?*

"This woman is the Samaritan woman from the Bible. She came to the well to draw water when she hoped nobody else would be there, just like you came here hoping everybody would be gone. She had been married five times and was living with a man who wasn't her husband," he said, holding the paper so I could see.

I took the bulletin and tore it in two. "This woman is not me." I spit the words at him.

"What are you looking for, Bobbie? Why did you come here?" he asked.

"Just to be alone," I answered.

"No, Bobbie. You came to find Him. You have been looking for Him, and He has been looking for you," Zach said as the tears escaped from his eyes. "He loves you, Bobbie. Jesus loves you."

"No, Zach. Nobody loves me, and I don't want anybody to love me. I am just fine," I said, shaking my head. "I don't need anybody."

"Then why did you come here, Bobbie?" he asked again.

"I just wanted to be alone. It is Christmas, Zach, and I am so lonely. I just wanted to be alone," I cried.

"He is here, Bobbie, waiting for you. Jesus has been waiting for you to come to Him all these years."

"Why would He be waiting for me? I have never done anything for Him. I don't read the Bible, and I don't go to church. Why would He want me?" My voice was getting louder, and I heard the words echo back to me from the walls. "Why would He want me?" I said more to myself.

"He died for you, Bobbie. He loves you, and He has been waiting for you. Yes, Bobbie, this woman is you. Jesus was waiting at the well for this woman." He handed me the torn bulletin and pointed at her. "Jesus is also here at this well, waiting for you." He spread his hands out, showing me he meant the church. "He has a Christmas gift for you, Bobbie. It is a gift that He paid a dear price for.

"You know John three sixteen: 'For God so loved the world that He gave His only begotten Son that whosoever believeth on Him should not perish but have everlasting life.' *Whosoever* means you, Bobbie. It means whoever believes in Him, whoever believes that He exists and whoever believes He is real."

I sat there quietly, trying to understand what Zach was telling me. I had heard the story all my life, but I never realized it was for me. I never realized Jesus died for me.

"I can't believe, Zach. I can't believe Jesus would die for someone like me. I am nothing but a drunk. I killed my baby, and I have pushed everybody away. How could He want anybody like me?" I asked.

Zach took a Bible out of his pocket and opened it up to Romans 5:8, "But God commendeth his love toward us, in that while we were yet sinners Christ died for us."

"God doesn't wait for us to come to Him. He comes to us. It was your sins that put Him on the cross. He is waiting right here for you.

You are a sinner, Bobbie, and so am I. But look what it says: 'While we were yet sinners Christ died for us.' He died for you, and He died for me. If you knew somebody who killed a man, robbed banks, and beat up little old ladies and when he went to trial the judge, asked if anybody would take these crimes away from this man and let him go free, would you give up Little Zach for him?"

I looked at him like he was crazy. "Of course not. That man deserves to go to jail," I said.

"God did. "He gave His only Son, Jesus, for that man, and He also gave Him for you. He died for all of us." He continued. "But that man has a choice, and so do you. You can either continue on this path of destruction you have put yourself on or you can accept His generous gift He is offering you."

Slowly, he turned the pages in his Bible. "The Bible says in Romans three twenty-three, 'The wages of sin is death.' Somebody has to pay for all your sins, for all your crimes. When a crime has been committed, someone has to pay for that. Well, you have committed a crime against God. Now you have to pay for that crime." He pointed to a place in his Bible. "Well, the end of this verse is, 'But the gift of God is eternal life through Jesus Christ our Lord.'"

I looked at him and told him things I had never told anybody. "I killed my baby, and I had an affair with Danny. I lied, and now look at me. I am just a drunk."

"Bobbie, Jesus can wipe the slate clean. He can give you living water like he gave this woman in the picture. He gave her living water, and she left her water pitchers and ran into town, telling everybody about Jesus. He can change your life, Bobbie, and He wants to because He loves you," he told me.

"What do I have to do?" I asked, fearful of the answer.

"Just believe," he said. "Romans ten thirteen says, 'For whosoever shall call upon the name of the Lord shall be saved.' Do you believe, Bobbie? Do you believe He died for you on that cross two thousand years ago? Do you believe He loves you?"

"Yes, I believe," I said quietly, welcoming the peace that was flooding my heart.

"Let's pray." Zach took my hand and led me to the altar, and he said, "Dear heavenly Father, thank You for leading Bobbie here tonight and allowing me the privilege of introducing her to You. Now, Bobbie, just ask Him. He is right here waiting." He squeezed my hand.

"God, I am not very good at this, but I am asking You to forgive me and give me Your living water. I know I am a sinner and that You died for my sins, and I am just asking You now for forgiveness for those sins. Thank You."

Zach hugged me gently and kissed me. I wasn't sure what I was supposed to do. I felt so light, so relieved. I felt like I could go out and conquer the world, but the most wonderful thing was the feeling that I was not alone anymore.

Epilogue

The three years were long and hard, but I knew I had to do the time for killing Billy Jo. After my confession to Chief Brown, I was sentenced to five years for manslaughter. I was to be on probation for the next two years.

I waited in the line with the other ladies. We were dressed in ragged old blue jeans and T-shirts that were ten times too big. The guard handed me my possessions and twenty dollars. My first thought was, *I have been here before, but at least this time I have shoes.*

The big iron gate shut behind me, and I stood there, waiting for the sounds of the locks, knowing it would be the last time I would ever hear them. I watched as the other ladies were met by their families and loved ones. We said our good-byes and promised to keep in contact. Some of those ladies were my sisters in Christ, and we made plans to get together soon.

The sun was shining, and I looked up at the beautiful blue sky and watched as two doves fluttered to the ground for a piece of bread someone had dropped near the picnic area. The trees were green, and the dandelions covered the fields like a blanket.

I saw an old truck that looked just like Oscar's sitting across from the prison, and I thought, *Wow. I wish Oscar was here.* I turned and started walking down the street, and I heard someone call my name.

"Bobbie."

Turning, I saw Zach standing behind me with tears flowing down his cheeks. I wasn't sure what to do. He picked me up and hugged me and started kissing me all over.

"I love you. I have waited three years for this moment to finally take my wife home," he said.

His words stunned me, and I couldn't say anything. Suddenly, the truck door opened.

Little Zach came up beside me. He looked just like his father, so tall and handsome. I touched his face with my hand and wiped the tears from his eyes.

"We have been waiting for you," he told me and then wrapped his arms around me. "We want to take you home." I hugged him to me and was amazed how tall he was.

Zach hugged us both and said, "We want to be a family again."

I looked toward the truck, but it looked empty. I was afraid to say anything, and Zach just looked away. I didn't know what happened to Mary that night. Nobody ever told me.

We hugged and kissed and started to talk all at once. Out of the corner of my eye, I saw Little Zach go to the back of the truck and pick up a blanket. When he handed it to me. It started moving, and then a tiny little head poked out.

"His name is Mutt. We thought you needed a new dog since Mongrel died," he said.

"I think he died of a broken heart," Zach said.

Behind me I felt someone tugging at my T-shirt. When I turned around, there was Mary, standing there with the biggest smile on her face.

"I still got it," she said, holding out her hand.

"Got what, Mary?" I asked, puzzled. Zach shook his head and shrugged his shoulders.

"Your kiss, the one you gave me when I was in the hospital," she said.

I hugged her close to me, and we piled into the front seat of the truck and headed home. Mutt started whining, so I held him close to me, and he cuddled up.

I lifted my eyes to heaven and said, "Thank you, Father, for making everything turn out right, no matter how much I mess it up."

Mary reached over to pet Mutt and then rested her hand on my arm.

God's Plan of Salvation

The Bible says there is only one way to heaven.

Jesus said: "I am the way, the truth, and the life: no man cometh unto the Father but by me" (John 14:6).

Good works cannot save you.

"For by grace are ye saved through faith; and that not of yourselves: it is the gift of God: Not of works, lest any man should boast" (Ephesians 2:8-9).

Trust Jesus Christ today! Here's what you must do:

Admit you are a sinner.

"For all have sinned and come short of the glory of God" (Romans 3:23).

"Wherefore, as by one man sin entered into the world, and death by sin; and so death passed upon all men, for that all have sinned" (Romans 5:12).

"If we say that we have not sinned, we make him a liar, and his word is not in us" (1 John 1:10).

Be willing to turn from sin (repent).

Jesus said, "I tell you, Nay: but, except ye repent, ye shall all likewise perish" (Luke 13:5).

"And the times of this ignorance God winked at; but now commandeth all men every where to repent" (Acts 17:30).

Believe that Jesus Christ died for you, was buried, and rose from the dead.

"For God so loved the world that he gave his only begotten Son, that whosoever believeth in him should not perish, but have everlasting life" (John 3:16).

"But God commendeth his love toward us, in that, while we were yet sinners. Christ died for us" (Romans 5:8).

"That if thou shalt confess with thy mouth the Lord Jesus, and shalt believe in thine heart that God hath raised him from the dead, thou shalt be saved" (Romans 10:9).

Through prayer, invite Jesus into your life to become your personal Savior.

"For with the heart man believeth unto righteousness; and with the mouth confession is made unto salvation" (Romans 10:10).

"For whosoever shall call upon the name of the Lord shall be saved" (Romans 10:13).

What to pray: "Jesus, I know I am a sinner. I believe that you died for those sins and I am asking for you to save me. Amen"

"But as many as received him, to them gave he power to become the sons of God, even to them that believe on his name" (John 1:12).

"Therefore if any man be in Christ, he is a new creature: old things are passed away; behold, all things are become new" (2 Corinthians 5:17).

Conclusion

John 4 (KJV)

Christ talks with a woman of Samaria and reveals Himself to her.

When therefore the Lord knew how the Pharisees had heard that Jesus made and baptized more disciples than John, (Though Jesus himself baptized not, but his disciples,) He left Judaea, and departed again into Galilee. And he must needs go through Samaria. Then cometh he to a city of Samaria, which is called Sychar, near to the parcel of ground that Jacob gave to his son Joseph. Now Jacob's well was there. Jesus therefore, being wearied with *his* journey, sat thus on the well: *and* it was about the sixth hour. There cometh a woman of Samaria to draw water: Jesus saith unto her, "Give me to drink." (For his disciples were gone away unto the city to buy meat.) Then saith the woman of Samaria unto him, "How is it that thou, being a Jew, askest drink of me, which am a woman of Samaria? for the Jews have no dealings with the Samaritans." Jesus answered and said unto her, "If thou knewest the gift of God, and who it is that saith to thee, Give me to drink; thou wouldest have asked of him, and he would have given thee living water." The woman saith unto him, "Sir, thou hast nothing to draw with, and the well is deep: from whence then hast thou that living water? Art thou greater than our father Jacob, which gave us the well, and drank thereof himself, and his children, and his cattle?" Jesus answered and said unto her,

"Whosoever drinketh of this water shall thirst again: But whosoever drinketh of the water that I shall give him shall never thirst; but the water that I shall give him shall be in him a well of water springing up into everlasting life." The woman saith unto him, "Sir, give me this water, that I thirst not, neither come hither to draw." Jesus saith unto her, "Go, call thy husband, and come hither." The woman answered and said, "I have no husband." Jesus said unto her, "Thou hast well said, 'I have no husband:' For thou hast had five husbands; and he whom thou now hast is not thy husband: in that saidst thou truly." The woman saith unto him, "Sir, I perceive that thou art a prophet. Our fathers worshipped in this mountain; and ye say, that in Jerusalem is the place where men ought to worship." Jesus saith unto her, "Woman, believe me, the hour cometh, when ye shall neither in this mountain, nor yet at Jerusalem, worship the Father. Ye worship ye know not what: we know what we worship: for salvation is of the Jews. But the hour cometh, and now is, when the true worshippers shall worship the Father in spirit and in truth: for the Father seeketh such to worship him. God *is* a Spirit: and they that worship him must worship *him* in spirit and in truth." The woman saith unto him, "I know that Messias cometh, which is called Christ: when he is come, he will tell us all things." Jesus saith unto her, "I that speak unto thee am *he*."

His disciples marvel. And upon this came his disciples, and marvelled that he talked with the woman: yet no man said, "What seekest thou?" or, "Why talkest thou with her?" The woman then left her waterpot, and went her way into the city, and saith to the men, "Come, see a man, which told me all things that ever I did: is not this the Christ?" Then they went out of the city, and came unto him. In the mean while his disciples prayed him, saying, "Master, eat." But he said unto them, "I have meat to eat that ye know not of." Therefore said the disciples one to another, "Hath any man brought him *ought* to eat?" Jesus saith unto them, "My meat is to do the will of him that sent me, and to finish his work. Say not ye, 'There are yet four months, and *then* cometh harvest?' behold, I say unto you, Lift up your eyes, and look on the fields; for they are white already to harvest. And he that reapeth receiveth wages, and gathereth fruit unto life eternal: that both he that soweth and he that reapeth may rejoice together. And herein is that saying true, 'One soweth, and another reapeth.' I sent you to reap that whereon ye bestowed no labour: other men laboured, and ye are entered into their labours." And many of the Samaritans of that city believed on him for the saying of the woman, which testified, He told me all that ever I did. So when the Samaritans were come unto him, they besought him that he would tarry with them: and he abode there two days. And many more believed because of his own word; And said unto the woman, "Now we believe, not because of thy saying: for we have heard *him* ourselves, and know that this is indeed the Christ, the Saviour of the world."

PS

Thank you, Father for your love and for your patience. While I am leading my life my way, you are always there, pulling me toward you with your loving kindness. You who made the galaxies, the stars, the mountains, and the seas are the same one who holds my hand and leads me each day.

Forgive me for not acknowledging you at times and for pushing you aside when I need you to be close. Forgive me for relying on me to get by and to solve all my problems. Thank you for loving me through it all.